A Story of a Rabbi

Obadiah Ariel Yehoshuah

WestBow
PRESS
A DIVISION OF THOMAS NELSON

WestBow Press books may be ordered through booksellers or by contacting:

WestBow Press
A Division of Thomas Nelson
1663 Liberty Drive
Bloomington, IN 47403
www.westbowpress.com
1-(866) 928-1240

ISBN: 978-1-4497-2832-8 (sc)
ISBN: 978-1-4497-2831-1 (hc)
ISBN: 978-1-4497-2833-5 (e)

Library of Congress Control Number: 2011917652

Printed in the United States of America

WestBow Press rev. date: 10/13/2011

Chapter 1

After a long bought with cancer Ezekiel's father took his last breath peacefully in his sleep at home. It was difficult but it was a gift nevertheless because he had suffered so much and didn't have much energy at the end. Raisa and little Aliya brought him breakfast in bed every day. Mordechi loved his little grand daughter and even in his last days would tell her that someday the whole family would leave Russia for Israel. He wanted to die in Israel feeling that he would be truly free when he touched the place that was given to his people by God. Aliya would sit next to his bed while he prayed from the Torah. One day when Mordechi was feeling up to getting out of bed he sat down in the chair and put Aliya on his lap. "Aliya one day you will grow up and have children of your own. Promise me that you will make sure that they keep the mitzvah of God."

Aliya was too young to understand the importance of what her grand father was saying so like most children she just nodded in agreement to make him happy. Mordechi wanted Aliya to have a much better life than he had. It was some kind of taboo to be a Jew. He wanted that she could live a life free from the stigma and actually be proud to be a Jew.

On the day that he died Raisa came in to wake him up as usual to see what he wanted for breakfast. At first he didn't answer her but she could see that he was awake. "Abba are you okay? What do you want for breakfast?"

Mordechi only looked at Raisa and said "Raisa where is Ezekiel?"

"He is just getting up. Today he starts teaching classes at the school. He is very excited about this. I'm sure he will come in and speak with you before leaving. Maybe you can come to the table and have breakfast this morning. The doctor said that it is good when you can get up and walk as much as possible."

"Raisa tell my son that I need him to come in and speak with me now. I need to tell him something very important."

"Okay Mordechi." Raisa wasn't sure what all the fuss was about but he never sounded like this before so she called out to Ezekiel to come into the room as soon as possible and went on straightening up the room. Ezekiel came through the door still straightening up his clothing. "Abba what is going on are you okay, do you need to see the doctor or something?"

"No son. I know that you are getting ready for school but I need to speak with you about this now. I don't have much time. I'm sure they won't be upset that you spent a few moments with a dying man."

"Father please don't talk like that. You have lots and lots of time left. Remember we are going to Jerusalem. We talk about it all the time. Don't talk like this."

"Ezekiel I need to tell you something very important before you leave today. Sit down it will only take a minute and you can go." Ezekiel sat on the chair by his bedside. "Ezekiel the time has come that I should leave you. I'm sorry that we didn't get a chance to get to Israel together. But it is important to me that you take the family and leave here as soon as possible. This place has changed and is no longer a place of refuge for our people. They tease my grand daughter in school. What will be next Ezekiel? You must get her to safety. I had a dream many years ago but I never told anyone about it. I want to say before God today that I am sorry that I did not heed the warning that I was given a long time ago."

"What warning father, what are you talk about?"

"Listen to me son. I had a dream and there was a great angel who told me that the Jewish people would be persecuted again. He said

2

that I should speak with the Jewish people all over the world to return to Israel for this would be the only place where we could be safe but I did not do it. Please Ezekiel do this for me. Do not make the same mistake that I made in not doing what I was asked to do. Remember that before the war we had a chance to get out of Poland but we did not heed the warning. Because of it many people died. If we do not heed this warning many more will die. The Jewish people including your uncle think that they are safe in America and other places where they live but in essence they are sitting ducks just waiting for the next time they are taken advantage of. Please Ezekiel promise me that you will take the family and leave here as soon as possible or something terrible is going to happen."

"Calm down father before we have to take you to the hospital. I will talk with you about this when I get home. But I promise that we will go to Israel. Right now you are sick and we cannot leave you behind. I will not leave you behind." He kissed his father and asked that Raisa not leave him alone. He didn't know what had gotten his father so upset but he just didn't have time to sit with him this morning. Raisa was standing next to the bed while her husband and his father talked but she said nothing.

"Raisa I'm not feeling up to walking today. I had a dream last night. I saw my beautiful wife and she was standing on a cloud and asking me to come with her. I felt that if I had walked out onto that cloud that I would have past onto heaven Raisa."

"Oh father. That is beautiful. But we are not ready for you to leave us yet. We still have not made it to Jerusalem. We must all go together. So don't talk about such things."

"Raisa please indulge an old man. Call Rebbe Isak and tell him that I want to speak with him. I don't think that I will make it much longer. It is time for me to give vidui. I want to go to Jerusalem but I won't be able to make it. But do not give up on the dream of our family. My brother Stephen will lead the family now. I have a letter that I have written to him. When I die make sure that he gets it. I have told him to take my little Aliya to Jerusalem she gets so excited when we talk about the homeland. She told me the other day that the children tease her at school about being Jewish. I have suffered because of this and don't want her to suffer for the rest of her life because she is Jewish. Promise me Raisa?"

"Okay abba. I will call Isak and have him come over as soon as possible."

Raisa left the room and headed straight for the bedroom to tell Ezekiel that his father is wanting to speak with the rebbe. They were both in denial that Mordechi would live a lot longer and someday the family would all go to Israel together. He was old and he was tired.

Ezekiel didn't know what to do. His father wanted to speak with the rebbe and he had to go to work. He didn't want to miss this opportunity to be with his father during such an important time in his life. Reciting vidui was to be done by all Jewish people before they died. It was an opportunity to make confession before God.

Rebbe Isak loved Mordechi. He had been a holocaust survivor as well. When Raisa called he said that he would be there right away. He could get someone to take over his class for a few minutes. He knew how Mordechi had suffered with the cancer and considered it an honor to be with such a beautiful soul at the time of his confession before God.

Mordechi had actually gotten out of bed and tried to wash himself in preparation for the rebbes' visit. He didn't want to be laying down when the rebbe arrived. Isak knocked on the door and Mordechi called out weakly for him to enter. Isak saw a very frail person sitting on a chair by the window. Mordechi could barely hold his head up and he coughed with every word that he spoke. He was definitely not the person that he once knew. It reminded him of the days when they were in the work camps and the people were just so skinny because they didn't have enough to eat.

"My son I came as soon as I could. How are you doing?"

"I've felt better. But I have been doing a lot of thinking Isak. I'm tired and my body doesn't want to stay much longer. I thought it was time for me to make confession. I had a dream the other night and I saw my beautiful bride. I just know that its time for me to go."

"Well that is a serious thing. I am here for you. Let me put on my tallit."

4

Mordechi took out his tallit and put it over his head. "Unto you O Lord my God and God of my ancestors, I acknowledge that my life and recovery depend upon you. May it be your will to heal me. Yet, if you have decreed that I shall die of this affliction, may my death atone for all sins and transgressions which I have committed before you. Shelter me in the shadow of your wings; grant me a share in the world to come. Protector of orphans and guardian of widows, protect my beloved family, with whose soul my own soul is bound. Into your hand I commit my soul. You have redeemed me, O Lord God of truth. Shema Yisrael, Adonai Eloheinu, Adonai Echad, Hear O Israel: The Lord is our God, the Lord alone. The Lord is God. The Lord is God. Thank you Isak."

"You are a good friend Mordechi. I know that you are tired but maybe you will recover and still take your family to Israel. This will make your son very happy. You know he talks about going to Israel all the time."

"I know. Little Aliya is just like her father. She eats, sleeps and drinks Israel. Isak I have something else to confess to you. Please do not tell this to my son until after I have gone. In this envelope here is a letter to my brother. Please give this to him. Also in the bank I have been saving up for many years for the chance to go to Israel. Since I will not make it I want Ezekiel to use this money to move the family after I have gone."

Isak could see that Mordechi was feeling very tired so he prepared to go. He took the information and told no one about it. He wanted to keep his promise to his friend. Raisa came in after Isak had left and helped Mordechi get back into bed.

After his classes Ezekiel rushed home to see his father and see how he was doing. He knocked on the door just in case he was sleeping. "Abba are you awake?" When he did not get an answer he pushed the door open gently so as not to startle him. There was a strange feeling in the room. Mordechi looked as though he was sleeping but when Ezekiel touched his fathers arm he didn't see him breathing. Immediately he felt panic set in and he started to shake him and call his name but there was no response. He called Raisa into the room and asked that she call the paramedics that he believed his father had died.

The paramedics didn't seem to be in any hurry. Ezekiel sat next to his father holding his hand for quite a while before anyone arrived. As the tears fell from his face Ezekiel prayed for his father as he waited, "Elohaynu veilohay avoteinu v'imoteinu, Our God and God of all who have gone before us, author of life and death, we turn to you at this time of great grief. We turn to you in trust and pray that Mordechi be granted perfect rest in your sheltering presence.

Much was left unfinished in his life, yet we know also the good that he tried to do. May those acts of goodness continue to give meaning to our lives and may the errors in his life be forgiven.

O God, protector of the bereaved and the helpless, watch over this family. Provide us comfort from the pain we feel at this time. Into your hand is the spirit committed; redeem it, O God of mercy and truth.

Adonai melech, Adonai malach, Adonai imloch l'olam va'ed God reigns; God has reigned: God will reign for ever and ever. Shema Yisrael, Adonai Eloheinu Adonai echad. Hear, O Israel: The Lord is our God, the Lord is one. Baruch shem k'vod malchuto l'olam va'ed. Blessed be God's name whose glorious dominion is forever and ever. Adonai natan v'Adonai lakach. Y'hiyi shem Adonai m'vorah. God gave and God has taken away; blessed be the name of God. Baruch dayan ha'emet. Blessed be the Judge of Truth." It seemed like an eternity as Ezekiel prayed over his father. His life flashed before his eyes. What to do now? It was all too much to take in.

Raisa didn't quite know what to do. She could hear Ezekiel praying over his father and she knew that he had gone. What would she tell Aliya? He was her whole world. She would not understand that her grand father was no longer with her. Ezekiel was grieving and she didn't know what to do. She called the paramedics and told them that they were not needed and instead called Rebbe Isak to have the funeral home come to pick up the body. It was customary that the funeral take place within twenty-four hours whenever possible. Special arrangements would have to be made. But Stephen his brother lived in the United States and so they would have to wait until he arrived to have the funeral.

Ezekiel had a very close relationship with his father and felt it unbearable to believe that his father, mentor and rebbe would no longer be there for him when he needed advice. His mother had died many years before. Life for his family was not always easy but he and Ezekiel shared precious but painful memories of how they survived those difficult times. His father and mother were by no means rich but they lived comfortably. Ezekiel was their only son.

Mordechi could barely fight back the tears as he remembered the beginnings of the occupation of German soldiers in Poland. Mordechi was just a young man still in school, he was about 13 years of age at the time. One day as he left for school there was nothing out of the ordinary on the streets, people were going to work, school and to shops to sell their goods. Mordechi remembered reaching school and as he reached his destination he ascended up the stairs to his classroom. He remembered reaching out to open the door when he was greeted by the angry face of his professor. He thought that maybe something was wrong but he had no idea what that something was. The teacher opened the door just as his hand hit the knob and yelled, "You dirty, stinkin Jew" and spit in his face. "Go away you stinkin Jew you do not belong here" he shouted at Mordechi as though he had done something terrible. This was the first time that Mordechi remembered that sick feeling in his stomach that his teacher didn't like him because he was a Jew and no other reason.

Fighting back the tears Mordechi stumbled down the stairs because the tears made it hard for him to see. He didn't want his mother who was still at home to see him crying so he made a detour to see a friend of his who had a shop not far from where his school was located. Mordechi had so much on his mind he had not noticed all the people running in the direction of the synagogue. He wiped his eyes and stopped crying long enough to see the smoke and hear the screams of the people who were walking quickly to see what was happening. He figured since he wasn't going to school that he would see what was happening. As he got closer to the scene he noticed that the synagogue was on fire. Who could have done such a thing? The synagogue had such memories for all the Jews in the community. It was just a year ago that Mordechi had his bar-mitva. He had become a man and looked forward to one day owning his own business so that he could take care of his father and mother when they got old. They were good parents and he wanted that they should not have to work for the rest of their lives.

What could they do? The crowd just stood their looking in awe at the sight of so many years of memories going up in smoke. From day to day more and more of this happened it became the norm for their community. Life for the Jews had changed forever. Mordechi could hear his father and mother talking when he went to bed about how the Jews could no longer own their own businesses. They had been stripped of the right to have bank accounts and could only have a certain amount of money at home at one time. Life became more and more difficult. His father and mother had exhausted all of their resources and since most of their neighbors were in the same boat they could not help one another. He remembered the day when they ate their last potato. He went to bed hungry after that.

The Jews were made to wear white arm bands with the Star of David on them. They were branded so that all the people would know that they were Jews. Mordechi knew several of the Polish shop keepers in the area. There was a very nice man who felt sorry for him and would let him come in and work in his shop so that he and his family could have something to eat. It wasn't much but at least they would not starve. It was a blessing from heaven. They were surviving.

Mordechi told his son that he prayed the day would never come when he and his children would have to go through what he and his parents went through. No one should ever have to suffer like they did. His father received word that all of the Jews would be moved from their homes to a ghetto that wasn't big enough for the rats let alone all of the many families that lived in Krakau. It's amazing how just when you realize that you don't have much the Germans took that away and you had even less. They didn't even have much time to pack. Mordechi's family didn't have much but what they had they had worked hard for. It was their memories, their life and they were proud to be Jewish. His mother and father packed up what they could. The Germans came through the place like a flood. They went from door to door making sure that all the families were vacating their homes. Some people had thought ahead of time and had found places to hide. Mordechi's friend Shmuel's mother had already planned on giving her son to some Polish people who were a part of the underground railroad. When things calmed down they would get papers for him and sneak him across the border. They were not worried about themselves so much but they wanted their son to live.

Some families hid in the floorings in their apartments and some of them hid right in plane sight under leaves under the trees. If the people didn't move fast enough the Germans started to shoot people for no reason at all. They were brutal soldiers who didn't seem to have a heart or a soul. People were killed because they were old. Many of the Hasidic Jews were targeted for no reason. Mordechi saw a group of them placed against a wall. They knocked off their hats, cut off their curls and shot them all in the head. Mordechi could not forget the brutality that happened during the German occupation. He kept wondering why this was happening and if he would ever be free again.

Life was unbearable in the ghetto. Instead of one family to an apartment there were three or four families to one apartment. There was no privacy and certainly not enough food to go around. The rations were never enough to sustain them until the next time.

Just when it seemed as if life were just about as bad as it could get they received word that they were going to move everyone from the ghetto to work camps. The people had enough by this time. They were being treated worse than cattle on a ranch. At least the cattle were free to walk and roam as they pleased. They were fed and taken care of but his people were literally starving to death. Mordechi wished that he could somehow get out of there and go to his friend. He knew that he could hide him out maybe until the war was over. He was a good man and hated what was happening but he was helpless. But Mordechi was afraid that he would be shot and never see his parents ever again. He just could not leave them so he stayed. Many had left the ghetto never to be seen or heard of again. They could only wish for the best.

The work camps were from the pits of hell. Mordechi would pray and pray sometimes that God would kill him so that he would not have to endure any more pain and suffering. He was young and strong but after days without food and much sleep he was starting to look much older than his years. People were being killed every day at the work camps.

Each minute seemed like an eternity. They were starting to hear terrible stories about other camps like Auschwitz. The Jewish people were being put on trains and sent to what was called death camps. They heard that the people would be stripped naked and sent into these baths where they thought they would be taking a shower and they would be all gased to death. They heard that the bodies were piling up so much that they were being thrown into ditches like trash. They were not even allowed the dignity of a descent burial like human beings. All of these people were somebody. They all had names, families. It was horrible to even think of such a thing. Many would not believe but Mordechi knew somehow that this person had told the truth. It made him sick.

At night when he slept he could see the faces of the many people that were massacred while in the ghetto. There was no mercy for his people and it wasn't getting any better. He would say his prayers at night and plead with God that he would stop the killing and they would be saved. He knew that God was watching the atrocities against his people and that someday things would change. One night Mordechi had a dream and it was like he was looking down upon the work camp and next to him was an angel of the Most High God. He said to the angel "why is this happening and when will it end?"

The angel told him "Remember the story of your people when they lived in Egypt?"

Mordechi said "yes I remember the story."

The angel said "the Nazi's are just like the Pharaoh. They are greedy and care not about other people. They do not fear God but the day will come when God will release his people from this bondage. He will repay for every life that has been lost and he will make the way for his chosen people to return back to the land that he promised Father Abraham thousands of years ago."

Mordechi felt a sense of relief. "How long angel of God will this take place, my people are suffering and many won't hold out much longer?"

"Do not worry about time just know that God will deliver you and you will tell your sons and your daughters that God is still their God and that he delivered you just like he delivered his people in the Bible days."

Nothing had changed but Mordechi held onto the words of the angel that God was still with his chosen people and that he would deliver them and that he would live. Mordechi and many others were given the task of hauling away the many bodies that were killed every day. There was not one day that Mordechi could remember that someone was not killed for one reason or another. As he stood looking over the pile of dead bodies, they looked like skeletons, not much meat on the people because they were literally starving to death he literally blacked out. It was like he was there but he wasn't there. The same angel that he saw in his dreams was standing next to him. He said "Mordechi can these bones live?"

Mordechi said "only you know angel."

The angel of the Lord said to Mordechi, "prophecy to the bones and say unto them people of God you will live again."

Mordechi thought that he must have lost his mind. How could those that have died live again? But he was too afraid this was the angel of God. He surely knew something that Mordechi did not know. Sickened at the sight of the mountain of bodies that lay in the ditch Mordechi found his lips moving and speaking from his heart said "People of God, Father Abraham was told by God that he would bring forth from his loins a people that would be as vast as the stars in heaven. He said that we would be afflicted but that he would judge that nation and they would come out with great substance. God has done all that he said that he would do and more for our people. This affliction that we are enduring now is the same affliction but God has promised that his people would be a royal nation and that the land that he gave to Abraham would be for our people forever. As the word of the Lord spoken through my mouth we will live and I said we will live according to the covenant that God has made with us."

Mordechi stood motionless at the great heap only to be startled by one of the other young men. "Mordechi you had better stop daydreaming before someone sees you."

It was then that he turned his head and saw the Nazi officer riding on his horseback to the mountain. They had been given orders to burn all of the bodies. The stench was the most aweful smell that it made you sick to your stomach. The burning went on for many days there were so many bodies. The flames rose high in the sky and the ashes were so many that it filled the air like snow from a blizzard. The people's hearts sank with fair and despair. This would be there life until they died or the war ended. Things had not changed but Mordechi had heard a word from the Lord and he would hold onto it until the change came.

Ezekiel had never seen an angel but that angel came to his father and gave him the hope that he needed.

Ezekiel Chapter 2 – The Throne of God, 4656

Ezekiel and his wife were his father's only surviving relatives besides an uncle that moved to the United States after the war was over. His father's brother moved to Russia like the rest of the family. After making some money he decided to move his family away from the terrible memories of the war. Ezekiel contacted Stephen right away and he promised that he would be on the first plane out that afternoon.

Stephen felt that with the passing of each of his relatives that a very important part of history was slowly but surely being forgotten. When he moved to the United States he felt like he was in a time warp. The Jewish community was thriving like they were before the war started. He served as a painful reminder of what they could have been experiencing. Although they knew what had happened to their people it was all so real when they saw the actual numbers that were printed on his arm. Stephen felt like he would never get over what had happened to their family. They had lost so much. His brother was now gone and a part of him died that day. What a special boy Ezekiel was. How he loved his parents and how they loved him. He could remember the day that he was born and they took him to the synagogue to be named by the Rebbe. His brother was so proud of his boy. The family name would be carried now from generation to generation. He wanted the best for his son like any father would.

When the war was over Stephen married his best friend. Shortly after marrying they had their first child Peter. When little Peter was born he was the apple of his father's eye. It was always comforting for his mom and dad to look inside his crib and see a child that was not scorched with the past like his parents. He was born free and would never have to endure being treated with such hatred like the Jews that lived in Poland during the war. Two years later his sister Sarah was born. A new generation had been born and Stephen made sure that his son and daughter knew who they were as a people. He wanted them to know that they did not have to be afraid of their Jewish heritage, that there was so much to be proud of. He would be attending the funeral alone because after many years of marriage his beautiful bride had already passed on to heaven.

It would be hard going back to Russia. Stephen had not made many trips to Russia but he would call his brother often and send packages from the United States. He had made some investments over the years and had done well. He promised his brother that he would make sure he and his family never went hungry or did without anything that they needed. He had kept his promise and had also sent Ezekiel to a yeshiva to become a rebbe. Stephen felt that if it were not for the hand of God on the Jewish people they would have all been wiped out. Stephen wanted to give Ezekiel a chance at life that he and his brother had lost.

LaGuardia Airport was packed with people from one end to the other. Stephen took a cab to the airport. He wouldn't be staying very long so he only took a carry on. The airport was like a war zone people traveling all the time. He was used to traveling for his business and had his secretary to print out his boarding passes. Hopefully this would make things easier on him. He hated standing on line.

There was still plenty of time before they would call for boarding the plane so Stephen went to have some lunch and a cup of coffee in a small café in the airport terminal area. He walked through the area where they checked passenger luggage to see whether you had a bomb in it or something. The airport was the worst means of transportation after the Twin Tower bombing. People wanted to be safe but it was bordering on ridiculous. You couldn't even take your toiletries with you because they thought it might be a liquid bomb. Stephen just wanted to get through the metal detector without having to take his cloths off. The attendants seemed nice enough but their seemed to be some hold up in front but he couldn't make out what was happening. The man in front of him turned around to make conversation. "I cannot believe what they are doing?"

"What's happening? Is there some type of problem?"

"Well apparently that lady has something in her bag and they want her to step out of the line. She's giving them quite a fuss it seems."

"Well I don't blame her this is ridiculous they act like we are terrorists or something."

"Yeah."

Just then the police officer grabbed the young lady and threw her against the chair that he had asked her to sit down in while they looked in her bags. Other officers were coming from all over the terminal. You would have thought that there was a bomb in that bag or something. If it was they sure didn't make any announcements or anything. The woman was screaming and crying. Two officers were standing over her with police dogs. They were salivating and barking. It was scarey and for a minute Stephen could not believe what he was seeing. But like all of the other passengers he just looked on with fright and thanked God it wasn't him being subjected to such cruelty. It reminded him quickly of when the Nazi's came to move the Jews into the ghetto they were treated the exact same way. Had the United States of America, the land of the free and the home of the brave changed? If so when did it change? This type of thing was not supposed to happen in the United States.

Stephen's heart was beating really hard he didn't realize he had started to sweat. After passing through the metal detector he went into the men's room to get himself together before sitting down in the restaurant. The waitress brought him a menu and he asked if he could have a few minutes before ordering. She said that she would come back in about five minutes to take his order. He still had plenty of time before boarding his plane for Russia.

As he glanced at the menu he could hear the news report on television. The Palestinian president and the president of Israel were meeting at Camp David with the president of the United States to talk about the crisis between the two groups and what would be done about it. Stephen tried his best to stay out of politics but many of the Jews who survived the Holocaust eventually moved to Israel. There was a saying amongst the people "see you in Jerusalem." Stephen thought from time to time that before he died he and his brother would both go to Israel and die there with their ancestors. But now he would have to go alone.

Stephen felt in his heart that the U.S. should stay out of the business of the Jewish people and let them make their own decisions. But for some odd reason the Israeli prime minister seemed to keep having these so called peace talks. What peace? There would be no peace as long as the Jewish people were not allowed to live in their beloved Israel without bombs killing their children as they walked to school. Unfortunately, the Israelis in Israel were fighting for their right to be a people. Why is it that they are still fighting after so many wars just to be free? Stephen felt that he would never get the answer to this question as long as he lived. But he made a promise to himself that he would do everything within his power to help his people no matter the cost. He had lived his life and his children were old enough to take care of themselves. They didn't need him any longer. He would talk with them when he returned that he would like to leave the United States and live in his beloved Israel.

Since he had lost his appetite somewhat Stephen decided on just a small sandwich and a cup of coffee. The waitress brought his order within just a few minutes. He said a quick prayer and that his flight would bring him to his family safely. He longed to see the face of his little Ezekiel now a grown man with a family of his own.

Stephen could hear the faint voice of the flight attendant calling for the boarding of flight 221 to Russia. He quickly paid his bill, took a few more sips of his coffee and made his way to Gate 115. There were already oodles of people waiting to get aboard the plane. Men, women and children were waiting with great anticipation. First were called those with children and disabilities to get on board first. Then all other passengers were allowed to board. Stephen decided that this old man with such great fortune should be able to fly first class for a change. There would be less people in first class and he would be able to stretch out a bit more. Losing his brother made him realize that his fortune was not as important as life. You should enjoy the fortune before life was not there anymore to enjoy.

Stephen was assisted by a very beautiful flight attendant named Marcia with his luggage. She reminded him of his beautiful angel. When his daughter was born he was the happiest man on the planet. She just smiled all the time and he wanted to give her everything that would make a little girl happy. And she didn't have a hard time asking for whatever she wanted. But he obliged.

After everyone had boarded the plane the captain came over the loud speaker for everyone to take their seats that the plane would be taxing down the runway any moment. Marcia stood up front as he gave instructions about air masks, how long the flight would be etc. Marcia had been working this flight for the past couple of years and was a season veteran for everything the captain would say and when. Stephen was putting on his seat belt and making sure he had said a prayer for safety he put his head back and decided to take a nap he had a long way to go.

Stephen was startled at the voice of the flight attendant Marcia asking him whether he wished to have a beverage and what he would like for dinner later on in the flight. "Sorry sir to bother you but would you like to have a beverage? We have tea, coffee, an assortment of sodas or if you would like an alcoholic beverage we have wine, champagne, vodka and rum."

"Well I don't think I will have anything just now. I'll probably take a little nap and have something later."

"No problem. But would you mind telling me what you would like to have for dinner. This way I can have it all prepared for you when you wake up."

"Sure what will you be serving?"

"Sir you have a choice of fish, chicken or steak. Which would you like?"

"I guess I'll have the steak please."

The video news was activated while Marcia was taking Stephen's order. Stephen put his head back to take a nap but was startled when he saw that in the international news for Europe a cemetery for Holocaust survivors was desecrated. The tombstones were broken, some caskets were opened and bones were strewn across the lawn and swastikas were drawn on tombstones that were still partially standing. He could not believe what he was seeing. Tears stung his eyes as they poured out. He didn't want anyone to see him crying so he quickly took out a handkerchief and dabbed at his eyes. As if his heart could be broken even more than it was at that moment. He was on his way to bury his brother and now this.

Marcia had been standing on the side watching the news report and noticed the reaction of the man sitting just to her right which was Stephen. She wanted to say something but didn't want to intrude. But since he wasn't sleeping she went to the cupboard and retrieved some peanuts and drinks and put them on the tray so she wouldn't look obvious. She also made for him a small plate with cheese, crackers and fruit. Maybe he just needed a friend, someone to show him some love and compassion.

"Hi. I'm sorry to bother you but I thought that maybe you would like to have a beverage and a snack. I noticed that you were watching the news instead of napping like you mentioned."

"Wow. Thank you so very much. Its nice to see that there are still some nice people in the world today. Did you hear what they just said on the news about the cemetery of Holocaust survivors?"

"Oh yes. I just cannot believe how people are being so hateful today. You know in the last three months a nun was beaten and raped in a church. Someone came in and found her almost dead. A female pastor was killed in the church and her body left for the congregation to find. Children are being kidnapped, raped and killed almost every day and now they are shooting people in the churches and people are lobbying to carry guns to church now. Sir I'm sorry what is your name?"

"I'm Stephen and what is your name?"

"I'm Marcia. I don't know what your religious affiliation is but I'm Christian. I'm just totally appalled at what I see happening in the world today."

"Well I'm Jewish Marcia. The reason why this has so much meaning to me is that I and my family survived the Holocaust. I'm going home to bury my only brother and this has increased the pain that I am feeling." Tears begin to stream down Stephen's face.

"Stephen a wise man once said this "in the last days before the Messiah comes that many shall come in my name, saying, I am Christ: and shall deceive many. And you shall hear of wars and rumours of wars; see that you be not troubled: for all these things must come to pass, but the end is not yet. For nation shall rise against nation, and kingdom against kingdom: and there shall be famines, and pestilences, and earthquakes, in diverse places. All these are the beginning of sorrows. Then shall they deliver you up to be afflicted, and shall kill you: and you shall be hated of all nations for my name's sake. And then shall many be offended, and shall betray one another, and shall hate one another. And many false prophets shall rise, and shall deceive many. And because iniquity shall abound, the love of many shall wax cold. But he that shall endure unto the end, the same shall be saved."

"He sounds like a very wise man. Marcia do you know how many people made a lot of money on the blood of my people? The Nazi's made a lot of money on the blood of the Jewish people and even some Christians died in the Holocaust as well. When will it all end? I'm tired Marcia. I'm an old man. I was just thinking about how my brother and I made a plan that we would one day return to Israel the place that our God gave to our people. Now that he has died I will have to go alone. I have made lots of money and have raised my children. I refuse to die in a country that doesn't care about me."

"Stephen I had the privilege of going to Israel. I felt a tugging from God that I should visit the place where Jesus walked. I don't know whether you know it or not but this Jesus that we Christian's believe is our Messiah was a Jewish man. Did you know that?"

"I have lots of Christian friends that I do business with but we agree to disagree about Jesus. I don't doubt that he was a Jewish man but as for the Messiah I'm not too sure about that. But you know Marcia all I know is that we need him now. Things have gotten so bad in the world. They don't have any morals. People don't care about each other. I didn't grow up like this. We loved each other and cared deeply for family and our fellowman."

"I understand Stephen. Well I'm here for you if you need to talk again. I will put this here for you if you would like to have a snack. I'm terrible I always eat when I feel depressed."

"Thank you Marcia. You are a good person. You remind me of my daughter."

Stephen felt he just wanted to put his head back for a moment and he slipped into a deep sleep. He had a dream unlike anything that he had ever had before. In this dream he could hear a voice like the voice of thunder, and he was standing upon a mountain and there was a man standing with him but he was not like any man that he had ever seen in life before. The man stood as tall as the trees. He had on a white robe with a golden sash around his waist like a belt. He had the deepest blue eyes that Stephen had ever seen and there was fire all around him like it would engulf him but the man was not burned. He stood with a sword in his hand. He made no movement, nor made any sounds but just stood looking off into the distance. The power was so strong I fell to the ground.

And he said to me "Stephen I am Michael, Captain of the host I must speak with you. I am the one who watches over Israel."

The spirit entered me and raised me to my feet. I heard a loud voice saying, "Stephen I have called you to go to my people Israel. You must warn them that the Messiah is soon to come but they are not yet ready for him. Before the children of Israel left Egypt they had sinned against God with the children of Egypt, they took their gods and forsook the God of Abraham, Isaac and Jacob. They ate what was not clean before God and sacrificed to idols. If Abraham had been there he would have been sorrowful for his children. Today they are no different. The children of Abraham have forsaken their God and have taken new gods. Instead of taking care of the widows and orphans they put their money into banks that will one day take all that they have earned. My youth run the streets and do not enter into the synagogue to give honor unto God. You rely upon military might, guns, tanks and other governments to protect you. Only the Lord thy God loves you like his bride and he will never leave you nor forsake you. Go to them and tell them that the Messiah will soon come and they must repent and prepare for his coming."

"Michael, Captain of the host how will we know that it is him? There have been many that have come and said that they were the messiah but our people are non the better."

"Remember the words of the Prophet Esaias, "For unto us a child is born, unto us a son is given: and the government shall be upon his shoulder: and his name shall be called Wonderful Counsellor, The mighty God, The everlasting Father, The Prince of Peace.

A virgin shall conceive and bear a son and shall call his name Immanuel. Butter and honey shall he eat, that he may know to refuse the evil, and choose the good.

Who has believed our report? And to whom is the arm of the Lord revealed? For he shall grow up before him as a tender plant, and as a root out of a dry ground: he had no form nor comeliness; and when we shall see him, there is no beauty that we should desire him. He is despised and rejected of men; a man of sorrows, and acquainted with grief: and we hid as it were our faces from him; he was despised, and we esteemed him not. Surely he had borne our griefs, and carried our sorrows: yet we did esteem him stricken, smitten of God, and afflicted. But he was wounded for our transgressions, he was bruised for our iniquities: the chastisement of our peace was upon him; and with his stripes we are healed."

Then said he unto me "I know what is in your heart. Remember that Moses was called of God when he was older than you are now. Do not worry about whether you can speak well or whether the people will respond to your message. It is not for you to make them listen but it is for you to give the message to the people. So you will not worry I will give you two scrolls one scroll will have several messages on them. You will give them as I tell you to and when these things come to pass they will know that you are a man of God. Take this scroll and you must eat it now. It will taste bitter in your mouth but it will be sweet when it gets into your belly. The other scroll you must guard with your life. You will take this scroll to Israel and give it to a person that I will tell you of when you get there. Trust in me and I will take care of you and tell you of many things which are to come."

With that the angel was gone and Stephen woke up from his dream. He looked around the plane like he couldn't believe what had just happened. He would have to tell Ezekiel about this but no one else. No one would ever believe what he would have to say. Stephen hid the scroll in his bag.

Ezekiel Chapter 3 – The Funeral

It is customary in the Jewish community to have the body buried within a day when possible but since family and loved ones were coming from far away it took a few days before the funeral could take place. Rebbe Isak was called right away to help the family prepare the funeral arrangements. Shalom took care of all the funeral arrangements for the members of the synagogue. He and his father owned their own funeral home. The body was removed from the home and immediately taken to the funeral home for Taharah or purification. Ezekiel had not asked for anything special to be done so Mordechi would be dressed in the traditional plain linen shroud call Tachrichim.

The wooden box that Mordechi would rest in would be simple. It was not their tradition to have flowers or fancy caskets. It was considered to be a waste of money. Mordechi was a simple man all of his life and valued every day of his life. The most important thing for him was family, friends and his love for God. He was so excited when his only son took to studying Hebrew and the Torah. Ezekiel would come home many times after studying to tell his father about the great things the Rebbe had to say about the sages from of old and the wise prophets that spoke to God and did his work on the earth.

After the body had been prepared for burial it was customary that someone stay with the body at all times. Mordechi had been a part of Beth El since moving to Russia so that Rebbe took care of all the arrangements. Ezekiel wanted to be the first to stand watch over his father. As was customary Ezekiel recited Psalm 23 in respect for his father. "The Lord is my shepherd; I shall not want. He makes me to lie down in green pastures; he leads me beside the still waters. He restoreth my soul: he leadeth me in the paths of righteousness for his name's sake. Yeah, though I walk through the valley of the shadow of death, I will fear no evil; for thou art with me; thy rod and thy staff they comfort me. Thou preparest a table before me in the presence of mine enemies; thou anointest my head with oil; my cup runneth over. Surely goodness and mercy shall follow me all the days of my life; and I will dwell in the house of the Lord forever."

Ezekiel tried not to cry but the tears began to flow and all he wanted was that this was not his father in this casket. What was he going to do with the rest of his life now? He had a family but he and his father had always talked about the family leaving Russia and going back to the holy land. Should he still go? He would have to speak with his uncle when he arrived after the funeral. He would now be father and confidant for the family. Stephen's plane would be arriving in the morning and the funeral would be held that afternoon, just enough time for him to rest.

When the plane touched down in Russia Stephen was relieved. He flew a lot but truly hated it most of the time. There were so many plane crashes of recent that he was apprehensive every time he put his life in their hands. It had been quite a few years before he saw Ezekiel and wasn't sure that he would recognize his nephew. He still called him little Ezekiel but yet he was a full grown man. He already had his luggage so he went to the information desk just in case Ezekiel had left some instructions for him there. As he walked through the terminal he remembered for a quick moment the first time he and his wife had boarded to plane for America. It was a bittersweet day but there was no turning back.

He saw a row of men and women with signs on large cards that would be picking up people from the airport. There was a man just at the end that looked just like his brother, it just had to be Ezekiel. He walked in his direction smiling and almost running. He finally looked in his direction and called out to him. "Uncle Stephen is that you?" The two men hugged and embraced one another. "It's me son, it's me."

Overwhelmed at the meeting of his little Ezekiel who had grown up to be quite a strapping young man, Stephen began to bawl like a baby. "Ezekiel I cannot believe that my brother is gone."

"Yes Stephen he has left us. He says that now you will be the keeper of the family. We will talk after the funeral. I'm sorry but we have all the arrangements made for this afternoon. We don't have much time. We need to get you to the house to wash and prepare."

" I know. I'm sorry I couldn't get here any quicker." The two men quickly drove over to the house so Stephen could take a shower and change his clothing. Raisa and Aliya were already dressed. Raisa had a hard time explaining to Aliya that her grand father was no longer with them. She had not had to deal with death of someone so close to her before. She was just a little baby when her grand mother died. It would be a long process and so Aliya asked many questions. Perhaps the funeral would help some. Rebbe Isak was really good at talking with little children.

The silence in the car was almost deafening. But little Aliya broke the silence by asking her mom if she could go and visit her grand father in the Garden of Eden. Raisa was caught off guard with this question. "No Aliya we cannot go to visit him right now but one day we will all go and he will be waiting for you there."

Aliya could not quite grasp why she could not go to this garden and see her grand father. But she didn't pose the question again. By that time they had arrived at the funeral home there were many people from the synagogue and the local neighborhood. Mordechi was well known and loved in his community. The family members were seated and the congregation all took a seat when Rebbe Isak came in the room.

You could here a pin drop in the room as the rebbe began to speak, "God full of mercy, who dwells on high, grant proper rest under the wings of the divine presence in the lofty levels of the holy and pure ones, who shine like the glory of the firmament – for the soul of our brother the Jewish people, the holy and pure, who fell at the hands of murderers whose blood was spilled in Auschwitz, in Madjanet, in Triblinka and the other camps of destruction in Europe, who were slain, burned, and slaughtered, and who were buried alive with extreme cruelty for the sanctification of the divine name. For we, their sons, their daughters, their brothers, and their sisters, will contribute to charity in remembrance of their souls. May their resting place in paradise – therefore may the master of mercy shelter them beneath his wings for eternity; and may we bind their souls in the bond of life. God is their inheritance, and may they repose in peace in their resting place. Now let us say – Amen."

I and the family of Mordechi thank you for coming today to remember a great man. I look at the life of my good friend and it reminds me of what life is really all about. Mordechi was a lover of family, friends and living a holy life before God as the Torah teaches us all to live. He was a good Jew and loved his people. His only hope was that one day he and his family could leave this place and live in Jerusalem. Many of us here today survived a most horrendous time in the history of the Jewish people. But Mordechi like most of us want to move on with our lives and build a better world in which our children will never have to be afraid to be Jewish. They will not have to lose their lives in a work camp or in a death camp. Let's not forget those who were there during the struggle. Let's not forget that there is a new generation that need to know about what took place so that it won't happen again. In his memory and for the memory of all those who died in the death camps and the work camps that as long as anti-semitism still exists in the world that we will aid in the struggle for freedom for our people to live in peace."

The rebbe came down and shook the hands of Ezekiel and Stephen, Mordechi's son and brother. The procession of cars was so long that you would have thought that some dignitary had died. Mordechi was truly loved by all in the community. The group moved on to the burial sight where they could pray and put their beloved son to rest. The rebbe and all the congregation joined together in the last prayer for Mordechi,

(May His great Name grow exalted and sanctified in the world that He created as he willed. May He establish His reign for His kingship in your lifetime and in your days and in the lifetime of the entire Family of Israel, swiftly and soon. Amen. May His great Name be blessed forever and ever. Blessed, praised, glorified, exalted, extolled, mighty, upraised, and lauded be the Name of the Holy One, Blessed is He beyond any blessing and song, praise and consolation that are uttered in the world. Amen. May there be abundant peace from Heaven. And good life upon us and upon all Israel. Amen. He who makes peace in His heights, May He make peace upon us, and upon all Israel. Amen.)

Mordechi was finally put to rest and the family and some friends came back to the house for a time together. Rebbe Isak had not seen Stephen in many years and had much that he wanted to say but this was not the appropriate time for catching up. He had to make sure that he spoke with him because Mordechi had asked on his death bed that he would speak with him and give him the envelope that he had prepared. Ezekiel was in such deep sorrow that when he got back to the house he locked himself away in his room for quite a few hours before he emerged to speak with anyone. Raisa understood how deeply he was grieving and so did the rest of the family.

Ezekiel Chapter 4 – The Letter

After the funeral Stephen felt the full weight of the responsibility of taking over the family. Ezekiel was grieving, Raisa didn't know how to comfort him and little Aliya needed love and guidance now more than ever. He called home to tell his son and daughter he really needed to stay in Russia for a lot longer than he had anticipated so he could help the family and get them back on track again. Ezekiel took some time off from work although he had just started teaching the classes at the synagogue. Rebbe Isak understood his situation and wanted to help out as much as possible. He came to the house quite frequently to visit with him and make sure he was taking care of himself and his responsibilities at home. He knew that he would come through eventually but he was worried nevertheless.

After a few days Isak came by to talk with Stephen and take him around the old neighborhood. He really wanted to have a talk with him about what Mordechi said before he died. Mordechi had a lot on his mind but was grateful to have some time with his old friend. He could not believe how the place had changed. "Isak I cannot believe how the area is growing. My little Ezekiel is not so little anymore and that little Aliya looks just like her grand mother. She would have been proud."

"I know. She is amazing. She loved her grand father. She will deeply miss him. They had a special bond and he took a lot of time to teach her the prayers and tell her about the sages and the struggle of our people. Stephen I have something for you that your brother gave me just shortly before he died. You don't have to read it now it is a private matter. But he really wants that you should take the family to Israel so that little Aliya can be a free Jew and not have to suffer the way that we did."

"It's funny Isak that you would speak of this. You might think that I am an old man that has lost his mind. But on the plane while coming here I had a dream Isak. It was just out of the Torah if you know what I mean. I spoke with the Angel Michael. He told me that God wanted me to go to Israel and that there was something that he wanted me to do. What Isak can an old man like me accomplish? I'm not good looking, I don't have a big college education, nor do I have great sums of money. I can't imagine what I can do for God. But you don't say no to God am I right?"

Isak wasn't quite sure how to respond to this but he was an holy man and still believed in the miraculous things of God. "Well Stephen many of our sages received revelation from God not in their early years but in their later years when they had lived life some and could understand what the people were experiencing at that time. Abraham and Moses were both old men when they received the word from God. So this is not unusual."

"But why me Isak? Now my brother on the other hand he was the great man of God. He was the holy one. I left here to pursue money and a dream to take care of my family financially. I have not been to synagogue in so long that I'm ashamed to even tell you. My beautiful wife would be so angry with me. Why would God want me to do anything?" Stephen put his head down into his hands.

Isak began to laugh. "It's not for us to know how God works Stephen. Maybe this is his way of getting you to get back to synagogue and the Torah readings. Read your Torah and you will see that there are many people in the Torah that were not good Jewish people. God is saying that its not about us but it is about him. Did he not use a prostitute, a Gentile to be a blessing to the children of Israel as they went into the promised land. If he could use the Gentiles then he could use anybody. There is definitely a need for reform amongst our people. We are no longer one body anymore Stephen like in the days of the

Torah. Something bad has happened. Perhaps God is going to use you and some others to get this back on track again. We have no Temple in Jerusalem anymore. The Temple was the center of Jewish life. All of this has changed and the Jewish people are lost. We need to get back to what Moses taught to us. Read the Torah Stephen it will guide you into all truth about what God wants you to do. If you need me I will be here for you. Who knows maybe I will go with you."

Isak returned Stephen back to the house he felt good that he had accomplished what his friend had asked him to do. He was interested in what Mordechi had to say to his brother but didn't dare to ask him what he had written in the letter. He would tell him if he wanted to at another time. It was so good seeing his good friend. Isak was busy with the synagogue and didn't have the time nor the money to travel to the States to see Stephen.

Stephen needed to connect with his nephew but wasn't quite sure what to do at the moment. He was grieving so and he had the right to grieve. The Torah speaks of morning but it should be only for a season. He would give him time to do this and then he had to get his mind refocused on life again. After dinner he retired to his room to read the letter that Mordechi had written to him. What was wrong with him he should have called him then he could have come right away and had time with his brother before he died. But perhaps he had no idea that he was so close to death. Stephen sat down in a reclining chair next to the window opening the letter with great care. This was the last voice of his brother that he would hear forever. Stephen pulled the letter out of the envelope like he was pulling the torah scroll out to be read at the synagogue. It must have been important if Mordechi wrote it down. He wasn't much on writing. The contents of the letter would be treasured forever. Mordechi wrote, "To my brother and friend forever, one day we shall see each other again in paradise. If you are reading this letter this means that I have passed on. I'm sorry that we did not get a chance to see one another before this time. I know that you have been very busy and that coming home sometimes brings back terrible memories for you. Business first I have been putting away some money for Ezekiel and his family to return to Israel. He has no knowledge of this but please retrieve it from my bank account and go with them to

Israel. Remember this was our dream. Do all that you can to help our people Stephen. I see things now that remind me of the days of old before our people were put into the camps. It is very unsettling to me and I am afraid for the Jewish people.

Most importantly Stephen you might not believe what I am about to tell you but what I am about to tell is the truth the whole truth and nothing but the truth. You know that I would never lie to you. Quite a few years ago I had a very unsettling dream. At first I had no idea what I was seeing. I thought that maybe I was having flashbacks from the war but I could see hundreds of people at what looked like a work camp and men, women and children were being put on these trains just like what happened to us. A voice kept saying they are going to the death camps, they are going to the death camps. I wanted to scream no, no not the death camps but there was no one to tell. They took them to these camps where many of them were put into large showers where they were gased to death. There were large pits with dead bodies in them. I could smell the stench, Stephen it was the same stench that we smelled when the bodies of our people were put into the pits and burned like garbage. Why was I seeing this? But what was even more unsettling was what I saw next. I saw large submarines, Russian submarines sitting in the waters on the coasts of the United States. They were just sitting there and waiting. I could hear a voice saying they have no idea that they are there. One day they will strike and the American people will be forced into labor camps and death camps like the Jews during the war. I wanted to wake up but I couldn't wake up. I saw hundreds of thousands of people going into the work camps and the death camps and they were all being given a number. The number was put either in their foreheads or their arms. It reminded me of the number that we were given when we entered the work camps and the death camps. Stephen if this is going to happen the American people and the Jewish people in America must know about what is about to happen to them before it is too late. Please Stephen get my family out of Russia and get your family out of the United States before it is too late."

Stephen could not believe what his brother was saying. Certainly there had to be some mistake. But he knew his brother. He would never lie to him about anything. If he saw this in the dream then he most certainly saw it. What could Russia be thinking? What if anything did this have to do with his dream? Maybe he was being asked to warn the Jewish people of another war to come that could take millions of lives like before. If so he would have to talk with Ezekiel and his children about this. Would they believe him? Would they think that this old man had indeed lost his mind? Time would tell.

Stephen sat speechless for a long time. He had no idea that several hours had passed by. It was not time to speak with Ezekiel about this. He had enough on his mind. This would most definitely be difficult for him to deal with. He would find the right time. In the mean time he would retrieve the money that his brother left and wait to speak with Ezekiel.

Ezekiel Chapter 5 – The Explosion

Weeping may endure for a night but joy comes in the morning. Stephen knew that was somewhere in the Torah and hoped that Ezekiel knew too. It was just a few days since his brother had been buried but he really needed to talk with Ezekiel about what his father had revealed to him. This was a very serious matter. The next morning Ezekiel seemed to be doing much better. He came down for breakfast which he had not done before. Little Aliya was full of life and energy as usual. She took one look at her father and said "father don't look so sad grand father came to me last night and told me that he was doing well and that he missed us all. He told me to be a big girl and take care of you and mommy. I promised him that I would take care of you. He also said to tell you that you need to learn how to go on without him." Ezekiel raised his eyes to look at Aliya. She was so young and pure. Even though she was just a young girl her eyes sparkled like the stars but she had a grown up way about her as well. He could not believe what she had just said. After all she was only five years old. She never made up things such as this. Could his father have really come to her and spoke to her? He wasn't sure but somehow the thought of it made him feel just a little bit better inside. He realized just then that he had a wonderful wife and daughter. He needed to get it together and move on. He owed them that. It didn't mean he didn't love his father but he had no right to die with him he was still alive and they needed him.

Stephen came down to breakfast and was glad to see Ezekiel sitting at the table with his family. Raisa was feeling good about it too. She was humming as she made the breakfast. It had been a long time since Stephen had family with him for breakfast. Stephen realized what he had been missing in his life. There were no children running around the house. No laughter or conversation for him every day. His children had their own lives so this felt good. The air was still a little bit thick but Stephen wanted to break the silence. "Ezekiel you are looking much better this morning."

"Stephen please forgive me for my absence I just needed to be alone to deal with my loss for a moment. I'm so glad that you are here. We need you now more than ever. Would you like to go over and see the new changes to the synagogue? It's been a while since you have been here. They have done many upgrades to the school for the children. Soon we just might have enough money for a school for the younger children Aliya's age. I just started teaching just before father died. He was so proud that I had accepted a teaching position their. It is very important to him that the children know the Torah. He is right about that."

"That would be wonderful." Stephen felt good that his nephew was coming out of his slump and he would be able to talk with him about serious matters soon. But he would tell him part of what his father spoke about in the letter. "Ezekiel I have something to tell you."

"What is it Stephen?"

"Well your father and I often spoke about one day taking our families to Israel. It was very important to both of us. I think that you may have shared in this dream with us but I had no idea that he was saving money for it. In a letter he wrote to me he said that he had been saving money for the day when we would go. Since he is no longer here he wanted that I retrieve this money from the bank so that we could all go. I don't know how much he saved but I was actually thinking about going back on the plane ride over here. What do you think about this?"

34

"Stephen I too wanted so much that our little family would go to Israel together. I had no idea that my father was saving money for the day. I don't know I guess in a way I wanted it to happen but never really thought that we would ever go. But I never wanted my father to think that. I mean where would we get the money? But here he was thinking ahead. I truly miss him. I guess we are going to Israel. Let's talk more about it."

"Okay. Let's go to the synagogue and then to the bank to see how much money your father saved up. But not to worry because I have some money saved up myself. We will do just fine Ezekiel. By the way I never got a chance to tell you how proud I am of you. You have taken such great care of the family."

"Thank you." All of a sudden there was a loud noise like a bomb had gone off. It was so loud and close too that the building they lived in actually shook. Stephen and Ezekiel looked at each other with such fright in their eyes. Raisa came running downstairs screaming. "What was that? Ezekiel please go out and see what has happened."

Ezekiel and Stephen were both afraid to go outside. They could only imagine the worse. As they opened the door they saw people running from everywhere. The synagogue and school were not far away so the two men walked in that direction. There was an old man screaming and crying coming from that direction, "they bombed the synagogue, the children are inside, they bombed the synagogue!"

Ezekiel was beside himself with fear and anger. He could not believe that such a thing could be happening in his day. He would have been working if he had not been at home mourning his father's death. He and Stephen stopped for a moment in shock and only looked at each other. They were afraid that he was right and how would they deal with it if it were true. Then Ezekiel began to run and scream down the street. "Isak, Isak". Isak was to be working that morning. Had he been inside? Had the children been inside when the bomb went off? He could not believe his eyes as he turned the corner where the synagogue and school sat. Someone had indeed set off a bomb in the school. He felt like it was the war all over again. There was lots of smoke and fire. The whole structured had not collapsed but it was well on its way. The children had not been there a few hours after their parents dropped them off when it hit. The school had only a few teachers but since the school was growing quickly Ezekiel was asked to be assigned to a group of students. The school was growing as the community grew. There were fire trucks and police officers emerging on the site as onlookers and parents rushed inside the burning building to see if anyone was still alive. Ezekiel told Stephen to stay outside and that he would go inside to see if he could help.

There were several classrooms but Ezekiel knew the building like the back of his hand. He could make his way although the smoke and fire made in virtually impossible to maneuver if you had not already known before. He was coughing uncontrollably as the thick, black smoke bellowed throughout the building like a cloud. Firemen were running hoses to combat the fire. He could hear the faint cries of children who were stuck under the debris since the ceiling had fallen in on them. It was amazing that anyone could have survived that explosion. "Help, help." He could hear just in front of him. "Who is that?" "It's me David. Help me I'm stuck."

"I'm right here David. It's me Ezekiel. I'll get you out. Just keep talking so I can follow your voice." The poor little boy was stuck under a desk. The ceiling had fallen and he had somehow been pinned down under the desk as it fell. It was a good thing because it probably saved his life with all the debris that had fallen from the ceiling. Ezekiel followed his voice and found him and several others in the same area. Such brave little soldiers. Ezekiel tunneled his way through the debris and the desks and helped the children out. One of the boys had a broken leg, Ezekiel picked him up and walked the children out. There was about five of them. They were all taken to the hospital for medical help. Ezekiel had not seen Isak or any of the other teachers outside anywhere. He began to ask of the people outside whether they had seen him. No one had remembered seeing him come outside at any time. Ezekiel ran back into the building. Slowly some of the teachers were being followed by students from their classes. The fire was being contained but he had to go in and find out what happened to his friend, he was not going to lose another person so quickly. This time he went into the synagogue because maybe he had been in there praying or something when the bomb went off. He often times would go in to the synagogue to pray before school started. The synagogue was a mess. They would have to rebuild the whole thing and they had just made upgrades to the place. As he walked through the rubble he would call out his name "Isak, Isak are you in here? Please my friend answer me if you are in here." He heard a faint cough over by the Torah cabinet. He could not believe what he saw next. Isak had been pinned down by a large pillar that had fallen on him. There was no time to waste because the fire had started to spark again and the smoke was getting thicker. Ezekiel had almost fallen one time and if he passed out he might not make it back out. All of the efforts were being concentrated on getting the children out. No one thought to check the synagogue.

Ezekiel needed help so he had to go back out and get help. But before he did he wanted Isak to know that he was coming back for him. He made his way to where Isak was laying, "my friend, hold on. I cannot move the pillar, please don't give up. I will be back with help for you." Isak could barely talk and he was bleeding from a large gash on his head. Ezekiel fought back the tears and made his way back outside to tell the firemen that there was someone trapped inside the synagogue and that he needed help.

The head fireman told three men to go with him and they brought oxygen to help Isak to breathe while they got him lose from the rubble that was on top of him. Isak seemed to have passed out in the mean time so they made it back just in time. A part of the ceiling had collapsed and the rest seemed like it was going to go anytime. They had to move and move quickly. They tied a rope around the pillar and all of the men used all of their strength to move it just a little while Ezekiel pulled Isak from out of the way. They brought a gourney in because his injuries were such that they didn't want to make it any worse. Ezekiel felt that he could breath now that his friend and mentor was alive.

He couldn't help but notice how the beautiful synagogue that held so many memories for him and the whole community was gone. It would take lots of time and money to fix it up or build a new one. Who would want to do such a thing? Without thinking he went over to the Torah cabinet which amazingly was still in tact. Only he would think let me get the Torah out of the cabinet before the fire reaches it. He ran for the cabinet tearing away parts of the ceiling that had fallen.

He had to break the glass cabinet open and retrieve the Torah but he managed to get it out safely.

In all the mayhem he had lost track of where Stephen was. When he was convinced that all of the teachers and students had been safely rescued he started searching for Stephen amongst all of the onlookers, parents and emergency personnel. He was a sight for sore eyes. He had really forgotten that he had the Torah scroll in his hands. When he finally saw Stephen he broke down in tears as Stephen opened his arms to embrace his nephew.

"Stephen Isak is hurt, take the Torah scroll back to the house and put it in a safe place. I will be going with him to the hospital to make sure that he is taken care of. I promise you I will not rest until I find out why this has happened to us. The government must find out who did this and make them pay."

Stephen took the scroll and went back to the house to tell Raisa and Aliya what had happened and make sure that they were safe. He knew that his brother was right. This was no longer the place for his family and they would have to get out soon or maybe pay with their lives.

Ezekiel Chapter 6 – The Mob

Ezekiel jumped into the back of the ambulance to go with his friend to the hospital. Isak was in shock from his injuries and was not aware that Ezekiel was there nor that he was on his way to the hospital to fight for his life. A million things was going through Ezekiel's mind as they entered the hospital. This bomb was intentionally set while innocent men and children were in praying. What kind of animal could do such a thing? It reminded him of the stories his father told him when he was a little boy. The burning of the synagogue was an outward sign of a system that did not want Jewish people within their society. Now the same thing was happening. He had often times said that what had happened to them before could not possibly happen again. But the truth of the matter was that it was happening all over again. It could have been his beautiful Aliya in that building. The children could have been killed. He had to do something but what? He had no idea what he could do.

Isak was in a terrible shape and the doctor said that he would have to have surgery but he would live. He had almost lost another father that day and it was too much to bare. While sitting in the waiting room they were already replaying the mass confusion of the day on the news. One news reporter said that Al Qaeda a terrorist organization said that the Jewish people didn't have a right to live on the planet and that this was justice for all the terrible things that they had done wrong in the past. What wrong have the Jewish people done to the world? The president of Iran also made some terrible comments that the Jewish people were lying about the Holocaust and that it never happened. Ezekiel was dumfounded at what he was hearing. Maybe he could be a voice for his community. He would talk with Stephen about contacting some of his friends in America and asking them to put pressure on the government to find out who did this and if there could be any justice for the children and teachers who almost lost their lives. There was an atmosphere of Anti-semitism creeping up in the world. It would only mean disaster for his people and if they sat down and did nothing then their destruction would be swift and sure.

Many of the students had been released to their parents with minor cuts and bruises but those who had more extensive injuries had been brought to the hospital. The parents were arriving and waiting in the emergency section just like Ezekiel. It was utter chaos. Mothers and fathers were crying as stretchers with wounded children were being brought in for treatment. One woman was hysterical and the nurse could not get her to let the child's hand go. Ezekiel stepped over because he knew her pain and gently put his hand around her and slowly removed her hand so that the nurse could take her into the examination room. She threw her arm around Ezekiel and cried like a baby. This was her only child. She would have died without her. "Come let's sit down here. She will be okay. Let them help her."

"Rebbe what is happening to our world? When children cannot go to school without getting hurt? Many of our parents and ancestors died in the work camps and death camps. We cannot live through that again. I'm going to get my daughter out of this country and go to America or Israel. It's no longer safe here."

"I know how you feel. Do not tell anyone Sarai but my family will be leaving for Israel as soon as possible. My father always dreamed of the day when we would all go but he died before we got the chance. But we are still here. For my family's sake and my father we will leave here soon and I admonish the rest of the people to do the same."

A group of the men had gathered together around the water cooler and one of them had started to get pretty loud. Ezekiel could not help but hear him from where he was sitting. He went over to see what they were talking about. "Gentlemen you are getting a bit loud. You will trouble the children. They have already had a very difficult time. You must all keep it together for their sakes."

"Keep it together, keep it together! Our children were blown up like they were not even worthy to be in the world. Why should we be calm? Who cares about us Ezekiel? We should all get together and burn this whole town down. They don't care about us so why should we care about them? They call us terrible names, we cannot hold our heads up like men and now they desecrate our holy temple. What's next? Will we be back in camps again? Will they put us in gas chambers again? Mark my words Ezekiel if something doesn't happen I promise you someone will die next time. I don't plan on it being me or my loved ones. If we cannot live here in peace then we will not live here at all."

The rest of the mob started yelling too. Ezekiel couldn't blame them because he was feeling the same kind of sickness in his stomach as they were. He wanted to protect his family. He didn't want to see anyone killed but the facts were clear that they were not wanted here.

"Simon I know how you feel but don't talk about hurting anyone. There are more of them than we. If we strike out at them it will only make matters worse. I will go to the authorities, the police, the press and anyone who will listen and tell the world what is happening to us here. Maybe that will get them listening. I don't really know what to do. My uncle Stephen knows some people in America maybe they have contacts to get some answers about what is happening.

"Ezekiel I hope that you are right. This will be good but I think that we ought to have a meeting amongst the community and come together on this thing. We have to do something. I feel so helpless."

Although Ezekiel knew no more than anyone else all of a sudden the parents started coming to him and asking if he could find out who did this, why were they being picked on and what could be done to make sure that it didn't happen again? Ezekiel was dumbfounded. Why he was being chosen he didn't know but all that he knew was that he wanted answers too.

The doctor came and told Ezekiel that Isak had come through surgery just fine. He would not wake up for several hours so he should come back to see him the next day. He felt good that his friend would be okay. He was sure that Raisa and Stephen were worried that they had not heard from him yet so he went home to give them an update on what was happening. When he opened the door he was greeted by his beautiful little Aliya. "Daddy, where have you been, we were all worried about you? How is Isak?"

"Hello darling, Isak is doing better. He had surgery today but the doctor said that he will be fine. I will go and visit with him at the hospital tomorrow."

Raisa and Stephen were standing by listening to what he was saying. "Stephen, Raisa the people are all worried about what took place today. I too am worried but I didn't want them to see it. Someone has got to keep a level head about all of this. But I have decided that the community must come together and we will call a meeting in a few days. This way we can all be on the same page. Many are talking about leaving, some are talking about fighting and the other's well I'm not sure what they are thinking. But I know that in most cases fear is talking and that will not be good."

Stephen was boiling inside. "Well do you blame them Ezekiel? They know what has happened to the Jewish people before. We are sitting ducks. It's them against us. No one seems to care about the Jewish people. I'm going to call a friend of mine from New York. He works for one of those big newspapers. He's a Jewish man. He cares believe me. He has gotten into a lot of trouble because he does articles in favor of the Jewish people maintaining Israel as a Jewish state and not a Jewish/Palestinian state. There is nothing in the Torah that states that we have to sell Jerusalem. We have given enough the Jewish people and its high time that the people of the world stop trying to exterminate us. He will come here and we will tell him our story about what happened here. He will tell the world."

"This is what I was telling Simon. We must find productive ways of fighting our cause. They want to burn down the place. If we start doing what they are doing to us then we are no better than they are. Murderer's is what they are. We are peaceful people and we are going to stay that way."

The next few days passed by without incident. Ezekiel and Stephen finally got a chance to take care of Mordechi's estate with the bank and work on organizing the community. The people were all afraid since the bombing. The authorities were giving out no good information and they were frustrated. Stephen made a call to his friend Benjamin, he had just returned from an assignment in Israel. The Israeli's were fighting to keep control of their land. Some soldiers had been taken and the whole community was in an uproar. Stephen was not at all surprised that he had not heard about the bombing. He was glad that no one had died but was interested in coming in a few days to see them and take down the story. In the meantime the two men organized a meeting at one of the churches. Ezekiel's good friend John was the pastor of a church and had contacted him to tell him that they could meet at the church until they could either rebuild the synagogue or rent a building for themselves. This was one of the issues that needed to be addressed. The school and synagogue were gone. Where would they meet now for meetings and what about the children? They would have to be put in regular schools or they would have to find another place quickly so they would not miss the whole school year.

The evening of the meeting John arrived early to open the doors, turn on the lights and set up some food that the church had prepared for the group. It was a gesture of love for the Jewish people. John understood his responsibility to love his neighbor and take care of those who were in need at a time of crisis. And this was his good friend he was glad to help. John was just a friendly man and when he saw Ezekiel one day in a book store he struck up a conversation with him. He so wanted to know more about the Jewish people and took the opportunity to engage Ezekiel in a conversation about the scriptures. He knew that the Jewish people read the Old Testament or Torah just like the Christian's did. He wondered what the Jewish people knew that the Christian's did not know. He and Ezekiel liked talking about the scriptures together. They learned much from each other. John realized that they both wanted the same things. Ezekiel had a family that he wanted to live for God and live in peace with his fellow man. John wanted the same thing. They would often meet at the bookstore and talk and have coffee together. So when he heard about the bombing he immediately talked with the congregation about the members of the Bethel synagogue using their sanctuary for meetings until they could get a building of their own.

Ezekiel and his family wanted to arrive early to make sure that the others felt comfortable. None of them knew John and the circumstances made it such that they needed to see someone to give them assurance that this was okay and not some kind of trap. Stephen walked behind Ezekiel and Raisa with the Torah scroll in his hand. They would have to get a cabinet but just having the Torah scroll with them at this meeting really meant a lot. John welcomed the family like they were coming into his home. "Welcome to Christ's church." The two men hugged each other like brothers. John shook Stephen's hand and Raisa. Aliya didn't know who this man was but her father was happy to see him so she gave him her best smile. John reached out and picked up little Aliya and gave her a big hug. "You must be Aliya. Your father has told me so much about you its like I've known you all your life." Aliya just giggled.

"Ezekiel I have in the fellowship hall a spread fit for a king. When you finish your meeting please help yourselves and don't worry about the clean up. My wife and the other ladies will come in tomorrow morning and take care of that. If there is anything left you can put it in the refrigerator. Just shut off the lights and close the door. Everything will be fine. They know us in the community. I hope that you will feel comfortable here." The tears started forming in Ezekiel's eyes. He knew that he loved this man but now he felt an even more special bond with him that he would do something like this for a bunch of people that he did not know. He was truly a great man and Ezekiel would never forget him for this. It was a testimony to the Jewish people that there was still love in the world for them.

After John left the families started coming in one by one. The whole congregation showed up for the meeting and even some whom they had not seen in quite a while. Ezekiel had never been in a church before. It was all so new for everyone. John's church was probably typical of most churches in the world they thought. There was a stage with a podium where he gave his messages. There was a large sign in the front and it looked like it was some scripture or something but it was not known to any of them. It read "For God so loved the world that he gave his only begotten son that whomsoever shall believe in him should have everlasting life (John 3:16)." Who was this John? Maybe these are the words of John his friend. Ezekiel would have to ask him what these words meant. The place felt very comfortable and the building was bigger than any synagogue that he had ever been in. There were three sections of seats in the church. The middle section was even too large for their whole congregation to fill up. Could there be so many Christians that they could fill up this whole building? Ezekiel was totally amazed. As the people came in and took their seats he walked to the back that lead to the fellowship hall that John spoke about. He was right. There was a table that had nothing but drinks, eating utensils, plates and desserts of all kinds. Aliya would be in heaven. There were tables with beautifully decorated cloths on them. On the far right was a spread fit for a king. Ezekiel had only seen so much food at some of their weddings. Why had John gone to so much trouble? His people were common people and didn't go to such a fuss. But this formed a place in his heart for these people that he never thought could be possible. He didn't tell anyone about the feast yet until the meeting was over.

After about twenty minutes Ezekiel felt that most of the congregation was present so he wanted to start the meeting. "Please everyone take your seats." The people were restless as usual and had a lot on their minds. "Let's get started. First we will have Stephen to read from the Torah. In all of the chaos I managed to save the Torah scroll from the fire." The eruption from the congregation was enormous. Many of the women started to cry. They could not have imagined that anything had survived and the Torah scroll's presence in the place that night meant that God was with them and the most important things like God and family had survived this horrendous situation. They started to applaud and shout. Stephen read from the Torah and Simon came up and prayed for the congregation and the meeting. He asked that God would be with them and help them to make good decisions for their families. He asked that God would forgive those who had set the bomb and that all would be well. He asked that there would not be animosity in their hearts but that what the devil meant for harm God would work it out for good.

The meeting went without incident. It was determined that they would continue meeting at the church. John had mentioned that they could also bring the children to the church for their classes. They already had a school and could give them a few classrooms for their classes. The congregation agreed that this would be a good thing until they could make other arrangements. When the meeting was over the men were calm and they all had a feast provided by their good friend.

Ezekiel Chapter 7 - Questions

zekiel was at Isak's side when he woke up. He had lost all of his relatives in the Holocaust. The community was his family. Walking into the room was quite difficult. Isak's face didn't look like him anymore. His head had swelled up like a watermelon. It was almost impossible to see his eyes. Both of his legs had been broken when the pillar fell on him. He had internal injuries but came through the operation with flying colors. He had been in a coma for a few days and Ezekiel wasn't sure that he was going to make it. There were monitors everywhere beeping and making noises. How could anyone sleep through all of the commotion? As he sat by his bed praying all of a sudden Isak starting groaning and groaning. But at least he was waking up. Ezekiel got the doctor and he came in to check Isak. "He might be like this for quite some time before he fully recovers. But this is a good sign. Just let him rest. This is what he really needs."

The doctor walked out of the room and Isak opened his eyes and gave Ezekiel a bit of a smile. "Thank you."

"No my friend. How are you feeling?"

"I've seen better days. The children? Are they all okay?"

"Yes. They are still afraid but this is to be expected. A friend of mine has allowed us to meet at his church for services and school. We don't have much money so I didn't turn him down. The rest of the members are okay with it surprisingly. They are very leary about everything and everyone. I don't blame them. Isak I need to tell you that my family and I will be leaving here soon. We don't want to leave the people like this but I'm afraid for my family. You need to think about what you want to do."

Isak turned his head and stared to cry. He was remembering the old days before the camps. "I don't blame them Ezekiel. Why Ezekiel can we not have peace? I am an old man. Can I not have some pleasure in life? Maybe I should go with you. But then who will take care of those who decide to remain here?"

Ezekiel put his head down. "I don't know Isak. But we deserve to have a life too. God gave us Israel. Maybe we should just go and fight for her instead of fighting for that which does not belong to us. We don't belong here. That's how I feel about it. Israel is our home. Let's go there. Even Stephen is ready to go. He has done well in America but that is not home. Israel is home Isak. Isak there is a newspaper reporter coming to do a story on the bombing. I hope you will be feeling better so you can give your side of the story. We must tell the whole world what is happening to us here. I don't know what good it will do but I just want the world to know that we are people too and that we should have rights just like everybody else."

The nurse came into the room to check on Isak. "Maybe you need to give him a rest. He really needs to rest." She wiped his forehead and left the room after taking down some numbers from one of the machines.

"Isak I had better go. I'll come back tomorrow to see you." Isak had fallen asleep before Ezkiel walked out the door. He didn't want to upset him. The newspaper reporter would be coming. He wanted him to rest and be ready to tell his story. The world had a right to know.

When Ezekiel left the hospital he went to the police station to find out why no one had been questioned yet about the bombing. Had they found out who was responsible for the bombing? It didn't make any sense. At least they could ask some questions. Maybe someone saw something that could be important to the case. Isak told him that when he came to work there was a truck sitting outside the school. The latest news report said that it was in fact a bomb inside of a truck that was responsible for the blast. But no one had come to ask him whether he saw anyone near the truck or anything. That was the thing about the Russian government. They kept quiet about everything. Ezekiel believed that the government themselves were responsible for the bombing. But he could not put his finger on why would they want to bomb the synagogue.

The officer didn't want to give Ezekiel the time of day. "We are working on the bombing sir. I don't know a whole lot about it but that there was a truck with explosives in it in an alley way next to the school. No one had come forward with any information but the investigation was not closed but still on going."

On going. Why had they not asked any of the survivors if they had seen anything? What was the cover up? They knew something but they weren't saying anything. Ezekiel refused to leave and the officer was getting more and more agitated. "Can I get a copy of the police report? Why have you not gotten any information from the people who were in the building? Maybe the children or one of the teachers saw something. What kind of investigation is this anyway?"

"Sorry but that information cannot be provided. We are still investigating and don't want any mess ups. Why don't you just let us do our job and I promise you we'll keep you informed if any breaks come up in the case."

Ezekiel knew that he would never hear from them. Maybe he'll talk with the newspaper reporter when he arrived. He couldn't wait to see how that was going to work out.

Stephen met Benjamin at the airport. He had not seen his friend in quite a few months. Benjamin was quite upset at what his friend was telling him. He had not been to Russia so he was excited about that but had rather that the circumstances be different. Benjamin didn't know what he was expecting but his vision of Russia was realized as they drove from the airport. There seemed to be a checkpoint every couple of blocks. What were they looking for? If the checkpoints worked then how could someone have gotten a bomb into the synagogue? Why did it go undetected? Benjamin was ready to take this on and hoped that he didn't ruffle too many feathers. Innocent children and men were almost killed and someone needed to answer to the charges.

The soldier waved the car through and Stephen and Benjamin made their way back to the house. "What is going on with this?"

"Oh I forgot you don't know a lot about living in Russia. They want to make sure they know your every move. It's like Big Brother personified a thousand times. The people are prisoners in their own home. The Jewish people are treated terribly here. I see why my brother wanted to get out of here. I wish that he had joined me in the States. At least he would have known what it meant to be free."

"Wow well I know I won't be moving here. So tell me what have the police told you about the bombing?"

Stephen turned his head to look at Benjamin. "Are you kidding me. They have told us absolutely nothing. No one has been questioned. All we have are what they tell us on the news. No one will ever come out and tell us anything."

"What kind of place is this? The people have the right to know. We will go and speak with the authorities and see what they have. We'll talk with the people in the neighborhood usually that is where the real information is."

Stephen and Benjamin arrive safely at the house. Ezekiel had just returned from the police station and the family was preparing dinner. Raisa was in the kitchen and Ezekiel was playing with Aliya in the other room. Stephen called out to the family that they had arrived. Ezekiel, Raisa and Aliya went to the door to meet their new guest. "Hey everybody this is my good friend Benjamin." Benjamin was a very tall man with a long beard and quite good looking. But his tall stature could be a bit overwhelming at times. Aliya looked up at him as though to say wow what a tall man. "You are very tall."

"Yes you noticed. Maybe if you are a good girl I will give you a piggy back ride after dinner."

"That sounds like fun."

"Sorry, don't mind her she doesn't mean any harm." Ezekiel didn't want Benjamin to feel bad about Aliya's comment. Little girls often times said what they thought without thinking about it. Raisa took his coat it had already started to get cold outside. Winters were brutal in Russia so he came prepared with hat and coat.

"That's okay. I was a kid once and I think that I said some things that my mother was embarrassed about. Thank you for inviting me into your home. I'm sorry about your loss. And now this. Please tell me what you all know about this bombing situation."

"A picture is worth a thousand words. Let's take a quick walk down to the school. The dinner is almost ready and we can talk then." Ezekiel wanted Benjamin to see the synagogue and school and he might be able to make some assessments of what he sees. The three men leave the house and walk the few blocks away to the school. Benjamin could not believe his eyes. He could still smell the remnants of smoke from the fire. He had brought his camera with him to take pictures so he could show them to a friend of his. He could only write a story but his good friend Gideon was a news reporter. He wanted to come but he already had a story that he was working on.

Neither Ezekiel or Stephen had been back to the site since the day of the fire. The officer had told him that there was a bomb in a truck. In all of the mayhem Ezekiel never even noticed a truck in the alley way next to the school. But there it stood. "Benjamin I went to the police station today to ask some questions. Look over here. The officer said that there was a truck with a bomb in it. This is how it was done. I had not even noticed this in all of the confusion. I was focused on getting the children and the teachers out that I didn't even see it."

The truck was blown to smitherines. The majority of the damage was done to the school but the fire eventually spread from the school over to the synagogue. The school was still salvageable and the synagogue. There must not have been a large amount of explosives but enough to do damage. The officer had not mentioned anyone in the truck so they put it there and left it to blow up at a designated time.

Ezekiel relived that day as though it had just happened. They walked through the rubble in the school and he showed Benjamin where he had found some of the children. He was so glad that no one died in the bombing. But still someone had to pay for what took place. God was watching over them that day. They walked through the large gape in the wall that connected the school with the synagogue. He wanted him to see where Isak had been standing when he was hit. The ceiling had just about fallen in. But there was still some small sections here and there that was still holding on. Ezekiel had tears in his eyes as he remembered tunneling through the debris to get at his friend, his faint voice crying out for help. He remembered breaking the Torah case to get the scroll out after the firemen had moved Isak from the debris. Amazingly the case didn't look so bad. He might come back and dislodge it and see if it could be saved. He had broken the glass but they could get new glass for it. They had not decided what they were going to do next but Ezekiel knew that he and his family were leaving when things were worked out. It was not the time to leave the community while they were hurting.

Benjamin was taking pictures the whole time that Ezekiel was talking. He had a very expensive digital camera that took pictures as well as he could made video's. This could be used on the news by Gideon. The people could see for themselves the face of this young man and his uncle who had actually lived through this terrible situation. "Let's get back. Raisa get's nervous now when I'm gone too long."

"Benjamin tomorrow we can go to the hospital and visit with Rebbe Isak. He is my very good friend that almost got killed in the explosion. He was in the synagogue when the bomb went off. He is in critical condition but he is out of the coma and can talk. He can give you a perspective that I cannot because I was not there when the explosion happened."

"Okay Ezekiel. That will be great. If the police won't help us then we will have to do some snooping around. There's a story here I can feel it." The men return back to the house for dinner.

Benjamin had a long flight and had a lot to think about. Why would the government bomb a synagogue and school with children in it? Could they have been targeting someone in the synagogue? The police work had been botched up. They left crucial evidence like the truck that held the bomb. It would hold crucial evidence. It could lead them to who owned the truck, what type of explosives had been used and other evidence. But obviously they were not interested in really solving the case. He was quite interested in talking with the Rebbe he might know something or maybe someone in the neighborhood. Time would tell but he was certainly interested in knowing.

Ezekiel Chapter 8 – The Reporter

Benjamin felt like a fish out of water. Whenever he had to cover a story outside of the States it was always difficult. His size didn't make things any easier. He was quite intimidating but being with the Rebbe and his good friend Stephen helped him a lot. The first stop would be to see the police detective that Ezekiel spoke with although he already figured he would not get any information from him. But a phone call to a good friend of his gave him a contact in the Russian intelligence office that would shed some light on what was revealed thus far in the investigation.

Michail had been working in Russian intelligence for many years. He loved his country but knew that there were many things that were not right with the government. He wanted to see change but it was slow in coming. The three gentleman sat in the waiting room for about twenty minutes while Michail finished a very important phone call. He was not at all what Benjamin thought he would look like. He had been watching too many movies perhaps. He pictured every Russian man like Stalin or something. He didn't know whether he should trust him or not but his source was pretty reliable and this was all that he had.

The receptionist escorted the men down a hall with many offices and half way down the corridor she opened the door to a very large office where a middle aged man very well dressed sat behind a desk.

Michail came from behind the desk to greet the men. "Welcome. Please have a seat. Doris bring these gentleman some coffee please."

The secretary walked out of the office to get the coffee and the three men sat down. Benjamin didn't think that the Russian intelligence had such lavish offices and was quite impressed with Michail's office. "I must be in the wrong business. I don't even get an office I only have a small cubicle with no privacy and I've been working at my job for almost fifteen years." The men just chuckle. Michail didn't smile for a while like it took some time for him to get the joke. He had that hard Russian demeanor. Maybe he wasn't sure whether he should be trusting them either.

"Let's get to the point. Michail my source says that you might be able to help us with some information on what the police have found out about the bombing at the Jewish school. Do you know anything or know someone who has some information?"

Michail sat down and took out a cigar box. "Would you like a cigar?" That most definitely meant that they were about to get the business. Benjamin didn't feel like getting the run around but remained calm. "No thank you."

"Okay let's cut to the chase. It seems that the bomb was set for someone in the school. The authorities are not sure who that person is yet. They are not talking about anything because they don't have the information. It seems like this person received some information from a very bad man who was allegedly doing business with the government concerning some arms deals. Unfortunately, the government had a leak in their intelligence. I think that someone is trying to clean up the pieces if you know what I mean." Benjamin almost fell off the chair when he said that.

"What? I'm not sure what you are saying. I'm sorry but I cannot tell you anymore than that. You need to speak with the people in the synagogue and find out what they know. If the government is looking for this person then they will find them. They will not stop until they get to them you know what I mean. They don't care who gets hurt as long as they achieve the goal."

Benjamin felt that Michail was giving him the business. This was a small piece of the puzzle. But from what he was saying someone in the synagogue had some information worth being killed for. Who was that person and what was the information? Since no one in fact had been killed then the government was still looking for this person. They would have to find him quickly before something else bad happened. But who could that person be? The three gentleman thanked the intelligence officer and left without drinking their coffee.

There was silence in the car on the way to the hospital. Ezekiel was exceptionally quiet and Benjamin wondered why. This was a very important piece of the puzzle. They would not have found that out from anyone because the person with the information was definitely not talking. Maybe the Rebbe knew something. He was growing more and more interested with every moment.

Isak was making progress and had a lot to say about the bombing. Benjamin had the camera rolling. He told the men that he had gotten to the school early that morning as usual. There was nothing out of the ordinary. He opened the school and the synagogue doors like usual and then he went in to pray as was his usual practice. After he had finished he could hear the other teachers and the students next door talking and laughing. He was finishing up prayer when he heard the blast. The sound was so loud that he put his hands up to his ears because they were hurting. It all happened so quickly. The pillar came tumbling down and the ceiling fell. There was smoke and fire everywhere. He got hit on the head. He wanted to get up but he couldn't. He was so worried about everyone. All he could do was pray and ask God to help them. Isak was feeling weak so the men didn't want to stay long. He looked up at them through the squinted eyes and begged that they would find out why this had happened. Benjamin assured him that they were getting closer and they would keep him posted.

Stephen was searching his heart. He didn't want to ask his nephew if he had in fact knew something that he wasn't saying but he would have to ask him. This was a very dangerous situation. The other teachers would have to be asked as well. How could he leave him out? Maybe he knew something but didn't realize it. He didn't say a word after the meeting with the intelligence officer. He knew his nephew if he didn't know anything he would have been saying so right away. His silence said a whole lot. He decided that he would not say anything in front of

Benjamin. He would take him aside and ask him and then if there was something to tell him they could do it together.

The three men arrived back at the house in time for Raisa had already prepared a big meal for the hungry group. Aliya was still intrigued with how tall Benjamin was and couldn't wait for another piggy back ride as soon as they walked through the door. "Benny, Benny pick me up." She couldn't quite say his whole name so Benny was the best she could do. Benjamin loved the attention.

After dinner Ezekiel took Raisa aside to talk with her. "Raisa come upstairs for a moment I need to speak with you."

"Okay Ezekiel." Aliya was busy spending time with her uncle and his friend. "What is going on Ezekiel?"

"Well sit down Raisa. I hope that you will not be too alarmed at what I am about to tell you. I thought I should tell you before I tell Stephen and Benjamin. Remember Mishenka the man whose father built the synagogue and school, well he had been working for the Russian government making guns for them. He had lots of friends in very high places who talked with him about things that the Russian government was planning against the United States. He told me that he wanted to get his family out of Russia because he was afraid for his life. Someone had tried to kill him probably so that he would not talk about what he knew. Before he could leave the Russian government brought him up on espionage charges. It was a three ring circus Raisa. He was innocent. He didn't do anything wrong. The intelligence officer that gave him the information has since left Russia and no one knows where he is. Perhaps the government has killed him or put him in some jail too. In any case we received information today that the bombing was to get rid of someone who the government suspects has some information about what they are doing. I have no such information. I only know that Mishenka was put in prison for no reason at all. We will have to get out of here or else they will kill me. I'm sorry Raisa."

Raisa could not believe what she was hearing. She knew how the government was about these types of things. They kill first and then ask questions later. They would have to talk with Benjamin maybe he could help. "Let's talk with Stephen and Benjamin. Whatever they say we will do?"

"You are a good wife. Let's put Aliya to bed and then we can all talk about this. We had better be careful. If they find out that it is me we will all be in danger."

Raisa went downstairs and got Aliya so that she could put her to bed. She wasn't ready to sleep so Raisa had to tell her a story and sing to her before she would go to sleep. Ezekiel had sat down in the living room with Stephen and Benjamin waiting for her to come downstairs so they could talk. The sweat was already beading up on his face before Raisa came down to join him in the living room. He couldn't wait any longer so he asked the two men if they would cut off the television so that he could talk with them. Stephen and Benjamin wasn't sure what it was all about but were eager to find out. Stephen looked at Benjamin and a crazy feeling came over them both. "Don't tell me Ezekiel that you know something about what's going on. Come on spill it. I had a feeling because at the office today you didn't say a word. I had a feeling that you knew something you were not saying." Ezekiel got up and starting pacing the room. His face had turned beet red. He didn't know quite how to put it into words. What would his uncle think about him? But after all he didn't have any idea that things were going to turn out this way. He should have told his father a long time ago what was going on with Mishenka. "Okay I wanted to wait for Raisa but she'll be down in a moment. I met Mishenka many years ago when we were just little boys. We used to play together. After the war was over his father made some bad decision and started working for the Russian government. Once you get in with them there is no turning back. I didn't like him any less because of how his father made his money. But he like his father chose to continue working for the government. Mishenka told me that he wanted to clean up the family name and do good things for the community and so he gave a lot of money for the rebuilding of the synagogue and the school. The community didn't know what they were into and I didn't tell them. We needed the money. I guess I will have to deal with God on that one. In any case he was trying to get out from under the government but that was not going to be easy. He had already moved a lot of money out of the company into offshore accounts. He and his wife had already bought a place in New York and were talking with the government about asylum. He knew a lot about military actions against the United States. He knew people in all forms of government. One of his biggest mistakes was talking about the government openly about what he knew they were doing. He should have kept his mouth closed but he was trying to do what he thought was right. It was a step towards redemption. The more he talked the more he got in trouble with the government. The government knew that he had a contact in Russian intelligence that was feeding him information. From what he told me his contact talked a bit too much about Russian military intelligence and what military intelligence had planned against the United States. Unfortunately he told me who this person is and that is the reason for this bombing. You may not have heard about it but they finally brought him up on charges and he is now in prison. He got his wife and family out of the country before all of this happened. They have confiscated all of his assets and I think they are cleaning up the pieces to get anyone out of the way that know why he is really in prison. He didn't do anything wrong but run his mouth against the government. I feel terrible because I have not had any contact with him since his imprisonment. I didn't want to get involved. I have a family. Now this. I don't know what to do now. If I speak out I will end up in prison just like Mishenka." Like a true journalist Benjamin had already taken out his tape recorder. If something happened to Ezekiel he wanted to make sure that he had the true story in his own words.

Stephen was dumfounded and could only comfort his nephew. Raisa had entered the room and knew from the looks on their faces that he had confessed to knowing what was possibly happening with the bombings. "I'll get something for us to drink." She went into the kitchen to get some wine. They were going to need it. Things were going to get difficult from here.

Ezekiel Chapter 9 – The Conspiracy Theory

Benjamin could not believe what he was hearing. But after a few years investigating stories all over the world it didn't amaze him when he heard that the Russian government could possibly be planning an invasion against America. The sad part was that they had an innocent man in prison whose wife was living in fear in America. But who was this Russian intelligence agent who had already left the country? Where was he and had he given any information to the F.B.I. or the C.I.A. about what the Russians were planning on doing? What were they to do next? He felt that the first thing he needed to do was to get Ezekiel and his family out of Russia before the police found out that it was really him that they were trying to find. If his editor agreed they would leave right away. He had to get the story out to America that they were in danger. Benjamin made a quick phone call to his boss. "Hey Parker I got a big one. We just might win the Pulitzer for this story man."

"Well what's going on? I thought you were just getting some story about a church burning or something. Come on hurry up I got things to do."

"Okay, okay. Well listen it turns out that the man who I was writing the story on is a Rebbe here in Moscow. He had a friend that's been put in prison on espionage charges. But that's not all. Turns out that this friend knew a Russian intelligence officer that defected and has left the country. He has information that Russia is planning on a future war against the United States. We have got to find out where this guy is get this information for the C.I.A. Our lives might depend on it." There was no sign of life on the other end. "Parker are you listening? I need some money to get this family out of Russia or else they are going to find this man and kill him. Can I count on you?"

"What in God's name is going on? Russian spies. I thought that we were done with this. Don't you know that Gorbachev has entered the country and the Cold War is over man. And you want me to tell the American people that their lives are in danger? Are you crazy? What evidence do we have? We can't just print a story like this. We have to have evidence. Does he at least know where the wife is? If she can corroborate the story of what has happened to her husband then we can put all the pieces together. Get me the wife and I'll bring the family over. We can get help for them too."

"Parker I don't know where the wife is!" Benjamin almost threw the phone across the room. He had no idea where the wife was. He didn't think that Ezekiel knew where she was either. But they would need her to testify and give information. "Okay Parker I'll keep working on it."

"Alright just keep me informed and don't get yourself in trouble over this. I'm interested in what the Russian's are doing too but I don't want to lose a man over this. I don't trust those people I don't care what the government says. I'll talk with you later."

Benjamin knew that something was brewing with this story. He didn't like the Russian's either and couldn't believe that he was now sitting in Moscow on a possible attack on the United States. They had already gone through 9-11 so any kind of possible terrorist activity should be investigated and the American people had the right to know what was going to happen. Benjamin wondered if there was any way that Ezekiel could get the information from Mishenko about where his wife was hiding. Maybe if they could get to the proper people in the government they might be able to negotiate Mishenko's release. It was a big shot in the dark but it was worth thinking about. If it was one thing that Benjamin had learned in his line of work was that anything could be done with the right amount of money. He would have to speak with Ezekiel about what his editor had said.

Life was getting more and more difficult and Ezekiel wanted now more than ever to just get his family out of Moscow and move to Israel. But the people had the right to have their story heard. Now it was not just about the Jewish people but about the American's also. He had an obligation to tell the government what was being planned against them. The Russian's would not be happy but the President and the innocent people of America would be amazed to know what was happening behind their backs. Mordechi had left them enough money to move to Israel but they would have to go to America first and tell this story. He needed to at least tell John and one of the members of the synagogue that they would be going on a trip. He would not say that they were leaving for good. The less they knew the better. John was a good man and his good friend Simon could lead the congregation until Isak got better. He was one of the teachers at the school. After they had reached safety the news would come out but his wife and child would be safe. He called John to set up a meeting the following day. Simon was at home so he went over to speak with him about the upcoming trip.

Simon was glad that Ezekiel was coming over to visit. Things were so crazy at this point and he really needed advice on what to do next for his family. He had a small business but he could take what small savings they had and start over. Things were not good for them there even before the bombing. But he was an old dog and he didn't want to learn any new tricks. He just wanted peace for his family. Agressa was Russian and had lived all of her life in Russia. Her family was there and she didn't want to leave them. He thought that maybe he would fit in better if he had married a Russian girl. It did help when he wanted to start his business. Agressa's father worked at a bank and was able to get him a loan. He was in over his head though. One day he would have to tell his good friend Ezekiel that he had been involved for a long time laundering dirty money for his father in law. He made himself feel better by telling himself that many of the businessmen had to do something illegal for the government in order to keep their doors open. What if the bombing was a warning to him to keep his mouth shut? He wasn't sure but he was at the point where he was afraid all the time. He had told his father in law that he no longer wanted to be a part of the laundering business and that he was going to take his wife and children and get out of Moscow for good. His father in law told him that if he tried to walk away that the men he worked for would kill him and all of the family. He begged Simon to stay and that everything would be okay. He would look for someone else eventually and that would get him off the hook. Then in time he could move away and no one would think anything about it. Then the bombing happened and Simon was very afraid. He could not sleep at night worrying about whether the bomb was a message to keep his mouth closed. Well closed it would be. Ezekiel knocked on the door and Agressa opened it with the biggest smile. "Come in Ezekiel, Simon is waiting for you in his study. He was just finishing up some work. I think that he has some good news for you about the synagogue."

"Hi Agressa. Some good news. I could use some good news. How are you doing today?" She had a big smile but he knew Agressa too well. She didn't have on any make up and her face was really puffy. Her eyes were red and she looked like she had just gotten out of bed. This only meant that she was not having a good day. He hoped that she and Simon had not been fighting again. She pressed him so to be like her father. Simon didn't really care much about money. He only wanted to have a good business and be wealthy to take care of all of her needs. She needed more than he could make. Her father had spoiled her and poor Simon had bought into the job of taking care of her.

The door to his study was open and Ezekiel walked in to see his friend standing at the window just staring out as though he didn't even know that he walked into the room. Ezekiel called out his name and Simon turned around slowly like an old man with troubles on his mind. "My friend, come in and sit down. Can I get you something to eat or drink?" There was a cigar burning in the ash tray. Simon said that he had quit so he must be having some troubles that was making him smoke again.

"No Simon. Please sit down. I have something to tell you. This is going to be very difficult for me." The two sat down. Simon sat at his desk and Ezekiel sat on a long couch just along side of the desk. He always loved that couch it was so nice and firm. It was like what a psychiatrist would have in his office for people to lie down on. He had seen it on television once.

"Well I'm just going to come right out with it. I spoke with the newspaper reporter about the bombing. He thinks that we should go to New York and tell the story to the people of America. This is the only way that we can get some coverage outside of Russia and people will know what is happening here to us. What do you think?"

Simon picked up the cigar and took a puff on it like a true smoker. "Well Ezekiel I think that if this is what you think is the best thing to do then go to America. I wish that I could go with you but I'm stuck here in this life. My Agressa does not want to leave here. I'm almost thinking about leaving her but what about the children. It's not their fault that there mother will not side with her husband but wants to stay stuck under her father. I cannot be a real man and leave my wife and children. She's not a bad woman. I love my children. You Ezekiel are a good man. You did the right thing and married a good Jewish woman. Little Aliya she adores her father and Raisa will stick by you through thick and thin." He looked like a broken man. All of his riches and he was miserable.

"Simon I feel so very bad for you. Maybe things will change in time. Agressa said that you had some good news for me. What is it? You don't seem very happy today."

"Oh yes. I was talking with Agressa and her father. I have some money saved up and he said that he would give me a loan from the bank to make the repairs on the synagogue. It's in bad shape so we just might bulldoze the whole thing and start all over. We can salvage whatever might still be good and then we will start with the rebuilding of the synagogue and the church. It's the least that I can do. I will put it to the congregation and anyone who wants to donate any funds that will be great. This makes me feel good. Ezekiel you might not know it but I have done some things in my life that I am not proud of. I hope that I can fix these things and make amends with God before the day comes when I have to leave this place. You Ezekiel are a true Jew and good man. I wish that I could say that."

"Oh Simon. I try to be a good person. But that doesn't mean that I have not made any mistakes in my life. I need to take care of some things too. Maybe when things get better we can sit down and talk about some things. In the mean time I'm going to tell John the pastor of the church that you will take care of things. Just in case he needs to contact someone about having meetings at the church. He is a good man. If you need to talk with anyone I have to say that he will talk with you any time. I had better go now. I need to get back home and see my family. I have been so busy I have not been spending much time with them. We have to get to packing as well. Thank you for what you are doing for our people. I'm sure they will be very pleased to know that soon they will have their own temple again." The two men rise and shake hands. Ezekiel grabs Simon and gives him a big hug. He wasn't sure whether he would ever see him again.

The trip across town to the church gave Ezekiel time to think about what he was going to tell his friend. Ezekiel loved John and he had done a great thing for his people. He took a big chance allowing them to use the church. Luckily the community and the church members didn't have a problem with them coming there for worship. Ezekiel had made a quick phone call to John to tell him that he needed to talk with him right away. John said that he would be in his office at the church and to come right over. Ezekiel made a note in his mind to go over to the synagogue and try to dismantle the Torah cabinet. He would have Simon get it fixed. They could then put it up at the church so the Torah scroll would not be handled by too many hands. It was sacred and Ezekiel was glad that it had survived the fire. When he arrived at the church John was standing outside just taking in some fresh air. "Hello my friend."

The two men shake hands and walk inside the church to John's office. "Thank you for seeing me in such short notice.

"Not a problem Ezekiel. I always have time for friends. I was just here working on my sermon for Sunday. But then I'm sure you understand that."

"Yes I do. John I have something very important to tell you. I don't want to say more than I need to for your safety."

"What are you talking about Ezekiel, my safety? What is happening?"

"Well John as you know someone put a bomb in a truck next to the synagogue. Thank God no one was killed. I could not understand what this was all about. But after some investigation we found out that the government was trying to kill me because they think that I know about some information given to a friend of mine through one of their intelligence officer about a possible invasion of America by Russia. I know that it sounds far fetched but it is true."

John could only scratch his head. "Ezekiel are you absolutely sure about this? Maybe it's not about you. Maybe it's someone else they were trying to get at. In any case what are you going to do? Is there anything that I can do to help?"

"Thank you John but no. I and my family are going to pack up and leave as soon as possible. I will contact you as soon as we get to America. I have already spoken with just one of my friends about this. No one else in the synagogue knows anything about it for their own safety. I guess this is good bye for now." Just then four armed intelligence officer came rushing into the office. "Are you Ezekiel?"

"Yes I am Ezekiel. You need to come with us. We need to question you at police headquarters."

"Question me about what?" The officers took hold of Ezekiel and pushed him out of the door.

"John please contact my wife and tell her what has happened."

"Listen you can't just barge in here. What has this man done to you? He has not done anything wrong. John didn't want to get in any trouble but he knew that Ezekiel was in trouble and that he had to get him some help before he disappeared like many others in Russia.

Ezekiel was taken down to police headquarters for questioning. He was feeling very scared and wasn't sure whether he would ever see his family again. He didn't have any money and that would not help him with the Russians. They would lie and say anything and he would not be able to help himself.

John called Ezekiel's house to tell his family what had taken place. Raisa answered the phone. "Is this Raisa Ezekiel's wife?"

Raisa immediately got nervous. "Yes this is Raisa. Who is calling?"

"Raisa this is John the pastor of the church. I am Ezekiel's friend. He came over here to talk with me to tell that you were all leaving Russia and why. But before we finished our conversation Russian intelligence officer came in and arrested him. They did not say where they were taking him or why. I will make some phone calls but you must find someone to help him. I will do all that I can."

Raisa dropped the phone and starting screaming. Stephen came running down the steps when he heard her screaming. He had not ever heard her cry this way even at Mordechi's funeral. John was still on the other end. He heard her crying in the background but stayed on hoping that she would pick the phone back up and say something to him.

Stephen put his arms around her to comfort her and was asking her what was wrong but she could not speak. He picked up the phone. "Hi this is Stephen. I am visiting from America who is this? What have you said to my niece she is out of control."

"Hi Stephen this is John. Ezekiel came to see me to tell me that he was leaving for America. Some intelligence officers have come and taken him away. I don't know what is happening but he needs help. I will make some phone calls. I'll let you know what I can find out but you must be very careful. If you have any contacts then please call them." John hung up the phone and Stephen tried to console Raisa. He didn't want the little one to get upset. Good thing she was out at a neighbors when the phone call came through. Benjamin had gone out to the store to purchase some personal items. He had promised a friend some souvenirs from his trip. Since they were planning on leaving in a few days he thought he would just go out and take a taxi around to see a few things. He needed some fresh air to think about how to find Mishenko's wife. Her testimony would be crucial.

Stephen didn't know what to do next. Benjamin had all of the contacts so they would have to wait until he had returned. In the meantime he tried to console Raisa. "Raisa please get a hold of yourself. We must not fall apart. Ezekiel will need for us to be strong." Raisa was not hearing anything he was saying. Her sobs got deeper and harder the more he talked. He could only just hold her until she stopped sobbing. In a small voice she tried to speak. "Stephen what are we going to do? You don't know how they are. Now that they have him they will not let him go. I may never see my husband again. I will not have anyone to help me raise our child. She worships the very ground that he walks on. She has lost her grand father. Now she has lost her father. This is too much for a child to bare."

"I know Raisa. What we will do is get you and Raisa out of the country. You will go and stay with my son and daughter. They will take good care of you. There is nothing that you can do here. I and Benjamin will stay behind. This way you will be safe with the child. We will come as soon as we can get a release for Ezekiel."

"Stephen I don't want to leave without him but I am afraid for my little Aliya. If something happens to her I will die Stephen."

"No you will not die. Go upstairs and pack a bag for yourself and the child. Whatever you cannot take you can get in America. I will take care of everything. Do not worry. Be strong Raisa. Pray and God will take care of this for his son. He has not done anything wrong. They will see and the truth will prevail." Raisa went upstairs to pray and start packing for the trip. She had not ever been out of Russia. She and Ezekiel were planning to leave for Israel but never did. There was always some reason why they could not go. But now everything was falling apart and she had to leave for America without him. How did this all happen? Aliya would be home soon and she would have to explain to her what is happening.

Benjamin came bursting through the door with packages of all sizes. There was stuff for people at the office and he always had to get something for his mother. He was still a bachelor but he had been seeing a nice young lady for a few months and thought it appropriate to get her a gift as well. She would be so happy. Stephen met him at the door shaking and hysterical. "What is going on?" He dropped the bags at the door.

"Ezekiel has been picked up by the police. John the pastor of the church was talking with him when they burst into the church and arrested him right there. I cannot believe this is happening." Stephen sank into the nearest chair and started to cry. He was worried about his nephew. How would they get him out of the hands of the government? They would not be trusted. Maybe when they realize that he doesn't know anything that they will let him go but they could not be sure.

"Okay Stephen let's start with our intelligence guy who we spoke with the other day. In the meantime we will get Raisa and the baby out of the country. Can she stay with your family there?"

"Sure. I told her to pack a bag and we will take her to the airport and get her out of the country. This way they will not be able to use her as bait to get to her husband. They are not beyond these kind of tactics."

Benjamin called the airport and made arrangements for them to leave that evening. He didn't want to waste any time. They were on to them and they would have to stay ten steps ahead if possible.

Chapter 10

Stephen went to the neighbors to collect Aliya so they could get prepared for the flight to America. She was a little girl so she would be excited about the trip. They decided not to tell her that her father was in trouble but that he would be coming to America really soon and she and mommy were leaving right away. Like all little children she was so excited about going on a plane. She had not even been to the airport before. There was so much to see and so much going on that Raisa had to keep a close watch that she didn't venture off. Stephen had called ahead and his daughter was preparing for their arrival.

Benjamin and Stephen could only go so far with her in the airport. Stephen gave her some money, her ticket and all of the papers she needed. She was scared. Everything was happening so quickly. But she sucked it up. She knew that Stephen would not stop until he had found Ezekiel. The family would be together really soon. She kissed Stephen and Benjamin and walked through the metal detectors into the terminal. They would have to wait until she arrived and called to know that she was okay. Stephen bought her a cell phone to call just in case anything had happened. It was one of the hardest things that Stephen had to do. Now it was time to find out what happened to Ezekiel.

The next day the two men called Benjamin's contact in Russian intelligence. He seemed to be giving them the run around this time. He wasn't as nice as he was the first time they met. He said that he didn't have any information about Ezekiel and that they should go to their local police station and see if he was there. This made them suspicious. Why did he not want to talk with them? What was he hiding? Benjamin knew that they needed help. He was not in America and knew no one. After a few phone calls he had the name of the Russian Ambassador to the United Nations. He could at least ask some questions and find out what was happening to Ezekiel. He was an innocent man and didn't have any information. He should be released and able to travel to America.

Dmitri's office was even more elaborate than the intelligence officer. Benjamin was somehow taught that the Russian's were all poor and that the country was crumbling. But all he could see was elaborately built structures with ceilings that had paintings that dated back to when Stalin was ruling the place. They sure spent a lot of money building back then. Even the transit system was unlike any transit system he had ever taken before. It surely made New York's transit system look like something out of the ancient times. You could almost eat off the floors. They had beautiful statues everywhere.

The two men could not keep from looking like children at Willy Wonka's chocolate factory. The architecture was unlike anything that Benjamin had experience and he had traveled extensively in his life. He had thoughts of moving to Russia it was so beautiful. What did a guy have to do to have an office like this? He could fit his whole apartment in that one room. His secretary even had a better office than he had at home.

Benjamin hoped that Dmitri would give them as much help as they needed. He had never spoken to an ambassador before. But he hoped he was a good guy. Ezekiel was in trouble and they needed to give him all the help that they could. The secretary kept looking up at them from time to time. What that meant they were not sure? But they were not leaving until they got a chance to speak with him. All of a sudden a tall man with a very tailored suit came out of the door and waved for the men to come into the office. "Hold my calls."

The secretary looked up briefly as the men walked into the office. Benjamin was relieved that they didn't get the brush off. The ambassador was extremely cordial to the men that they could not believe it. "Have you gentleman had breakfast yet? I could send for something if you would like?"

"Oh no. We don't need anything. But thank you so very much for asking. We don't want to take up too much of your time. Let me please get to the point. I came here from America to investigate the bombing at the jewish synagogue that took place less than a week ago. To date my friends nephew has been taken by the police for interrogation about what we don't know. We need someone to make a phone call and find out where he is and why they are questioning him. Do you think that you can help us with this?"

"Well. Let me see if I can contact someone. Please give me a moment."

While Dmitri was making the phone call Benjamin and Stephen were praying silently and basking in the beauty of the room. Dmitri picked up the phone and dialed a number. Who he was talking to Benjamin wished that he knew. Within a few minutes of the conversation Dmitri informed the men that Ezekiel was being brought up on charges of espionage. He said that they believed they had enough information that he would spend the rest of his life in prison. They needed to arrange for a lawyer to represent him at his trial.

When Stephen and Benjamin left the office of the Ambassador they knew that they would have to fight with everything they had or else Ezekiel would spend the rest of his life in prison for a crime that he did not commit. The next step would be to get to the jewish community, the Christian community and on television to shame the government. They wanted the international community to know that they were holding an innocent man against his will. Stephen would go to the jewish people and to John to speak with the Christian community. He would find some news reporters that were not afraid of the government to tell Ezekiel's story on the television and in the newspapers. They would know that they were not going to get this one.

Stephen knew that he might lose his shirt over this but he had to save his nephew from being put into prison for the rest of his life. He asked around to find the best lawyer in Russia to take his case. Most of the lawyers did not want to touch the case. They were afraid that they too might lose their reputations and that in the end they would not win the case anyway. Daniel was a jewish lawyer. He had worked on several cases of this type before. It was not going to be an easy fight but they would win. Stephen was instructed to go to the jewish community and organize the people to picket outside of the police station and when the trial started they would be there to speak on behalf of their son. Benjamin made a few phone calls and could only find a few news reporters and newspaper reporters that would even print his story. But one would be better than none. Daniel had some contacts and would be going to see Ezekiel in the holding place where he was being kept. He had the right to representation and they would not deny him of that but Daniel knew that they would use every means to undermine his defense. The one man that could clear him was himself in prison. They would never let him get an interview with Mishenko. In the end they would have to negotiate his release through the government themselves. In the meantime he would tell Ezekiel to be patient.

After the initial meeting Stephen spoke with the jewish community about what was happening with Ezekiel. Ezekiel was loved by all in the community and despite their fears they would come out and demonstrate in front of the police station. At first the police didn't react to the demonstrators and allowed them to assemble. But after a few days when the demonstrators went from just a few jewish people to a large crowd of both Christians, Jews and some Russians who just hated the governments way of shutting people up they began to act. The newspapers and television reporters had Ezekiel's picture on a few times a day. Benjamin was happy to see that the community was coming out to help. This was democracy in action. Communism was dead but the Russians had not gotten the memo. They were still using the same tactics as in the days of Stalin.

Daniel could not believe what he was seeing when he was taken back to Ezekiel's cell. They had not just interrogated Ezekiel but he could see that they had beaten Ezekiel to get him to say things that were not true. Ezekiel was laying down on a cot in a small cell not big enough for the two of them to walk around in. He was probably hungry and he definitely needed medical attention. Daniel became angry and started shouting for an officer to come to the cell. "Officer, officer. This man needs medical attention, food and water. You'll pay for this. Get somebody in here right now."

An officer came to the cell where Ezekiel was being held. "I don't know anything about this. He was fine when I saw him my last time around. He might have gotten into a fight with one of the other inmates. I will have him taken to the infirmary and the doctor will take care of him."

"You had better get him there right now. I will talk with your superiors about this." The officer didn't seem too moved by what he said. But he did have some officers come and take Ezekiel to the infirmary so that the doctor could take care of his wounds. Daniel didn't leave Ezekiel alone. After the doctor worked on him he sat near his bed writing down everything that was happening. When the doctor walked out of the room Daniel carefully took out his cell phone so that he could take pictures of Ezekiel to show the world what was happening in the prison's of Russia. It was the only way that the international community could see first hand the brutality that took place in the prisons. Many prisoners died before coming to trial. He was lucky that Ezekiel was still alive. He had to be careful because the Russians had cameras all over but he had been successful at this before. If he failed they would both be in prison and he could not be any help to Ezekiel.

Ezekiel had finally woken up and was moaning. He had some water and gave him just a little. His mouth was swollen and had cuts on them. It would be difficult for him to drink but he need not get dehydrated. Through the small slits in his eyes Ezekiel managed to look up and saw an older man that he had not known. Very slowly and with great pain he managed to speak. "Who are you? Where am I? Where is my wife?"

"I am Daniel Ezekiel. I am your lawyer and you are in jail. As far as I know your wife and daughter have been sent out of the country by your uncle Stephen to be safe. She left right after they picked you up at the church. We are going to do everything possible to get you out of here right away. But Ezekiel that might not happen right away. If not I will need for you to be patient with me. We will get you out of here. I know that you are innocent. When you get better I need you to tell me what you know. Who is Mishenko? Did he give you anything before he went to prison? Is there any way that you can contact him while you are here? Benjamin wants to contact his wife so that she can help us. Maybe we can get him released as well. I'm sorry that I'm going so quickly but they are gonna boot me out of here in a few minutes. I know a lot of the officers that work here. They are not all bad people." Ezekiel tried to sit up. His ribs were broken and he had a very bad headache.

"Daniel thank you for your help. Mishenko and I grew up together. His father had been working government contracts since after the war. They made a lot of money working for the government and had been very good to the community taking care of those who were less fortunate. We didn't ask any questions about what exactly he was doing. It was not our place. In any case Mishenko told me one day that he had a friend in Russian intelligence that was going to defect to the United States to tell them that Russia had been spying on them. He himself had gone several times to America and brought back intelligence. They were in fact planning a future war against the America. The intelligence officer defected and Mishenko was eventually put in prison for espionage just like they are doing to me now. I don't know how much more Mishenko knew but he might have had more information than he told me about. I feel bad Daniel that I have not heard from him since he went to prison. I hope that he is still alive. If this doesn't work out I will be in the same place as he is. I don't know anything not that I know of anyway. And no he never gave me anything. Maybe he gave something to his wife. She left here and went to America after the trial."

The prison nurse came in to watch them. She was probably standing outside the door the whole time but Daniel didn't pay her any attention. Since she was watching Daniel decided that he would let Ezekiel rest. Maybe he could think of anything else that might help his case. Daniel knew that no matter what he said that he would be convicted and sent to prison. If God came to speak they would find a way around it.

Daniel was stuck between a rock and a hard place but he had to do the very best that he could for Ezekiel. The government wasn't wasting any time they already had his hearing scheduled in two weeks. He would bring in anyone who would testify that Ezekiel was an upstanding rabbe in the community. He would show that he was a good father and husband and not involved with anything against the government. He himself would have to testify what Mishenko told him. There wasn't much else. That would be the first round and they would proceed accordingly after that. He had a few new tricks for this case.

Daniel was about to make a few phone calls when someone knocked at the door. He didn't have any clients scheduled for the afternoon so he had no idea who that could be at the door. When he answered the door there were two men at the door. "Yes can I help you."

The two men did not look Russian or Jewish. He had never seen them before but was interested in why they were there. It was quite interesting that they were both dressed in long white garments. There was an amazing glow about their appearance and for a minute Daniel thought that these were angels coming to see him. He sure needed some divine intervention. They didn't say much at first they only stood there looking at Daniel. It was kind of weird but he would go with the flow. They just walked pass him and came into the house. The one closest to him started to speak first. "Daniel we are angels sent from heaven." Daniel could not believe it. He had never seen an angel before in his life. He didn't quite know what he was supposed to do. "Listen to us for we have something important to tell you."

Daniel didn't speak or move. He was afraid now. Was he going to die or something? He had this case it wasn't time for him to die. Ezekiel was counting on him. "The man Ezekiel is a very important man. We need you to do all that you can to help him. But we also want you to know that we are working along with you. You are not alone in this. Ezekiel has been called to help his people as well as to go to America and tell them of the danger that is coming to America."

Daniel was listening intently but managed to get a few words out of his mouth. "Danger, what danger are the American's in? The two angels look at one another as if to say should we tell him more. They both turn to look at Daniel again. "Many believe that the Cold War is over but it is not. The Russian's plan a major attack on the United States. They have for many years now been sending intelligence officers to listen in on the conversations of the President, Congress and the Department of Defense. Let us show you something." Just then Daniel felt like he left his body. He could feel himself lifted out of his body and he and the angels were now standing outside of the Pentagon. "Do you see that man sitting inside of his car?"

"Yes I see the man."

"He is a Russian spy from the Russian Embassy. He has put a bug in the Pentagon and he sits outside of the office listening in on conversations and taking notes. He will send the information back to Moscow. America must know that this is happening so that they can take better precautions and prepare for war with the Russians."

Daniel felt sick to his stomach. Now he understood why Mishenko and Ezekiel were being taken out of population. The government didn't want them to get this information to the public. If they did this could cause terrible problems between the United States and Russia. The climate was already bad in the world. All they needed was World War III. Daniel was caught up in the moment and didn't realize he had returned back to his home. He looked around but the angels were no where to be found. But they had said that they were with him and to help Ezekiel the best way that he could. He would have to speak with some of his friends and see if they would at least be character witnesses for Ezekiel. Mishenko was involved with some shady characters but Ezekiel was nothing but a rabbe and school teacher. He didn't know anybody in the government. He was not in allegiance with intelligence officer. This would help some but not nearly enough. He would start his investigation in the morning after talking with his friends in the intelligence community about Mishenko's case. He had to know what the government knew about what the intelligence officer told him. The police were all poor and it would not be difficult to get some blood money together to get some answers.

Chapter 11

Daniel didn't want anyone to think that he had lost his mind so he didn't tell anyone about his experience with the angels. He had to do something in the natural too to help with Ezekiel's defense. He spoke with several of the people from the synagogue and asked that they help with a testimony of how important Ezekiel was in the community. His wife had been taken out of the country and Daniel understood his uncle's fear that something would happen to her and the child so he could not count on her testimony that Ezekiel was a good husband and father. He had plenty of people who were willing to testify on his behalf. He was worried about Ezekiel so he decided that he would go and visit him again to make sure he had been fed and taken care of. Before he went to the jail he had to get the pictures from his phone to Benjamin so that he could get the pictures out of the country. With the use of computers this was very easy to do. He was taking a very big chance doing this because the government would surely retaliate against him for his actions. He could risk going to jail but he would have to keep the faith.

Stephen had invited Daniel to come over to the house for lunch. He wanted to know how Ezekiel was when he visited him. He was hopeful since they had a lawyer now that his nephew would get a fair trial and be exhonerated of the allegations against him. On the journey to see Stephen Daniel's phone rang. It was a phone call from one of his contacts at the jail. Apparently Ezekiel had been moved to an undisclosed location. The government had made a move that even Daniel was questioning why had they moved him. It was not even time for his trial. He saw this before. The next step would be that they would have a secret trial without a lawyer present and there would be nothing that Daniel could do. He made a quick call to a friend of his in the intelligence department. He didn't call him very much only when he was desperate. Ezekiel was already in bad shape and he was afraid that he might be killed and never heard from again. This was not unusual. Time was of the essence. He would have to work quickly to find out where he had been taken. He called Stephen to tell him that he had made a break in the case and that he would not be able to come over but that he had some work to do. Stephen said that he understood and to keep him posted as soon as possible. Daniel didn't have the nerve to tell him that he didn't even know where Ezekiel had been taken. This would only make him worry.

After several phone calls Daniel thought that he had made a breakthrough when he opened his mailbox and received a letter from someone that they had some information that would be helpful in this case. There was no name given but that the person would contact him in a few days. Daniel needed some help because he was at a dead end. The next morning after the mailbox incident he got a phone call from a man that he did not know. He said that he needed to meet him at the old synagogue. Daniel said that he could be there right away. Simon had gone to the synagogue as he had told Ezekiel to see what they could salvage and what would need to be done to refurbish the old synagogue. He noticed that the Torah scrolls cabinet had been smashed but it could still be refurbished so he brought some tools and began to dismantle it from the wall. This was no easy feet because the cabinet was quite large. He knew that Ezekiel would be happy. He was more worried about the community than his own life. He wanted to help Ezekiel but wasn't sure how. He didn't want the rest of the community to know about his dealings with the dark side. He still wanted that to remain a secret.

Daniel had not even taken the time to come to the synagogue where all of this began. He could still smell the odor from the smoke. Nothing had been touched as if it only happened a day ago. Simon took him outside to show him where the van sat that had the actual bomb in it. Daniel was amazed that anyone lived through such an explosion. "Did they all survive?"

"Yes. Rabbe Isak is the only one who experienced extensive damage from the incident. He was in the sanctuary praying when it happened. One of these large pillars fell on him and he had surgery. But he is doing quite well now. I cannot bare to tell him what is happening to Ezekiel it just might kill him. Ezekiel is like a son to him."

"I understand. But tell me why have you asked me here?" Daniel had a lot to do but needed all the help that he could get.

"I am a business man and want to help the community. I told Ezekiel that I had some money and that I would rebuild the synagogue and school. This is the heartbeat of this community. I came to assess the damage and noticed that the Torah scroll cabinet could be fixed. When Ezekiel came through here during the fire he broke the cabinet in order to save the scroll. We are very grateful to him for this. It was a sign that there is still hope for us here in Russia. You know that they hate the Jewish people. We survive by the grace of God. To make a long story short let me show you something." The two men walk over to where the cabinet once sat. "This is where I took the cabinet down."

Daniel could see that there was a hole in the back of the cabinet space. Large enough for something to be put behind the cabinet. "Did you find something behind the cabinet? Come on man speak up?"

"Hold on now. I need to talk to you first about this. I took the stuff home and put it in a safe place. I have a safe at home where I keep my important papers. I knew Mishenko as well as Ezekiel maybe even better. He told me that one day he was going to take his family and leave Russia because he and his father had gotten in with the government over there heads. I was just a friend so I kept my mouth closed. I really don't know how much Ezekiel knew about him but this is the point. Mishenko built this synagogue and I guess he decided that he would take some precautions just in case the government found out about him he could use it as leverage but he never got a chance to."

"What are you saying? What did you find?"

"In the back of the cabinet there was a briefcase. It had pictures, ledgers of bank payoffs and lots of information that implicated a lot of very influential people in the government. You can come to my house and get it tomorrow. You must be very careful because these people are dangerous. No one knows about the briefcase but me. I have told no one. I believe that they blew up the synagogue in hopes to kill Ezekiel because they think that he knows something that he probably doesn't even know. I am not a good person. Ezekiel is as good as gold. He doesn't deserve to be treated this way. Do not tell anyone about this. As long as they think that he has information he will stay alive."

Daniel sat down on what was a pew bench. Part of it was burned but it still was solid enough to hold his weight. He didn't know what he should do next. He had to get this information but how could he use it without getting himself and Ezekiel killed. "Simon if you can get a copy of this information made without letting anyone know please make a copy and keep it just in case something happens to me. If something happens to me take the information and get it out of the country. Take it to America and give it to the F.B.I. At least they will know the truth about what has happened here. Until then don't do anything. I will come and see you tomorrow evening. Thank you for all of your help. I hope that we can use this to get Ezekiel and maybe even Mishenko out of prison."

Daniel had to think carefully about how to proceed from here. Ezekiel had been moved and he didn't know where he was. Now he has this information that maybe could be used but these guys were dangerous. They would have no trouble killing him and Ezekiel and taking the contents of the briefcase and destroying it without anyone's knowledge. He wondered how high the conspiracy went. Mishenko definitely knew what he was doing but he didn't think it through. Daniel didn't want to make the same mistake. He would have to be a bit shrewder than Mishenko.

This case was becoming more than Daniel wanted in his life. For a moment he thought to take the briefcase to America and give it to the government and then just disappear but he thought about the angels and knew that he would never be able to live in peace until this whole thing was resolved and Ezekiel was set free. Benjamin and Stephen were doing all that they could.

Chapter 12

Ezekiel had been sleeping in his cell when an officer came to tell him that he was being moved. Ezekiel was still groggy from the drugs he had been given he was somewhat delirious. "Where are we going? Does my lawyer know about this?"

"Yes he knows all about it. Don't worry." The officer escorted Ezekiel along with a bunch of other prisoners into a van. Ezekiel was frightened and could only think the worse. His ordeal was only getting worse. He wondered whether he would ever be a free man again. He thought of his wife and daughter and hoped that they were safe. He would pray and hope that one day he would be delivered. He looked at the other men that were in the van. He didn't know why they were there but he would not pass judgment because he was an innocent man. The men all seemed to be in their own world. No eye contact was accomplished and the silence could be cut with a knife. Vladimir sat next to Ezekiel. He couldn't help but notice that Ezekiel was bleeding from his head and neck. "You must have gotten someone pretty mad. These police they are brutal. You will learn to keep your mouth closed and tell them whatever they want to know. I have been to prison many times. It's not so bad once you learn the tricks. I have friends inside. You stick with me and I will help you. No problem." Ezekiel just turned his head slightly to look at the man next to him. He didn't understand why he would want to help him he didn't even know his name or anything about him. One thing Ezekiel knew was that he didn't want anyone to know that he was Jewish. He just felt that it would not be well for him.

"I didn't do anything. When they picked me up they beat me up before we even got to the station. They think I have information about a government conspiracy or something. I don't know what I'm going to do. I think that they will ship me off to Siberia and I'll never see my family again."

"Oh man. Now that's some important stuff. Me I'm just a drug dealer. This time I'll be here for a few years. I don't have any other way of making a living so I keep selling the drugs. This for me is just a short time off the streets. My people will take care of me inside and after I do my time I'll be back at it again. This is nothing. I'm Vladimir. I know people. If I can help you I will. In my line of work its important to know people." Vladimir looked like a ruthless character. He looked like one of those guys that worked out at the gym every day and took steroids. His arms were huge and he had a neck that was enormous. But he wasn't there for killing anyone so Ezekiel hoped that he had made a friend. He had never been to prison and needed to get to Daniel to tell him where he was. Maybe Vladimir could help him. He would take his advice though and keep his mouth closed. The police wanted information but he didn't have any information to give them.

The prison was only about fifty miles outside of Moscow. When the van arrived the door opened and the men filed out one by one. It was a typical prison. There were guards in towers as high as the trees. The barbed wire would make it next to impossible to climb over the fences that lined the whole perimeter. The group was ordered to file one by one into a holding tank before entering the prison. Even though they had been checked before entering the jail the police wanted to make sure they had no drugs or weapons on them before entering the prison. Each man was taken into a room and ordered to take off all of their cloths to be checked for drugs or weapons of any type. Ezekiel had never felt so violated in his life.

After the check each man was given a blanket, some linen for the bunk and a few personal items. How they would survive with just these things Ezekiel didn't know? All he wanted at this point was to lay down and sleep. They had arrived just in time for dinner. After being assigned a cell the group lined up for dinner. The officers acted as though the inmates were in the military. Everything was done in military fashion. When they arrived at the dining area each person stood behind their chair and had to wait until the officer instructed them to go up and get a tray and get their meals. Ezekiel didn't know what he was supposed to do so Vladimir told him to stick close and he would show him the ropes. He still didn't know why Vladimir was being so nice to him. All he could think was that he needed a friend. He had to get news to his family that he was in prison but that he was okay thus far.

After the men got their trays and meals they were allowed to come back to the table but they had to stand behind their chairs before they could sit down. The officer gave the order for them to sit when he was ready. It must have been some kind of tactic to keep the men in submission. Ezekiel just followed suit with what he saw the other men do. There wasn't much time for talking either. The officers walked around watching their every move. The food wasn't the best but Ezekiel knew that he would have to eat what was prepared. He would have to pray that God would forgive him for eating that which was unclean for him. There would be no special diet prepared for Jewish people here.

He was glad when the meal was finished. He just needed to lay down. His head was hurting terribly. If Daniel could come and see him maybe he could get him some medical attention. His injuries were not healing properly. If he got an infection that would not be good for him. He was lucky though to get a cell with Vladimir. Maybe God was looking out for him. He was like a big brother. Vladimir couldn't stop talking about his exploits in the drug world. Ezekiel wasn't much for talking but he listened as much as he could before drifting off to sleep.

The morning seemed to have come too quickly. At four o'clock in the morning the men were awakened by the sound of a loud siren bellowing from the prison system. Vladimir told Ezekiel that it was time to get up for breakfast. Ezekiel could not believe it. His head was still hurting and he didn't have much energy for whatever they were going to be doing at four o'clock. He had fallen asleep in his uniform so he only needed to brush his teeth and wash his face. When he looked in the small mirror over the sink in the cell he looked in the mirror to see a face that he barely recognized. The few days in jail had already taken its toll. He had not seen the bruises on his head and neck. The world should know how people were being treated in Russia. If the Russian's got their way they would take over America and put all the people in prisons like this one. It was so dark and cold. There was no sunlight, nothing beautiful happened here and people were being held against their will.

Ezekiel paid more attention to his surroundings this morning. He was very tired and sick when they arrived from Moscow. The prison was a lot larger than he noticed last night. When the officer came around each man had better be ready or else they would be beaten terribly and would not be allowed to go and eat breakfast. After breakfast was over it was time for each man to be assigned his job. Vladimir was right he did have contacts behind the prison walls. He asked the officer in charge if he and Ezekiel could work in the machine shop. He told Ezekiel that he liked working in the shop because the officers always needed parts and he would use his influence to get whatever they needed. The prisons worked on a barter system. The government was not good about taking care of the inmates. They allowed that family members could bring food items, cigarettes, televisions, chairs or whatever the prison needed. Vladimir figured that the reason they kept bringing him back was because they needed him. He was right he did have great contacts on the outside. He waited for any opportunity to get what he wanted. Sometimes he sabotaged the machines just so he could make phone calls to get parts that he broke.

The day actually wasn't so bad. Being able to work made the day go by faster. Vladimir didn't have much of a singing voice but he like singing. He talked constantly and asked a lot of questions. Ezekiel wasn't sure whether he should trust him but needed to know whether he was for real or not. "So slick you got some government contacts or something? You said that the government put you here because you know about some conspiracy. I know some people in high places too. Maybe we can help one another."

"No I didn't say that I knew people. What happened was that a friend of mine knew these people and they put him in prison for espionage against the government. I wish that I could find him maybe he could help me out of this mess. I really don't know a thing."

"Yeah you really don't look like a thug. Hey I tell you what there is this lady she came in here one time to do a story about the prisons. From what I heard it really put some heat in the government to make changes in the prison system. Personally I don't see any changes but maybe if you get in touch with somebody like her she can help you get out of here. Maybe you can say you are sick or something and they will put you in the hospital. I've seen guys do that."

"Really." Ezekiel could only hope that it would be so easy for him. They wanted him out of the way. They would probably kill him first.

After a week in the prison Ezekiel was waiting for the right moment to ask Vladimir to make a phone call to Daniel to tell him that he was in prison and that he needed help. He wasn't sure whether he could really trust Vladimir. He would have to trust someone. Vladimir was a drug dealer and although he had connections he was still on the inside. While at work Vladimir had to make a call for some parts and after making his call he looked around and gave Ezekiel a cell phone. Ezekiel could not believe that he had somehow gotten a cell phone into the prison. He had not even told him about it. He just smiled. "Hurry up. If we get caught we will be separated and I will not be able to help you."

Ezekiel took the cell phone and dialed Stephen at the house. The phone rang and rang. Ezekiel's heart was beating so hard in his chest he thought he was going to have a heart attack right there. There would be no need for help. He would be put in a bag and sent back to his family. After quite a few rings someone finally answered the phone. "Hello this is Stephen."

Ezekiel was so happy to hear his voice but knew he had only a few minutes. He had wedged himself in between the machine so that no one would be able to see or hear him. The officers were always watching but Vladimir had good connections so they could do relatively what they wanted while at work. "Uncle Stephen this is Ezekiel. I can't talk long I'm in prison. They moved me from the jail in Moscow. You must tell Daniel so you can get me out of here."

Stephen couldn't believe that he was talking to Ezekiel. He started yelling for Benjamin to come downstairs. "Benjamin, Benjamin. I have Ezekiel on the phone."

Ezekiel was scared to death and Vladimir was looking out but he was grabbing for the phone at the same time. It was time to end the call. "Stephen I have to go. Tell Daniel I'm in prison." Ezekiel ended the call and got up as though he was picking something up from off the floor. No harm was done and Vladimir put the phone in his pocket and the two men went back to work.

"What is he saying?" Benjamin was grabbing at the phone too. He wanted to ask Ezekiel where he was and how he was doing. He could not believe that the government would do such a thing and take the man to prison without even so much as a trial. He would have to get in touch with Daniel right away and tell him that they had in fact heard from Ezekiel and that he was in prison and needed help.

Daniel was feeling stressed out and spent a few hours at the gym taking it out on the treadmill. He needed to clear his head. His cell phone went off and he almost shut it off but looked at the number just in case it was an emergency. The number was from Stephen's house. "Hello this is Daniel."

"Daniel this is Stephen. You need to come over right away."

"What's happening? You are talking too fast. I'm at the gym right now. Can it wait?"

"No Daniel. I need you now. We just got a phone call from Ezekiel."

"You what? Where is he? I'll be right there." Daniel didn't even bother to change his cloths. He jumped in his car and drove directly to the house. The traffic was terrible but it only took him a few minutes to get to the house. When he arrived he could see that Stephen was reasonably shaken up. He had not told him that Ezekiel had been moved. He would have some explaining to do.

Benjamin tried to keep his composure but Stephen was all in Daniel's face. "Did you know that my nephew was in prison or is this news to you?" Daniel turned red and didn't answer quickly so that gave him away right away.

"I'm sorry Stephen but when I went to the jail I was told that he had been moved. I didn't want to tell you about it until I had figured out what had happened and what we should do next. Really I'm quite stumped. I'm glad that he called. If he calls again ask him where he is and then we can work from there. The good thing is that he is still alive."

"Is that all you have to say? My nephew's life is in danger. We have got to do something." Benjamin tried to calm his friend. He understood that this was a very precarious situation and that it would not be easy to get through this whole thing. He would have to make some more phone calls in hope that someone would help them. Daniel left the house with his tail between his legs. He was stuck between a rock and a hard place and he didn't know how to get out. He understood how Stephen felt. If it were his son or nephew he would be afraid too. The government was not to be trusted.

Daniel needed a fresh perspective on this case so he went home and took a shower to change his cloths. He was planning on calling a good friend of his for dinner. She always had good ideas for the hard cases. She also had contacts in the American Jewish community that might be able to help. Tsilia was an activist extraordinaire. She loved taking on the government. She too had family that lost their lives in the Holocaust. It was her life work to make sure that people were not being treated unfairly. He wasn't sure how much he should tell her for her own good but he knew that he could trust her. On his way to pick her up he would go and get the briefcase. No one knew about it as far as he knew. The police would have come after them by now. That briefcase had information that would implicate not only government officials but other businessmen as well. They would not want their faces on the local television news. It was a way of getting things done but Daniel didn't feel that was the way to go. He made a quick call to Simon to make sure that he was home as he pulled up to his house. He couldn't believe that a businessman of Simon's caliber could own such a luxurious home. He wondered what kind of business he was in. Maybe he was a part of the conspiracy too. But he didn't want to get into his business. To date he was the only one that was helping him. But he would surely keep his address and phone number for further use. He was sure he was into something.

Simon answered the door. It didn't seem as though his wife and family were at home that evening. All the better he didn't want anyone seeing him come to the house. Daniel stepped into the house. It was immaculately kept up. You could eat off the floors in that house. Simon was doing pretty well for himself. He did say that he was putting the money into fixing up the synagogue and the school. That would take a pretty penny because the place was demolished. He would have to spend a lot of money to get it fixed up. Anyway Simon lead him into his office and the two men sat down for a drink. Daniel had a difficult day and he didn't usual drink alcohol but felt the need for a drink that evening.

"What happened to you? You were supposed to be here a week ago. Since you didn't show up I've been analyzing the contents of the briefcase. How have you been since we met last?"

"Not so good. I found out that they moved Ezekiel from the jail. I had not told Stephen because I didn't know what I wanted to do next. In the meantime Ezekiel managed to make a phone call home from prison. I had egg on my face something awful."

"Don't feel so bad Daniel. This is not an easy situation. I hope that he is doing okay and that this will be over for him very soon. Believe me I know what it is to be in a place you don't want to be in. I can't get into it right now. But one day I will be leaving this place. It is corrupt. You need to review these tapes and ledgers. There is stuff on politicians, the Russian mafia, the Jewish mafia and the police. It's more than I can believe. Mishenko was in over his head." Simon lit his cigar and handed the briefcase over to Daniel.

"You said what? I'm almost afraid to take this. I don't want to die for this guy. I'm only a lawyer. What was this Mishenko into anyway? No wonder they are holding onto Ezekiel. By the way Simon you look like you might know some important people. Do you know anyone that might be able to get some information on where Ezekiel is being held." Simon didn't say anything right away.

"Uh maybe I might know someone. Let me make some phone calls and if I find out something I'll call you right away."

"Come on Simon. Stop worrying about yourself. I know that you have a family and a life but there is an innocent man out there that might lose his life. Think about his wife and daughter. Maybe if you are in hot water yourself if we can get Ezekiel out then we can help you too."

"Your right Daniel. I will make some phone calls and get some information. Just give me a minute. We'll get Ezekiel out of this. It will take a little time but we have a lot of leverage here. I won't do anything without telling you about it first. I know how these people think."

Daniel left that evening with renewed faith that Ezekiel's life would be spared and he would be with his family soon.

Chapter 13

Vladimir was a good guy but he didn't quite know how to keep his mouth closed. After work the inmates were allowed some time outside in the recreational area. Ezekiel noticed that there were cliques and everyone stayed in their own group. Victor was a drug dealer and there was bad blood between him and Vladimir. Vladimir kept picking at him for no reason at all. Victor was sitting on the side with his boys laughing and talking. Vladimir said "you know Ezekiel I hate that guy. For some reason I can't get it out of my mind that he is the reason for my being put back inside again."

"How do you figure that out?"

"Well I had a big shipment of drugs coming in. No one was supposed to know about it but at the time of pick up there were police all over the place. I was told by a friend of mine that Victor's boys found out and because he was jealous he told on me. I would never do that to him. There's enough money on the street for everyone. I'm not that kind of guy. I'm gonna cut him. He'll never tell on me again."

"Vladimir you are already doing two years don't add anymore time onto it. Come on just let it go. Look at him it didn't do him any good. He's in here too."

"Ezekiel you don't understand. If he is that kind of trash then we don't need him. Look at him he thinks he's some big shot. Don't worry no one will know that it was me. I'll get him. My boy Yulenka is going to start a fight. During the fight I'm going to stab him. No one will know the difference. You stay back or else you will get yourself hurt."

Vladimir motioned to Yulenka and Ezekiel saw the man walk over to Victor and start talking with him. He couldn't hear what they were saying but Victor jumped up and hit the guy right in the mouth. The whole prison was in an uproar in just a few minutes. The inmates started fighting amongst themselves and the officers started running from all over the place. Vladimir ran over to the crowd and pushed through. He took out his pick and stabbed Victor several times and he fell dead in the crowd. No one even saw him do it. Ezekiel stayed back like he was told. He didn't want to get involved and would never tell anyone what Vladimir had told him.

The prison was a mess. The inmates were fighting and blood was everywhere. The police had on full military gear. It was unlike anything Ezekiel had ever seen in his life. Utter chaos had occurred. Some of the inmates had gone inside of their cells and pulled out mattresses and started burning them. Ezekiel just wanted to get out of there before someone got hurt. When the crowd got calmed down the officers were furious and everyone would pay for what had happened.

Victor and five other men died that day. Vladimir didn't shed a tear or feel any remorse for what had happened. It was all in a days work for him. This was no life for anyone. How could a man be so good and so evil at the same time? Ezekiel understood that Vladimir felt that Victor had put him in prison but to take another man's life was beyond his comprehension.

The whole prison was on lock down until further notice. The inmates were only allowed to come out for work and meals. The tension started getting really bad after the officers started to pick at the inmates. They were being beat with sticks and clubs for no reason. They made the inmates run around the compound in the cold with no jackets on for hours just laughing at them for no reason. Many were made to clean the floors, walls and machine shop areas on their knees with nothing but a toothbrush. The officers thought of anything they could do to punish the inmates. The officers wanted to make sure that the inmates knew they were not happy with what happened and that they were being punished. This went on for weeks and weeks until they finally stopped the punishment. Ezekiel and many of the inmates had gotten sick and were not receiving any medical attention.

Vladimir was getting nervous. There was talk amongst the inmates that someone said they saw him kill Victor. He would have to keep a low profile or else things might get bad for him. He could pay the guy off but then that would be an admission of guilt. He had several hiding places in the cell for his cell phones, money, girlie magazines, cigarettes and other items. If he were caught he would have gotten several more years added onto his sentence. One evening on a tip the officers came in and raided the cell without the knowledge of the inmates. Everyone was taken outside and every cell was ransacked for contraband. Vladimir did the unconscionable and didn't get rid of the pick he used to kill Victor that day. When the officers retrieved the pick they immediately shackled Vladimir and took him to solitary confinement until they could get him to break and tell what he had done. Ezekiel was all alone now. No one bothered him as long as he had his bodyguard. Now he wasn't sure how well things would go for him.

Fortunately Vladimir had informed Ezekiel where he kept all of his personal items. Amazingly the officers had not found much of what he had hid. They had only looked at the obvious places. Vladimir had a trap door in the floor directly underneath his cell where he kept the phone and his money. They never knew it was there. Since he was gone for a while Ezekiel took the phone out one evening and called home. He now knew what prison he was at so Daniel could see if he could arrange for him to get out of the prison. The officers had stopped the random punishment. The inmates were now able to sleep at night again. The officer made his rounds every two hours so Ezekiel made believe that he was sleeping and as soon as the officer passed his cell he took out the phone and called Stephen. The phone rang and rang for a few minutes and then someone finally picked up the phone. "Hello who is this?"

"Benjamin is that you? This is Ezekiel I only have a few minutes. Please tell Stephen that I love him and to tell Daniel that I am in Penal Colony #5. Tell him to get me out of here. They never even gave me a trial." Just then Ezekiel heard someone coming. "Hold on." He put the phone under the cover just in time for the officer to walk by again. He wasn't sure why he was coming back because he never did that before but he was sure that he didn't hear him. He didn't want to get caught because Vladimir would kill him and also he would be in big trouble. The officer passed his cell and Ezekiel had to end the call right away. "Benjamin are you still there?"

"Yes Ezekiel I'm still here. I will give him the information. Don't worry we will get you out of there as soon as we can." With that Ezekiel shut the phone off and replaced it in the floor where Vladimir kept it. After he had jumped into the bunk an officer came to open his cell. Did he hear him after all? What was happening? "Ezekiel, Ezekiel you have a new bunk mate?"

A young man about his age walked in with his pillow, sheets and other affects given when you arrived at hotel Russia. He looked like he was scared out of his mind. Ezekiel knew how he was feeling and was glad that he was put in with him instead of one of the ruthless criminals that lived there. He looked up at the guy and said "Hi I'm Ezekiel. What's your name?"

At first the young man didn't want to speak. His words got caught in his throat but he managed to get his name out. "I'm Mark."

"You better get some sleep. They wake us up early in the morning. What you in for?"

"Vehicular homicide. I killed a family in an automobile accident. You?"

"If you ask them espionage. But I didn't do anything wrong. I don't even know anything about what the government is doing? But anyway it's a long story."

"Well I have nothing but time. I won't ever get out of this place. But for what its worth you don't look like a spy." The two men smile.

While Mark got his bunk ready to sleep now Ezekiel was really worried about Vladimir. He didn't have much conversations with the officers but he would have to ask Officer Zubkov what happened to him when he went to work the next day. He was the officer that watched over the shop. Vladimir had done many favors for him. This one was over his head or else Vladimir would not have been taken away and put in solitary. He had gotten cigarettes, alcohol and just about anything that they wanted. It was a shame that they could not help him now. But Vladimir had crossed the line and taken a life.

That morning he showed Mark the ropes just as he was shown by his friend when they arrived a month earlier. Ezekiel could not believe that one month had already gone by since they arrived. He ached to see his wife and daughter again. He didn't know why he was in this predicament but tried to make the best of it. He thought about how difficult it was for his father and his ancestors when they worked in the camps. This was a five star hotel compared to the conditions they lived in. Vladimir had made sure that he had some real food to eat every day. He used his influences to benefit him and he still wasn't sure why. He sure wished that he could do something to help his friend now. Mark came to work with him in the machine shop. He couldn't believe that the officer allowed him to do this when he asked. He was afraid to ask but was happy when he said yes. Mark had made a terrible mistake but Ezekiel believed in redemption. The Torah taught that people should be forgiven. He wasn't a bad man but the alcohol impaired his judgment and he was the cause of the loss of life. For this he had to pay but he really was a nice guy.

Officer Zubkov was standing in the shop doing his round as usual when Ezekiel decided to ask him about Vladimir. They were allowed a cigarette break but Ezekiel didn't smoke so he would usually go outside and get some fresh air for a minute till the break was over. Instead this time he managed the courage to ask about his friend. "Officer Zubkov if you don't mind have you any word about Vladimir?" The officer always had a smug look about him but he really was a nice guy compared to some of the others.

"Vladimir has been accused of killing Victor Mikhailovich. Bunch of drug dealers. Vladimir had it good around here. If he had just done good he could have been out of here in a few months. But instead he had to settle the score with Victor. Piece of trash that Victor. He was a rat but not worth the time. Now Vladimir will serve a life sentence. He will be in solitary with only one hour outside a day. Don't make the same mistake. Keep your nose clean and stay out of trouble. Hey do you know his contacts we need some things for the shop?"

"Well he asked me to make some calls sometimes for him but I don't know whether I can do that now. If you can get some things to him I'm sure he won't mind my making some phone calls for him. Like he will need some smokes and some food. Can you get these things to him in solitary?" The officer looked down at his shoes and then into the air.

"Maybe. It all depends on what you can do for me. I need some smokes too and a few other things. You get them and I'll see what I can do."

"Okay. Also can you get me into see him? Then he can tell me other people who can help get you what you need. He was the man not me. Get me to see him and then we can talk about what you need."

"Okay. This is what we will do. Tonight when the lights go out I can take you to see him. You tell him that I need things and that I will help him if he helps me. That's it. Only one visit." Ezekiel could not believe what was happening. Maybe one of his contacts could get word to Daniel. He had already talked to them a few times but he needed someone to help from the outside. He didn't care who these people were. His life was in danger.

That evening the officer did exactly as he said. The other officer's were drinking and playing cards most evenings after the inmates went to sleep. The place was quiet and Officer Zubkov had been there for years no one would question what he was doing. He took Ezekiel down a long flight of steps into another part of the prison. Ezekiel would not have even known that there were other cells down there. After a long walk down a dark corridor he stopped at a cell. The Officer knocked on the door and called Vladimir's name. "Vladimir this is Officer Zubkov. Wake up. There is someone here to see you."

He opened the door and shined a light into the cell. Vladimir was hunched down like a rat. There was no bunk or anything. There was a tray on the floor. Only remnants of what he had for dinner. He was sure that he was starving. Ezekiel went into the cell to talk with his friend. He looked like a small child sitting in a fetal position like that. He no longer looked like the man that he once knew. They had beat him savagely. He remembered his ordeal before getting to jail. The officers had broken him but there still was a speck of fight still left in him. "Vladimir it's me Ezekiel." One of his eyes was almost closed shut.

They had used a whip on his back. The sores were still fresh. Some looked like they were healing but then fresh ones on top. His mouth was cut open which would make it hard for him to eat. Ezekiel fought back the tears. "My friend can you hear me?"

Vladimir reached out his hand to Ezekiel. He hugged him like a long lost brother. He had realized the error of his way. Taking Victor's life was not worth what he was enduring. "Ezekiel they are going to kill me in here. I don't know how much more I can take."

"I know Vladimir. Listen I can't stay too long because I might get all of us in trouble. Officer Zubkov says that if you will let me make some phone calls to get him some things that he will get you food and cigarettes. I can get some things to help heal your wounds. At least it will make things somewhat better for you. See if you can find a place to hide the items. We can get you magazines and a phone. At least you won't go crazy in here. If you do well maybe they will let you out of here soon. Keep the faith. Will this be okay?"

"Yes, yes. Ezekiel the phone has several numbers in them. Call anyone of them. But my brother call him first. His name is Aleksis Voronkova. He is an even bigger person than I was on the street. He can get you anything that you want. If you need anything you just tell him. He will be closer to you than a brother. I promise you that. Don't forget me Ezekiel."

"Don't worry Vladimir. You are my brother. You took care of me and now let me take care of you." The tears fell down the faces of each man. Ezekiel left the cell and the Officer returned him to his cell. The next day he made a call to Aleksis Vladimir's brother to get the items the officer needed and also to get some things for Vladimir. He knew that he would have to be very careful who he spoke to and when. He didn't want anyone to know the arrangements that were made. Vladimir's life depended on it. How could Aleksis help him he didn't know but he would think about how to play that card later on.

Within a week Aleksis had a private meeting with Ezekiel. Ezekiel had never been in on the meetings with Vladimir when he was in the cell with him. He thought it quite amazing that the Russian's allowed family members to not only visit their loved one's but also to bring them food and other things. This helped them because the inmates were able to get things that they could not get. It reminded him of the stories his father told him about how before they went into the camps that the Jewish businessman who had money also had contacts that could get them food, clothing, and other items that they could use for selling and also to barter for tickets out of the country when others could not.

Aleksis looked just like Vladimir. He was a bit taller and older. By looking at his clothing you would have thought that he was some kind of banker or businessman. What a drug dealer looked like Ezekiel didn't know but this was not what he expected. He didn't know who Ezekiel was but he knew that was Vladimir's brother as soon as he walked in the room. He jumped up kind of nervous but knew that this was a friend so he didn't have to worry. "Hi I'm Ezekiel."

"Please I have not heard from my brother in quite a few weeks. What is going on?" He looked at the dirty chair before sitting in it and put a handkerchief on the seat before sitting down.

"Aleksis Vladimir killed Victor. They have him in solitary confinement. I asked the officer if I could help him. He would only do it if you brought him cigarettes and other items that he wanted. I managed to get a meeting with Vladimir and he said that I should call you. Aleksis he is alive but they have beat him terribly. When you come next time I need to have another phone and some items for the cuts and bruises. They beat him with a whip and his back is all tore up. He'll make it though. He is strong. If you have any influence at all you need to help get your brother out of here."

If looks could kill Ezekiel would have died that day. Aleksis jumped up and started shouting and throwing things around. Ezekiel understood his anger but he had to calm him down. He didn't want to mess things up for Vladimir. They were his only hope.

"Aleksis calm down. Please. We must be very careful. You are your brother's only hope."

"I'm sorry Ezekiel. He is my little brother. What a stupid thing he has done. I told him to watch his temper but he didn't listen to me. Now what am I to do? Don't worry I will get you whatever you want. These officers they are the scum of the earth. They look down on us because we sell drugs but they use us for what they want. But that's okay. I let my brother come in here to teach him a lesson. He is hard headed and doesn't listen very well as you know but he is good as gold. Now I will let him stay here for a while but I can get him out of here whenever I want. The government of Russia is crooked Ezekiel as you already know. Anyone can walk out of this prison as long as they have the right contacts and the right amount of money. Trust me I know people in high places."

"Aleksis I need your help too. I didn't want to ask so soon but if you can get in touch with someone for me I would appreciate it. I was taken from jail and put in here without a trial. The government thinks that I know something about some leak in the intelligence agency. I don't know anything about it. Please get to my lawyer. His name is Daniel Reznik. Tell him where I am. If you can help him please get me and Vladimir out of here before they kill us."

"Okay. I'll see what I can do. I gotta go. Tell my brother I love him. Don't tell him that I'm gonna get him out of here. He needs to learn a lesson. Maybe he will finally get control of himself and live right when he comes out. In the meantime the package you sent for is with the officer. You take care of my brother. I will take care of you."

This was the best breakthrough that Ezekiel had in weeks. He knew that his family was working on his case but time was of the essence. Officer Zubkov was a great asset to Ezekiel. As long as he gave him what he wanted he allowed him to see Vladimir and get him the supplies that he needed. He didn't know whether his brother would make good on getting him out of prison or whether he would die in solitary. Either way the days were turning into months and he was still in prison.

Chapter 14

Daniel was beside himself with worry about Ezekiel. He hoped that his friend Tsilia could give him some angle that he wasn't thinking about. He would check the contents of the briefcase but he didn't want to jeopardize Ezekiel's release or his life by moving too quickly. Tsilia's car was parked outside of her house when he arrived. She was a good friend from law school. Tsilia had worked hard and finished at the top of her class. But at a young age she rose quickly to the top of her law firm and realized that she did not go to law school to make a big salary, spend countless hours in the law library defending drug dealers, shady businessman and corrupt government officials. So after fifteen years in the most influential law firm in Russia she packed her bags and opened her own office. He should have called her sooner but he had no idea the gravity of Ezekiel's situation.

Tsilia heard a car pulling up to the house and went to the window to see if it was Daniel. She always had an eye for Daniel but he was too intimidated to ask her out when they were in school. But they did become friends before leaving school and kept in touch over the years. She put the finishing touches on her outfit and hair hoping that she might finally catch his attention.

Daniel had not seen Tsilia in almost a year. He hoped she wouldn't be angry that he had not kept in touch like a good friend would. He had gotten boggled down with clients. He hoped she would understand. Now he needed not only a friend but a true colleague that knew the ropes and also had a few tricks up her sleeve. These people played a vicious game and they didn't plan on losing.

Daniel parked the car while Tsilia looked on. She hardly recognized him he had lost quite a bit of weight. He looked great. Armed with wine, roses and candy she couldn't help but blush. She had waited quite a few years for this day. Never mind that he probably needed some advice she had all the advice he needed. Tsilia opened the door before he even knocked. "My, my what did I do to deserve all this?"

Daniel smiled his boyish smile and took Tsilia in his arms and gave her a kiss like she was the most beautiful girl in town. "What can't a man bring gifts to his favorite girl." Tsilia sure hoped that he meant that. She had a thing for him but it wasn't nice for a girl to tell a man that she liked him before he did. She would wait forever. This one was kind of slow so she would have to be patient.

The couple moved into the living room and sat down on the couch. Daniel had not been to Tsilia's home since she moved from the swank apartment in the city. "Nice place you have here. Tsilia I'm sorry that I've been so busy. It's not easy to find good friends like you."

"Your right about that. I understand. I'm a lawyer too. I've been working on a few hard cases and I've been very busy myself. How are things going with your practice? I've got more work than I can handle. Maybe we need to join forces."

"Wow that sounds great. We will have to talk about that over dinner. Are you ready to go?"

"Sure. I hope this restaurant is better than the last one we went to. I like exotic food but I don't like things moving on my plate. Let's just go get a steak or something."

"Sure that sounds good. There are plenty of places that have a good steak. So tell me what kind of cases are you working on these days?"

"Well I'm working with this family that was in a car accident and their son lost his legs in the accident. I'm just trying to make sure that the insurance company doesn't take advantage of them. I don't usually work on this type of case but they don't have any money. They are poor and if someone doesn't help them they will end up on the street. I just can't let that happen. You know how these things work. The insurance company doesn't give a crap about these people. It's just a matter of money for them."

"I know Tsilia. I have a doosey for you. I hope that you either know someone or have some tricks up your sleeve that I can use to help this guy."

"I don't know. What is the problem?"

"Well this young Jewish Rabbe has been falsely imprisoned because the government believes that he was a co-conspirator with another Jewish businessman that had some very serious information given to him by a Russian intelligence officer. The businessman was sent to jail for espionage and now I'm trying to get this guy out of prison. He had absolutely nothing to do with the government. He doesn't know anything about what the intelligence officer told the businessman and to boot the government is hiding him out in prison. They didn't even bother to give him a trial. I have never seen anything like this before. I just absolutely don't know what to do."

"Well Daniel. Sounds like you are in over your head."

"You think."

"I'm sorry. I see the passion you have for this case."

"Yeah. And to boot I had these two angels that came to me and told me to make sure that I help this guy. Can you believe it? I'm sorry do you believe in that sort of thing."

"You mean real angels. Well yeah I believe in angels. I've never seen one. But I'm sure that people do. I'm sorry Daniel I have not seen you in a year and you come back into my life with espionage and angels and my word. This is a bit much to take in. Let me have a drink and maybe I can think clearly."

Daniel stopped the car at the restaurant and a young man dressed in a nice suit came to open his door. First he opened Tsilia's door and she stepped out looking elegantly. Daniel opened his own door and took the ticket. The young man drove off in the car and the couple walked up to the restaurant. Daniel had not called for reservations so he hoped they had a table available. The restaurant was surprisingly empty for a Saturday evening. A nice waiter walked up to the couple "would you like a table by the window or a booth?"

"A booth would be nice. Thank you."

Tsilia was ready for a drink. She had a feeling that this was going to be a very interesting evening. This case that Daniel was talking about sounded like something from a James Bond movie. She would help him as much as possible but she was going to make him pay dearly for her services.

After they were seated Tsilia didn't wait to order the biggest drink on the menu. She had a hard week and now this. But she had a thing for Daniel and was after all a bit intrigued about this case. She remembered hearing about a case about a Jewish businessman that was spouting his mouth off about the government and then they pounced on him. Everybody knew that he must have had some information on the government. He and three of his associates were imprisoned for espionage. His wife left the country end of story.

"So tell me about this young man of yours."

"Well Tsilia as far as I know this rabbe is clean. His parents were Holocaust survivors. They didn't have much money. They have no contacts. His uncle paid for him to go to college and he just accepted a job working at the school connected to the synagogue. You may have heard that a few months ago the synagogue was bombed. No one was killed but now he is in prison fighting for his life. I have to help him Tsilia. I figured that maybe you might have some connections you know. I saw him once in jail. The next thing I know he's calling from prison to tell us that they have moved him. How can they just take a person to prison without a trial?"

"Daniel the Russian government doesn't care about the law. They do whatever they want to do. Right now they are trying to take over Georgia. So do you think that they will not take your one little jewish man and put him in prison. I'm wondering why he's still alive. They could have killed him by now. They must be looking for something that they think he has. They will keep him as long as they don't have what they are looking for."

"Ok. I'm following you. Well say we find out what they are looking for then what do we do?"

"Well Daniel it all depends on what they are looking for. Well let's assume we have what they are looking for and we make arrangements with the appropriate people to get him out of prison. I would say that there is a chance that he still might not live. If they are ruthless enough to set a bomb then they don't care about his life. So you had better be very careful with these people. It would be easier to break him out of prison than to negotiate with criminals. They have no morals. So do you have any information?"

"Tsilia you know that I trust you. I just don't want to get you involved in something that might get your hurt. I would never forgive myself for that."

"Thank you Daniel but I think that I'm involved already. I know people that you don't know. They will know what to do. Tell me what you have."

"Well actually I'm not sure what I have yet. But all that I can tell you is that this has something to do with a war that Russia is planning on America."

"Are you crazy?" Tsilia nearly drinks her whole drink in one gulp. "A war. Come on Daniel. This is a bit much even for you. How in the world did you find these people?"

"I didn't find them they found me. I was just minding my business. Well a friend of a friend told them about me. Said that I was the best lawyer he knew. Can you believe it? I wish I had never met these people. And now I got these angels following me. I guess they knew that I would chicken out of this whole thing. I don't know what to do. But somehow he has gotten in touch with his uncle a few times and we know where he is. How can we get in to the prison to speak with him?"

"Getting into the prison is not difficult. We need to get him out of the prison. These people are not going to give up Daniel. I think we need to go over the information you have. If it is worth it I can get in touch with some people in America. We can get them to come over here and work a deal to get the guy out of the country. But what you need to do is to make a copy of all the material. We will turn the information over and then when we get him out of the country we can turn it over to the American government. They will not be happy but we might be saving millions of lives. See this is the case I live for. It's kind of dangerous but I believe in justice." "You make it sound so easy Tsilia."

"It is in a way. The thing we need to do is use the right go between. Someone very high up in the American government. Listen the Russian's are a bunch of crooks. All they want is that information back. We can use it to get the guy out of prison. We get him asylum in America. End of story. Listen there must be some very important people implicated in this thing. If they want to protect their reputation they will keep their mouths closed. They are not going to want this information put on national television. It will ruin them. It's the oldest trick in the book. This is why I got out of the firm. This type of thing went on all the time. I feel sorry for the businessman. He should have kept his mouth closed. But for now we have to get the innocent guy free and maybe save millions of lives as well."

"Okay Tsilia. Listen I'm sorry about dinner. I didn't mean to mess the whole thing up talking about work. Let's talk about something else for a change. I forgot to tell you how beautiful you look in that dress. Is it new?"

Tsilia was eating up all the attention the love of her life was bestowing on her. For the first time in months Daniel felt that Ezekiel would actually see the light of day. He and Tsilia had a good time together but he still wasn't sure whether he should involve her any more than he had already. She was a great person and a good lawyer she helped a lot of people and deserved to have a good life. But he had to face the fact that she had contacts that he didn't have. All he wanted was to get Ezekiel free and go back to his life.

Chapter 15

Daniel had not done much dating in his life. He didn't look at himself as much of a ladies man. There was something intriguing about Tsilia. She was smart and had accomplished a lot in her few years on the earth. She had a passion for people and put that before making money. She had a true blessing on her life despite leaving the firm she was doing quite well on her own. Daniel would have to think long and hard about joining forces with her. He realized though after seeing her that he wanted to see her again. Whether there was a spark of interest he wasn't sure but it would be nice. He wasn't getting any younger he would be blessed to have a beautiful wife like Tsilia.

It had been a long day and Daniel wanted to get Tsilia home so he could finally get a peak at what was in the briefcase. Poor Ezekiel was depending on him and to date he had made no progress in his case. The community had stopped coming to the police station. He didn't much blame them. They were not at all moved by the compassion of the people to see justice done in this case. The government was holding the cards but Daniel hoped that they had some good cards in that briefcase. Simon said that he would make a few phone calls and now Tsilia was entering the army to see justice done for the weak.

It was his hopes to just drop Tsilia off and come back to see her in a few days after he had looked at the contents of the briefcase and then they could go over its contents together. But Tsilia asked him to come in for a drink and he didn't have the guts to turn her down. It had already been one year since he had seen her last and he needed her help. He didn't want to hurt her feelings so he obliged her the drink. After contemplation he brought the briefcase in with him. They could look at it together.

Tsilia noticed Daniel getting the briefcase out of the backseat. She had other things on her mind and couldn't help but ask what the briefcase contained. "A man has to take time off for fun don't you think?"

"Sure but I have something to show you. This briefcase is supposed to contain some very confidential information that might help us with the case. I wasn't going to show it to you but I thought better of that and figured we could look at the contents together. Perhaps I can get a good night sleep for once if you can give me some points on what to do next for this case. I really need to get something going for this young man."

"Okay. Bring it in. We can go over it together." Tsilia really didn't want to do any work but Daniel seemed like he was really frazzled about this case. If she could get him some help then it would be for the good. It was just good spending time with her long lost friend again."

The couple entered Tsilia's home and Daniel got a chance to really see how lovely her home was. She was an even better decorator than she was a lawyer. She would definitely be a great catch. She had her own place, business and she was absolutely beautiful. Daniel sat on the couch and immediately opened the case while Tsilia went into her room to change into something more comfortable and take off her shoes. Daniel was surprised as soon as he opened the briefcase. There were several ledgers, tapes, memo pads, a gun with a silencer which scared him to death. He hoped that no one had been killed with that gun. He pulled the contents from the case one by one and put them in piles on the coffee table. He hoped that Tsilia didn't mind. He found underneath its contents a trap door in the case that contained lots of money. He was sure that Simon had not seen the trap door otherwise the money probably would not be in the case. What in the world was Mishenko planning on doing with this money and all this information. One ledger contained names, phone numbers, addresses and payment amounts. He was obviously paying some very important people money for what he wasn't sure. Or maybe he was accepting payments. Daniel wasn't quite sure which one it was.

Tsilia came out of the kitchen dressed in jeans and a shirt. She looked like a young girl again the way she was dressed. When she saw the contents of the briefcase she almost dropped the glasses and the wine bottle she was holding. "Sorry what in the world is all of that?" The table was full of money and the gun was on the table as well. She was quite startled. She was reminded of some of the cases she worked while at the firm which included some very shady characters. That was one of the reasons that she left. She didn't want to lose her life for the sake of one of the scum bags.

"I'm sorry Tsilia. Please sit down and let me explain. Ezekiel's friend Simon is paying for the work on the synagogue and the school. When he went to see what could be saved he was going to take down the Torah scroll cabinet. They have this cabinet that holds the scroll. Ezekiel saved the scroll the day of the bombing. In any case Simon found this case in the back of the wall behind the cabinet. He called me to come and pick it up. He said that he examined the contents and there should be something in this case that would help us get Ezekiel free. I also asked that he make a copy just in case something happened to me."

Tsilia was very nervous now. She wanted to help but when she saw the gun and the money it frightened her. She wanted to think about it but now she had already gotten in too deep. She might as well help. She only hoped that she would not live to regret it.

Mishenko was obviously afraid that one day he would be in trouble with either the government or the people that he worked for so he hid all of this information as perhaps an insurance policy but he got caught first and never got a chance to retrieve it from the synagogue. The pieces of the puzzle are coming together but Daniel still had not the full picture. The ledgers showed that Mishenko was either paying or receiving large sums of money from lots of people. It would have been good to have a talk with him but no one knew where he was or his wife. Maybe the contents might give some information where she had relocated to. Whether Mishenko was still alive was a big question as well.

Mishenko did however leave a video tape with some information on it. It was like how some people do when they are about to die. They make a video tape of what they want to tell their loved ones before they die. Mishenko was a smart man only he got caught. Tsilia and Daniel decided to review the tape. Perhaps it could tell them what Mishenko was into and maybe where his wife was hiding. Tsilia popped the tape in her recorder and they both sat back to watch.

Mishenko was a young jewish businessman. In his tape he talked about how he had a very good friend Dmitry Golikova who worked as a Russian intelligence officer out of the Russian Embassy in America. He met him through his father who made many different types of guns for the Russian military. They were involved in many different things such as money laundering, sex trafficking, drug sales and contract hits. After quite a few years of spying on the American government he got caught sitting outside of the State Department. They had been watching him for some time but waited for the right moment to arrest him. In exchange for his life he accepted a bargain to turn over evidence on the Russian government to the State Department what Russia was doing and why. How this could help Ezekiel now Daniel did not know. According to him the American government already had the evidence against Russia. He needed more to help Ezekiel.

He then went on to say that he was sending his wife and children out of Russia to be with Dmitry because he was able to get asylum for them as well. So if he could find Dmitry he could find Mishenko's wife. What she could do for them he didn't know but he had to get all of the pieces of the puzzle. Ezekiel's life depended on it.

The most intriguing piece of information he spoke about was received not from the intelligence officer but from another source. This source told him that the government planned on using what was called the E.M.P. (Electro Magnetic Pulse). This piece of equipment would knock out all the power in the United States. All life in America would cease. There would be no electricity to power the computers that literally make everything happen in the world. There would be no contact by television, radio or telephone. America would be helpless. In the two week period that the power would be down America would be hit by several submarines. They would be hitting Washington, San Diego, New York City, Miami, Seattle, San Francisco and Las Angeles. Daniel and Tsilia looked at each other and could not believe what they were hearing. Could this possibly be true? This sounded like Russia wanted to take over the United States of America.

When the take over is complete the scientist will be taken back to work in Russia. Many of the people will be put into work camps for the government. Those people who try to fight against the government will be killed. There will be a new system of government by which every person will be given a number. The number will be put in the forehead or the arm. Daniel felt sick to his stomach. He was a jewish man and he had a disdaine for any system that involved a number. The Germans had this system and his people were made to have a number. He would have to get Ezekiel out of prison and get this information to America. Their lives literally depended on them getting this information.

According to his source Russia already has planted in America many, many Russian soldiers as well as intelligence officer that were watching the government, and the cities. There were already in place bombs in all of the cities ready for the take over. In the briefcase Mishenko had detailed plans and locations where the bombs had been placed. He also had information concerning the collaboration of Russian intelligence with Iran and other Islamic nations. Russia wanted to be the number one nation of the world and the muslims wanted to get rid of the jews and take over Israel. A blood pack had been made between them with Iran and Syria. They would have to have control of the United States in order to help the muslims. As long as the United States stood with Israel they would not be able to accomplish their goal of taking over Israel.

Daniel couldn't absorb everything Mishenko was saying but he was trying to put it all together. He and Tsilia just looked at each other as though this was some kind of sick joke. But if it were true then the world was preparing for World War III. Daniel took the contents and put them all back in the briefcase. He and Tsilia were quiet for quite sometime. He didn't know what to say. She tried to break the silence. "Daniel I think that we have stumbled on something that is bigger than both of us. We need to get this stuff out of the country as soon as possible. First thing is don't tell anyone else what we have learned. This Mishenko has no reason to lie about all of this. He is spending the rest of his life in prison right now probably because he was trying to tell the people what was about to happen. His lawyer probably did the best that he could."

"Yeah. But now how can we help Ezekiel. Tsilia God is looking at me to help this man and I don't know what to do. Now we have the true story about what is going on here. We need to get Ezekiel out of prison somehow and get him to America. From what I know they had enough time to get his wife and daughter to America but now we have to get him and this information to the American government. Do you know anyone with any pull that can get to Ezekiel and get him out of prison for any reason? Then we can sneak him out of here. Maybe we can charter a boat secretly and take him to Alaska or Canada. We just have to get him out of Russia. Then we can tell the rest of the world what we know. Tsilia we might have to leave Russia as well. Are you ready to do this? If not you can act as though you don't know anything. I won't blame you. You have a good life here and people depending on you. I don't have anything to lose. I can leave here anytime. We won't be safe. Who knows they can be watching us right now."

Tsilia didn't say anything for a few minutes. She was doing well in her life. Her law practice was finally on its feet and she didn't have a care in the world. She was doing what she wanted to do and that was helping people. So many times while working with the firm she felt as though she had a higher calling than defending the rich. She felt in her heart that there were a group of people in world that didn't have money to pay for an expensive lawyer but deserved the same legal defense than they had the privilege of retaining. This was more than she could have ever imagined but a school teacher was in prison for no other reason than he knew someone who was living dangerously. He didn't deserve what was happening to him. But maybe Ezekiel was being called of God to expose what Mishenko was trying to expose before he went to prison. While Mishenko had been in the wrong at least he was trying to do the right thing in the end.

Tsilia cared a lot about her friend and could not imagine him going through this all alone. She had never thought about leaving Russia but if that is what it took she wanted to also tell the world that her government was actually planning World War III. This was history in the making. Tsilia took Daniel's hand in hers and said, "Well I guess you have a partner. I want to see the day when Ezekiel get's out of jail too. I know how you feel about this case. You want to see justice done and so do I. Do you have a safe at home?"

"No. Do you have one here?"

"Of course. I've had to hide some very important stuff. Why don't you let me keep the briefcase here. You don't want to keep driving through town with it. If they are on to you I will have to keep it as leverage to get you out too. Don't worry this safe is hidden so that no one will find it."

"Okay. If you feel safe. I don't want anything to happen to you Tsilia. I've gotten accustomed to you being around. And I would feel terrible if I got you into anything that could hurt you."

"Oh don't worry. I've dealt with some crazy people in my time. I think that I can handle myself."

"Okay. Well I'm gonna go now. I'm really tired and there is so much that I need to think about. Let's get together in a few days. You think of a strategy and if you know anyone that can get me some information on Ezekiel that would be great."

"No problem. I want to be careful so give me a few days. I have court on Monday but I should be wrapping up that case. You be careful."

Daniel stood outside of Tsilia's house for quite sometime. The night was cool but it was tranquil and quiet. There were very few cars on the road so he was sure that no one had followed them. He didn't feel good about leaving the briefcase with Tsilia but he didn't have a safe and it was in good hands. He had not told her who had the other copy of its contents so he still had access to the information if they were on to them.

Chapter 16

Daniel was watching every car as he drove home. He had wondered whether he was making the right decisions. He didn't know Simon but yet he left a copy of the contents of the briefcase at his home. He hoped that since Simon had given him the briefcase that he had to be a good guy. That remained to be seen. Tsilia was a good friend and he trusted her but if the government found out about the briefcase she could be put in prison or killed. He would never forgive himself if this whole thing blew up in his face. There was so much information in the tape that Daniel felt overwhelmed. He wasn't much on praying but he was scared and felt that only God was going to be able to get Ezekiel out of prison. But God was asking him to get Ezekiel out of prison and he didn't know how. Daniel starting to feel overwhelmed said, "God if you want me to get Ezekiel out of prison you're gonna have to help me. I need some divine intervention because I'm in over my head." After Daniel prayed his holy prayer his cell phone began to ring. It was three o'clock in the morning. Who in the world could be calling him at this hour. It might be Tsilia or Stephen so he decided that he had better answer the phone.

"Yes. This is Daniel. Who is this?"

"You don't know me but my name is Aleksis Voronkova. You don't know me but I have a message for you from Ezekiel. He is in prison with my brother. My brother is now in solitary confinement for killing a drug dealer in prison but Ezekiel called me and he is taking care of my brother. I told him that if he takes care of my brother that I will take care of him. He asked me to call you and tell you that he is okay."

Daniel almost dropped the phone. "Please, please tell me your name again. Can I call you? Can you get a message to Ezekiel? Is there any way that I can get into the prison to see him? How does he look? I'm sorry I'm just beside myself with this case. They moved Ezekiel without telling me. He is in prison without ever having a trial."

"Well I understand. He looks fine. My brother has been taking care of him. Vladimir is a good guy. He loves people and took to your client for some reason. I will be seeing him again because I have to take him some medicine for Vladimir. Apparently the police beat him pretty bad. In any case I don't know about getting you in there. If his lawyer comes with me that will look suspicious but if someone who they don't look at as a threat comes that will probably be okay. I'll call you. Don't call me just in case they are watching. You understand?"

"Yes Mr. Voronkova. Thank you so much for calling."

Daniel looked up to heaven and said "thank you God."

Divine intervention was what Daniel needed. But for some reason he felt like he knew that name Voronkova. But he couldn't put it together where he had heard the name. Maybe it was on television or in the newspapers. He would have to ask Tsilia if she knew the name. But he was certain that he had heard that name before. In any case he had to figure out who was to go into the prison and see Ezekiel. It would have to be someone who they would not be suspicious about. Maybe that pastor friend of his would be the right person. He didn't know who Voronkova was but a Christian pastor would be a good cover. If they looked into him there would be no problem there. He didn't want to send Benjamin or Stephen because they were too close to the case. He would call him first thing in the morning and have a talk with him. He would call Stephen as well and tell him what he was planning.

Daniel went into his bedroom to take his cloths off. It had been a long night. He was happy that he had finally seen his good friend. He wished that it was under better circumstances. Tsilia was a real trooper. Sleep came quickly the alcohol made sure of that. Daniel wasn't sure whether he was asleep or awake but he was having a conversation with a Rebbe. He didn't know the man but he was sitting in a synagogue with him. The Rebbe called himself Elijah. Could this be the Prophet Elijah from the Torah. Why would he be coming to see Daniel? He was sure it had something to do with Ezekiel. Who was this man that the prophet would come on his behalf?

"Daniel do not be afraid I am the Prophet Elijah. I have come to give you a message. You prayed that God would give you help with this case. But I need you to know that there is more at stake than one man. The whole Nation of Israel is at stake." Elijah was a tall man, and his eyes were as flames of fire. He wore a garment that was probably worn back in the Torah days and he had sandals on his feet. Daniel was in awe that he was standing before such an important person. Elijah looked out over Israel. "Do you know where we are standing?"

"No Prophet Elijah where are we standing?"

"My son this is the Mount of Olives. Do you know that King David came to worship the Lord on this very mountain?"

"I'm sorry Prophet Elijah I should have known this but I do not read my Torah like I should?"

"I know my son. I weep for Israel because many of my sons and daughters have forsaken their traditions and the Torah of which holds all life and truth. I have something very important to tell you. It is I that was spoken of in the prophets that said "behold I will send Elijah the prophet before the coming of the great and dreadful day of the Lord. And he shall turn the heart of the fathers to the children, and the heart of the children to their fathers, lest I come and smite the earth with a curse. Daniel the Messiah is soon to come. The prophet wrote "And his feet shall stand in that day upon the Mount of Olives, which is before Jerusalem on the east, and the mount of Olives shall cleave in the midst thereof toward the east and toward the west, and there shall be a very great valley: and half of the mountain shall remove toward the north, and half of it toward the south." "Daniel when the Messiah comes he will put his feet upon this very mountain. It is a very sacred place. But before this happens I will be sent to speak to the people of God. Why is this necessary? It is because the children do not know God any longer. They have done what their ancestors have done and that is put their trust in idols, and a government that does not care about them. Also there is one coming upon the earth that has been sent by the devil himself to take over the world. The one that is to come hates the Jewish people and will like Hitler design a government to not only annihilate the Jewish people but anyone who does not want to be a part of his governmental system."

"But what does this have to do with me?"

"You are called Daniel to take this message to the people of God. The time is winding down and the people must prepare for what is about to take place in the earth. I will be here soon. The time will be increased because the Lord is troubled about what he is seeing in the world. His children do not know him. He cries over Israel every day. He is ready to come and save his people from annihilation."

Daniel didn't quite know what to say. The two men looked at the beauty of the land that was before them. He thought about how David had walked and prayed on that very mountain. Without realizing it the prophet had left his side and Daniel woke up with a feeling that his life had now changed forever. Daniel had stopped going to synagogue years ago. He felt bad that the prophet Elijah was indeed coming to turn his heart as well back to the fathers and to prepare for the coming of the Messiah. There was definitely a need for God to make changes in the world.

Daniel didn't get much sleep that morning. He had the strange call from a man that had talked to Ezekiel. He wasn't sure but he had a feeling that the name was familiar but he wasn't sure where he knew the name from. He slept for a few hours and wanted to make a call to Stephen. This would be very good news for him and then he would have to make contact with the pastor to see if he would be willing to go in and see his friend. Daniel was sure that it would not be a problem. If he was a true friend he would want to see him. The phone rang several times before someone answered it. Stephen answered the phone. "Stephen this is Daniel."

"Hi Daniel. Have you figured out what to do next? My poor niece is beside herself with worry for her husband. I hope you have some good news."

"Well as a matter of fact I do. I received a phone call this morning from a young man who talked with Ezekiel in prison. He says that Ezekiel has been helping his brother who has been badly beaten by the officers there. He said that he promised Ezekiel that he would help any way that he could. I think that it would be a good idea if we can get that pastor friend of his to go in and speak with him. I can't go because they will be suspicious. I don't think that it would be a good idea to send you or Benjamin. This might cause too many suspicions. What do you think?"

"Yes, you are probably right. Tell Ezekiel that we are all praying for him. Raisa and Aliya are doing fine but they miss him and are worried about him. I've told her that we have everything under control and that he will be coming out soon and we will all be together. I don't want her to worry you know."

"I understand. So I will get in touch with the pastor this afternoon and see if he is willing to go and see Ezekiel. I just want to know that he is truly okay. I've been thinking also about how we can get Ezekiel out of prison. They are not going to let him go. We might have to see if we can pay somehow to get him released. A friend of mine seems to think that if we can convince them that Ezekiel really doesn't know what they think that maybe a high level official will be able to negotiate his release but with some financial help. You see what I mean?"

"Yes I understand. I don't have a lot of money but I have some. I am willing to use whatever I have to get my nephew out of prison."

"I know you are Stephen. Hold on though. I might have a few contacts as well that could come up with some money to help with this." Daniel would use the money that Mishenko kept in the briefcase if necessary. The conversation was brief but Daniel knew that he had finally given Ezekiel's family some hope that one day he would be released from prison. Unfortunately it would not be easy to accomplish.

Before calling pastor John Daniel wanted to touch basis with Tsilia to let her know about the phone call and that he was going to ask the pastor to go in and see about Ezekiel. She might know who this Voronkova was. She knew lots of people. Tsilia had decided that it was the weekend and she wasn't going to do any work. She and Daniel had stayed up until the week hours of the morning viewing that tape and she wanted to ponder over what to do next. She had just finished preparing lunch when the phone rang. "Tsilia this is Daniel. What are you doing?"

"Hey Daniel. Nothing much. Trying to get over my hangover. I don't do much drinking. But I enjoyed myself. We will have to do it again really soon. What's up?"

"Well you would never believe what happened when I got home. I received a phone call from a Mr. Voronkova. Does that name sound familiar at to you?"

"Voronkova. I hope you don't mean who I think you mean?"

"What do you mean?"

"Well if it is who I think you mean. He and his brothers are a part of the Russian mafia. His brother has been in jail countless number of times for drug trafficking. His brother Aleksis is the elder brother and manages to stay out of jail but only because he doesn't take the risks that his brother does. He has other people to do the work for him. But on the other hand Daniel if he called you then he will actually be an ally. If anyone knows the system and a way around it he is the guy."

"Well check this out. Apparently his brother Vladimir is in prison with Ezekiel. He was beat up pretty badly by the police and Ezekiel is taking care of him. Mr. Voronkova said that he will help Ezekiel. He is being appreciative of the fact that Ezekiel is helping his brother. Can you believe this? I couldn't have planned this myself."

"So what do you want to do next?"

"I asked him if he could get someone into the prison to see Ezekiel for me. I want to call his pastor friend and ask him to go in and see Ezekiel. I will feel much better if someone I know says that he is doing okay. I don't know what to do but I think that we need to ask this Mr. Voronkova if he can talk with some of his people and find a way to sneak Ezekiel out of prison or pay him out. Then we can get him out of the country and to the United States. Tsilia they are not going to let him out any other way. We also need to get this information to the American government. There is a lot at stake here. I don't know what they will want in return but we will find out."

"Keep in mind Daniel that these people are dangerous. They can just as easily turn on you and tell the authorities what we are planning then we will all be in prison. But one thing I know about Voronkova is that he is in bed with the government. Otherwise he would not be able to keep his business going. He has to pay a lot of officials, police, businessman and lawyers. If anybody can pull off this release it would be him. Just be careful. Let me know if you need me for anything."

"Okay Tsilia. I'll be in touch. Let's have dinner in a few days." Daniel could not believe that he would have to negotiate with a known mafia person for the release of his client. But what else was he to do. The government was not just going to hand Ezekiel over. They were convinced that he had connections with this Mishenko. God was watching over him because he was still alive. His next move was to get someone on the inside to see Ezekiel and see what information they could get that might help. They couldn't just walk him out the front door. But Daniel was sure the day would come when he would be free.

Chapter 17

Daniel needed to get in touch with pastor John right away. He didn't know when Mr. Voronkova would be getting in touch with him again. He needed to know whether John would go into the prison and talk with Ezekiel. He got his number and sat down to call him in his office. Pastor John said that he would be happy to meet with Daniel. He had been worried about how his friend was doing. He sounded like a very nice man so Daniel wasn't worried that he would go into the prison to meet with Ezekiel.

Daniel had never been in a church before. It was a new experience for him. He wondered how the two men became friends. When he finally met with John he met an individual that cared deeply for his friend. He and Ezekiel were both men of God and that was what drew them to each other. They were both young, had families and loved the scriptures. A brotherhood had developed so when Ezekiel needed some place to take the congregation pastor John had not hesitated to open his doors for his friend.

Pastor John took Daniel into his office so they could be alone. There were several members of the congregation there that day. There was going to be a funeral there the next day so they came in to prepare. He had pictures all over his office of his family. Things were progressing rapidly in Daniel's life and he was beginning to think that maybe he should start a family and get right with God. He just had not thought much about God or settling down until now. He couldn't help but think that John had it all and he had nothing.

What should he tell John? How much should he tell him? He had already involved his best friend in this mess and now this pastor who had a family and a congregation that depended on him. But what were friends for? If he really loved his friend then he should be there for him? Pastor John had left Daniel in his office to get them both some coffee. Daniel was glad it gave him a moment to get himself together. He didn't want to come off too abrasive the first time he met the man. John put the coffee on his desk and poured Daniel a cup. "I hope this is okay. I'm not really good at making coffee. My secretary usually makes the coffee when she comes in during the week."

"Oh that tastes just fine. John as you know I'm Ezekiel's lawyer. I'm sorry that I am just talking with you. I've been trying so hard to figure out what to do for him. It has not been easy. His uncle is mad at me and he should be. It's just that I've never had to deal with a case like this before. But I think that I might be getting some leads finally. I should have come to speak with you right away about what transpired the day that he was arrested. Please forgive me."

"It's okay Daniel. I have no idea what it is like to be a lawyer. The day that Ezekiel was arrested he came to tell me that he had decided to leave here and go to Israel. But first I think they were going to America to tell the people what had happened with the synagogue bombing. He told me that a friend of his had told him about an intelligence person who spoke with him that Russia was planning on starting a war with America. I wasn't exactly startled by what he had said. But shortly into the meeting the police came in and arrested him. I was shocked at the whole thing."

"Why were you not shocked by this whole thing?"

"Well Daniel. Ezekiel is named after a very important prophet in the Bible. The prophet Ezekiel had some very important things to say about the coming war between Russia and Israel."

"Okay. But what does that have to do with America and Russia?"

"A whole lot Daniel. Don't believe everything you hear about the Cold War. Russia has always wanted to be the greatest nation in the world. She will always be in a race to be better and stronger than the Americans. Not only do the Christians believe in World War III but many others believe it as well. This is what I believe. I believe that history will show that America has sided with Israel. If the Bible is correct and Russia will come up against Israel they will have to fight the United States as well. So it figures that Russia will have to come up against the United States first before she can get to Israel. This is just my thinking. But make no mistakes that according to scripture Russia and her allies from the Muslim community will come up against Israel."

"Wow. But if everyone knows about this war between Russia and Israel then why all this?"

"I'm not sure. Maybe Ezekiel's friend knew more than we know. Maybe there is more to this than meets the eye about this whole thing. It might be personal. Maybe this guy ticked off somebody and he thinks that Mishenko told Ezekiel about it."

"You might be right. It seems to get weirder with every person that gets involved. I have something to ask you John. Ezekiel has found a friend in prison. His brother called me the other day to tell me that he is okay. I want to get someone in the prison to see Ezekiel but he didn't think it was a good idea that I should go or someone from the family. The police might get suspicious. Would you be willing to go into the prison and see Ezekiel? Just talk with him and let us know that he is okay."

"Of course Daniel. I miss my friend and I'm worried about his well being. I'm not afraid of the police. I've not done anything wrong. You set up the meeting and I'll be there. What are your plans after that?"

"Well this Voronkova seems to be in the Russian mafia. I'm thinking that maybe he might have some connections that can pay Ezekiel out of prison. After that we will have to get him out of Russia right away. Please don't tell anyone about this. We don't want to compromise the plan. I'll be in touch. And thank you for your insight on this case." Daniel gets up to leave after shaking John's hand. He had a lot to think about but soon he would have more information once John got a chance to see Ezekiel.

Daniel took the long way home. His meeting with Pastor John gave him a lot to think about. He had never heard anything about World War

III. What was the world coming to anyway? He couldn't understand why the nations of the world could not get along and help one another. What wrong did Israel do to the Russians and to the Muslim world that they hated the Jewish people so much? Anti-semitism was on the rise and Daniel believed that the day was coming soon where no Jewish person would be safe anywhere but in Israel. But what did that mean for him? He was living in Russia and never thought that he would have to leave. But now his mind was turning toward either America or Israel. If there was to be a war against America and Israel would he be safe anywhere? The thought of it troubled him like nothing else ever had.

Daniel needed to unwind and felt the need to talk with a young man who worked at the gym that had been talking with Daniel for many years now about the New World Order. Daniel really thought that Jeremy was kind of crazy so he listened to him but didn't put much stock in what Jeremy was saying. Now he felt that maybe he needed to speak with someone who knew more about what was happening in the world than he did. He pulled the car into the parking lot only to see Jeremy preparing to leave for the day. He rushed over just as Jeremy got into his car. "Hey Jeremy where are you going?"

"Hey Daniel I was just going to get some lunch. Come with me I have something to tell you?"

"Sure man. I wanted to talk with you about something? I hope you don't mind."

"No. You know I love you man. Guess what?"

"Well I had a meeting with a very interesting person last week. I have not seen you around so I didn't get a chance to tell you about it. Well you know I've been telling you for years now that the Jewish people had better put together an underground railroad to get the people back to Israel when the hard times come. I'm telling you man that life as we know it is going to change and very quickly. Listen this guy tells me that he got it from a good source that soon the whole world is going to change the currency as we know it. Right now this whole problem we are having with the financial system in America, China, France and the rest of the world is all a part of the conspiracy." Jeremy looks at Daniel waiting for a reaction.

"What conspiracy Jeremy? Why the need to change the money? I don't really understand. Please I don't know as much as you do. That is why I am here. I have a source that says that Russia is planning a war against the Unites States. What do you think?"

"Oh man that's all a part of it. Oh man. I can't believe that you are finally opening your eyes. I've been trying to tell you for years now that there is a new government coming that is supposed to take over the whole world."

"Okay I'm listening. Start from the beginning? Who is this guy you had a meeting with? And what did he tell you?"

"Okay. Well we are here at the restaurant. Let's get a table and order quickly. I don't have much time. We are short at work today. If I'm back late they just might let me go this time." The two men walk into the restaurant. It wasn't too crowded so the waitress was able to seat them right away. The two men sat in a booth by the window. Passing on the street was a long line of military vehicles. Jeremy just looked out of the window in amazement. "See Daniel. Look at that. I wonder what that is all about? They are doing things right under our noses and we don't have a clue what we are in store for. But let me get to the point. This man is a true prophet of God. You see people don't believe that there are real prophets in the earth now. They think that the prophets stopped with Jeremiah and Isaiah and the rest of the prophets but that is not true. Okay this man has actually seen the Lord. He comes to talk with him all the time or he sends an angel you know. Come on don't look at me like that. You are Jewish you are supposed to know about these things." Daniel started laughing but he didn't mean any harm. He didn't want to get Jeremy going so he didn't mention talking with the angel and with Elijah it would have just got him going.

"Okay he said that an angel of the Lord came to him and told him that the world was preparing for a war. Now to corroborate what the angel told him a good friend of his in intelligence told him that what the governments are doing all over the world are preparing by forming armies comprised of people that live in the community. For example there is a guy in Europe that has it on good authority that the guys who just write tickets on cars are being given more authority by the government. They are being given cards that give them the authority to come into a person's home to search it and they are also being given authority to apprehend and arrest people. This is being done in America as well. The new president is calling for ordinary citizens to have the right to formulate a military police organization to police their own communities. Sounds like communism to me. The reason for this is that there is a war coming and the soldiers will be out of the country so they will need regular citizens to maintain control in the country. I know this is a bit over the top but it's absolutely true."

"I don't know Jeremy. But you know when the Nazi's were in power that's what they did. They indoctrinated Jewish men to police their own people. I hate those men who did that but they were trying to survive I guess."

"Okay. That was a good point. You see they call this New World Order the Fourth Reich. What Hitler did was nothing compared to what is about to come upon this earth. Daniel we are truly living in the last days before the Messiah comes to set up his kingdom in the world. Look at the world in which we live. The Russian people are oppressed. Many of them are leaving the country. Have you not noticed?"

"I guess not. I've kind of been in my own world. I'm sorry Jeremy. I don't know what to do that's why I came to you. I started thinking about things recently and personally I'm afraid."

"That's okay Daniel. This is a good place for you to be. Let me tell you what happened to me. I too was living in my own world. All I cared about was going to work and making a living for me and my family. The Russian government doesn't care anything about its people. All they worry about is having the greatest military in the world. You cannot have a great nation without the people. We are just puppets in this country. I hate it. Well to make a long story short a friend of mine tried for years to talk with me about Christ and how he was coming back to set up his kingdom here on earth. I didn't want to hear anything about it but more and more I started thinking is this all there is to life. What is going to happen to me after I die? I hoped that there was more to life than this. So I started reading the Bible I felt like that I had nothing to lose. I focused a lot on what Jesus was saying and how he was a light in the midst of the darkness of his time. The people were sick, hungry and had no hope. Even the religious people of his time had gone to the dogs so to speak. He came to tell the people that God the Father still loved them and that their leaders had fallen and should not be trusted. His message was about the Kingdom of God that God had for them since the foundation of the world. It was only because of the fall of man that took it away from them but only for a time. You see Daniel God never meant for man to govern themselves. God was their King but man decided to govern themselves. This is the reason why things are like they are now. Man is not responsible enough to govern themselves. Just look at the world as we know it today. Just look at this nation. The number of men and women in prison for terrible crimes like murder, prostitution, drug trafficking and the list goes on and on is rising every day. The people have no moral basis and have no hope for a good life. They are living like animals. Good moral people don't have a chance in the world anymore. I'm afraid to let my children go out and play in the neighborhood for fear that someone will snatch them off the street and I'll never see them again. This is not how God wanted life for his creation to be. Please start to read your Bible again and go to synagogue or you can come with me to church someday. The only hope for the world is the Messiah and he is coming back soon. If we are not ready then we will not be a part of the new Kingdom that he is coming to set up."

"I hear you Jeremy. I do need to get my life in order. I don't know about you but I need some help. I have something interesting to tell you. I wasn't going to mention it but you sound like you can take it."

"Sure what is it?"

"I had a dream that the Prophet Elijah came to me to tell me that he was coming back to the earth to speak to the people like it said in the Bible."

"Wow Daniel. God is trying to tell you something. But this is not just for you he came so that you would spread the message to others as well. Don't be afraid Daniel. Remember that in the Bible the Prophet Joel said "And it shall come to pass afterward, that I will pour out my spirit upon all flesh; and your sons and your daughters shall prophesy, your old men shall dream dreams, your young men shall see visions." God is alive Daniel and he is taking the time out to speak to you and threw you for your people and the world to hear what he has to say to

126

us so that we can get through these hard times. Listen to him. It's time for you to make a change in your life and stop thinking about yourself and start thinking about your people."

"But I'm nobody Jeremy. I don't have money or power or anything. What can I do to help my people?"

"Oh Daniel. The Lord says "not by might, nor by power but by my spirit." He is saying that you don't have to have anything. Just have a willing heart to do what God tells you to do. He'll make sure that if you need money or whatever you need he will provide it for you. Did Moses have money or power? He grew up in the house of the Pharaoh but after he killed a man he had to flee for his life leaving the power and riches behind. And then when God called him in the desert he said I am a man who cannot speak well. So God told him to let Aaron do the talking but he didn't tell him he no longer had to do what he asked him to do. Joseph was just a young man when his brothers sold him into slavery. After a time working in the house of the officer of Pharaoh the officer's wife tried to seduce Joseph but because he would not sleep with her she cried out that he had tried to rape her and he was thrown into prison for many years. But the Lord delivered him out of prison because the Pharaoh had several dreams that he needed interpretation of them. Joseph was given this gift by the Lord and because of this was not only released from prison but became a ruler over the land of Egypt. It was because Joseph was in this position that when there was a famine in the land and his family came for food he was there to meet that need. The Lord has always spoken through dreams and visions to not only his people but the Gentiles as well. So now he is talking to you. It's not about you it's about Him. Just go with God Daniel he will take you all the way."

"Wow Jeremy. For the first time in days I feel like a weight is being lifted off of my shoulders. I have this really big case that just seems to be getting bigger every day. I feel now that God has been telling me all along that he is with me and that he is going to give me the help that I need to free an innocent man from prison. Just like Joseph, Ezekiel will be freed I just need to rely on the Lord. And also in these tough times in which we are living the Messiah is going to come and deliver the Jewish people from the hands of their oppressors. We just need to keep the faith."

"Yes my brother. On that note I have got to get back to work. It was good talking to you. If you need me you know where to find me. I'll drop you off at your car. Come on."

The two men left the restaurant in good spirits. Daniel had found the answers to some questions that were plaguing his heart. But he knew that things were not going to be easy but that he was not alone.

Chapter 18

Daniel was on cloud nine hundred and ninety nine on his way back to the apartment. He knew in his heart that everything was going to be okay. He still would feel much better after Pastor John had seen Ezekiel face to face. He wanted him out of prison as soon as possible. Now all he could do was pray.

Ezekiel was taking it all in stride. Despite his situation his relationship with Vladimir had been the biggest blessing for him. Officer Zubkov had a request but this time for some of the inmates who did not have family members to bring them any personal items. He told Ezekiel that there were many inmates that were sick from one thing or another. The cells were cold and damp and this left many of the inmates sick and getting sicker every day. He understood his position. He would have probably done the same thing. The Russian government used this system so that they would not have to use their money to take care of the inmates. They left it up to the individual and their family to take care of their needs. The poor officer didn't make much money and so this was a way that he could get some personal things for himself and his family as well. Times were hard and everybody knew it.

It was easy now to make phone calls because Zubkov had made a request. Whenever Ezekiel could he would sneak a phone call home just so they would know that he was still alive. If Ezekiel got caught by another officer he would be in big trouble though. Vladimir was in need of that medicine so he made a phone call to his brother to see when he was coming and to give him the new list. He was really a good guy despite what he did for a living. Ezekiel had no idea that Vladimir was not just a small time drug dealer. All he knew was that this was his friend and he really didn't care what he did for a living at that point. All he saw was a man in need. Aleksis was always available for Ezekiel's calls. "Aleksis this is Ezekiel. I need to see you really soon. Vladimir is not doing very well. I've asked Officer Zubkov many times to get him to a hospital but he said that they will never allow him out of this prison. You have got to get me some stronger medicine. If you know any doctor friends tell them the problem and ask them for something to help him. His back is not healing well due to the conditions in solitary. It is unclean down there. I need more clean bandages and antibiotics to fight the infection. If we don't do something he will die in here. Also the Officer is asking for some medicine for the other inmates. Many are sick because it is cold and damp in the cells. We will have an epidemic in here soon if something is not done. The inmates are talking about strike again if the Russian government doesn't do something about the conditions in this place. Again than you for the extra blankets it is really keeping me from getting sick too."

"No problem Ezekiel. If my brother dies in that hell hole I'll never forgive myself for it. I could have kept him out of that place but he never listens to me. I only wanted to teach him a lesson. I hoped that maybe if he stayed in there for a while he would appreciate his freedom and do what he was told. Now look at him. I've got to think of a way of getting him at least to a hospital for a few weeks. I have friends in high places. You let me handle that part. How are you doing?"

"Well I hate life but I pray for the day when I will be released from here. I have done nothing wrong. I miss my wife and daughter. When I get out of here I'm going to America to tell the people about how terrible I was treated in this country. I don't want to make things hard for the rest of my people but maybe they will wake up and see that the Russian government doesn't like our people. Nothing will ever change that."

"I'm sorry Ezekiel. You sound like a good guy. Me I'm a bum. I've been in this life for a long time now and there is no turning back for me. Oh I spoke with your lawyer. He wants to send in your pastor friend to see you. I told him that would probably be okay. I will bring him with me in a few days. It will take just a few days to contact a doctor friend of mine. He will give me some clean dressings for Vladimir and some stronger medicine. In the meantime I will make some phone calls. I will get my brother to the hospital. Don't worry about that. Tell him for me that I love him and that he will be out of there for a time soon. He will have to return but I will work on something soon for the both of you. I'm not sure what it will be but just get ready you will be free soon. My brother is no saint but no human being should die in a place like that. Tell the Officer I will take care of his list. I'll see you in a few days."

Ezekiel told the officer that Aleksis would be there in a few days with the supplies that he ordered. Ezekiel asked if he would take him to see Vladimir that night to make sure he was okay and give him the message from his brother. After quitting time Ezekiel went back to his cell to just have a snack. He wasn't very hungry and the food was starting to taste worse every time he went. The budget was low and the prison was going down fast. The inmates were feeling desperate and fights were breaking out every day.

Ezekiel layed down for a quick moment. It was funny but Ezekiel had not thought about asking Aleksis to bring him a Bible. He didn't think that a person like him would care about bringing him one so he didn't ask. But one of the new inmates had several brought in by his wife. He called himself the preacher. He spent his time outside ministering to the inmates. He felt that the reason he was in prison was to save the lost prisoners. Every time Sophia came to visit she brought in more and more Bibles. This really intrigued Ezekiel. The Bibles were handed out to any inmate that wanted one. As a Rebbe he never thought about going into a prison and teaching the people about God. It was genius. He didn't want to be nosey but he wondered what a man of God was doing in prison. He just watched the young man and found out that his name was Samuel Jabotinsky. Samuel and his wife and family were on their way home from a meeting. Samuel was driving and being very tired he fell asleep at the wheel and caused a terrible accident. There was no loss of life but the court wanted to punish him for some reason. He was somewhat quiet at first but then he began slowly but surely to minister to anyone who would listen to him. Ezekiel missed his talks with Pastor John and thought here is someone who believes in the word of God. He wondered what was in his heart. So one day Ezekiel went over and offered him a bar of candy. Samuel just looked up at him and reached out his hand to take the candy. He couldn't believe that someone was offering a gesture of friendship. "Thank you. Sit down." Ezekiel sat down next to Samuel. "I'm Ezekiel."

"Hi I'm Samuel. Say do you have a Bible? I can get you one if you would like to have one."

"Actually no I do not have a Bible. I noticed you giving out these books and one of the other inmates said that you were a preacher and that you have given him a Bible. I'm Jewish but I do know that you have some of the same books in your Bible as we do in ours. I would really appreciate it if you don't mind."

"Of course not. So what is a Jewish man doing in prison if you don't mind my asking?"

"Well it's a long story. But I'm here on false charges. My lawyer is working to free me but it's taking some time."

"Of course. I'm not worried that I am here. All things happen for a reason don't you think?"

"Well that might be true but I'm not here because of anything that I've done. I miss my family and my daughter is growing up every day without her father and my wife is worrying about her husband. Where is the justice in that?"

"I think of it this way. God knew that both you and I would go through this but he did nothing to change it. Why do you think that is?"

"I'm not really sure. I never thought about it that way."

"Well you should. It will take a lot of stress off of you. God knew that this would happen to you and he didn't change it so that you could learn some lessons that you would not have learned otherwise. Remember the man Job in the Bible?"

"Yes I remember Job. What about him?"

"Well look at what happened to him. Job lost his family, his riches and a very profitable business. Then on top of that he lost his health. It was a test to see whether he would love God despite what he had and also a test to see whether he had faith in God or in himself. In the end despite everything Job continued to worship God through the good times and the light at the end of the tunnel brought forth a new family and blessings from the same God who allowed him to go through the test. Does that make any sense?"

"Yes it does. Job was a righteous man but he still had to go through some hard times in life. My parents went through the Holocaust and all they wanted for me was that I not have to go through any hard times in my life. I guess that really was not a realistic expectation in the world that we live in. I too wanted that for my daughter."

"I understand. I too am a father and want the best for my children. Here take my Bible. I have another one in my cell. Read it and it will give you peace. But I think that you already know that. There is much more to my Bible than the Jewish Bible. If you want read some of it. Jesus has a lot of good things to say. If you have any questions I am right here." Samuel went inside for dinner while Ezekiel sat and held the Bible like it was a newborn baby.

Ezekiel thought he would take a little time and read the Bible for a while and take a little nap. Officer Zubkov promised that he would take him to see Vladimir after everyone had gone to bed. It had been months since he had scriptures to read. He would say his prayers privately before sleeping but it was not the same as having the Torah to read every night like at home. He knew that when he got out of prison that he would make sure that he taught his little Aliya how to read the Torah. He now understood how very important it was. One could take it for granted when it was right there. But now that he didn't have it he understood how precious a gem that it really was.

Ezekiel opened the Bible and realized that there were two sections in the Bible, the old testament and the new testament. He would have to ask Viktor what the new testament was all about. He was quite familiar with all the books that were in the old testament section but none that was in the new testament. He really didn't know much about Jesus except the few conversations that he had with Pastor John. He still didn't think of Jesus as any thing but a prophet. He sounded like some of the sages that he was taught about. It wasn't hard to find his words though because they were all in red. He brushed through some of the pages just skimming and he found himself reading a passage of Jesus that said "The Spirit of the Lord is upon me, because he hath anointed me to preach the gospel to the poor; he hath sent me to heal the brokenhearted, to preach deliverance to the captives, and recovering the sight to the blind, to set at liberty them that are bruised. To preach the acceptable year of the Lord. This day is this scripture fulfilled in your ears." So Jesus really did believe that he was the Messiah. Ezekiel was intrigued by this but closed the Bible and fell into a deep sleep.

Ezekiel found himself having a dream that he was in a place unlike any place that he had ever been in his whole life. Had he made this whole thing up or was it a real place? He saw in front of him a great city and this city had a wall great and high, and had twelve gates, and at the gates twelve angels, and names written thereon, which are the names of the twelve tribes of the children of Israel. Ezekiel saw them all and the one said Juda and another said Reuben and another said Gad and yet another said Aser and another said Nephathalim and another said Manasses and then another said Simeon and another said Levi, Issachar, Zabulon, Joseph and Benjamin. On the east three gates; on the north three gates; on the south three gates; and on the west three gates. And the wall of the city had twelve foundations and in them the names of twelve men of whom Ezekiel was not familiar. There names were Simon, Andres, James, John, Philip, Bartholomew, Thomas, Matthew, James, Lebbaeus, Simon and Matthias. Perhaps he would meet someone who would tell him who these men were. And the building of the wall of it was of jasper; and the city was pure gold, like clear glass. And the foundations of the wall of the city were garnished with all manner of precious stones. The first foundation was jasper; the second, sapphire, the third, a chalcedony; the fourth an emerald; the fifth, sardonyx, the sixth sardius, the seventh, chrysolyte, the eighth beryl, the ninth, a topaz, the tenth a chrysoprasus, the eleventh, a jacinth, the twelfth, an amethyst. And the twelve gates were twelve pearls and the street of the city was pure gold, as it were transparent glass.

Ezekiel didn't know what to do but continued to walk on the streets of gold. He felt that he was going to fall into it because it was transparent like glass but this didn't happen. As he walked down the street he could hear this beautiful music playing and people singing. He hoped that soon he would see someone to tell him where he was and how he had gotten to this great city. All he knew in his heart was that he never wanted to leave this place. It was the most beautiful place in the world. It was light and there were trees with all manner of fruit everywhere. But these trees were different it was like the fruit and the trees were alive and they were praising God in song. The grass was unlike any grass that he had ever seen before. Each blade of grass had what looked like a precious stone like a diamond or an emerald inside of the grass. This had to be paradise. Where was his mother and father? Would he see them? Had he died? What was he doing here in this great city?

All of a sudden he saw a man coming towards him. Perhaps he would know what this place was and why he was there. Ezekiel walked quickly so that he could get to him. "Excuse me sir but what is this place?"

"Hi Ezekiel this is heaven. I am Moshe I was sent to meet you. I have a message for you from the Lord."

"The Prophet Moshe. Heaven. What do you mean?"

"Do not be afraid. You have nothing to fear. Please come with me I have something to show you." Ezekiel could not believe what he was hearing. Could he really being talking with Moshe the greatest man that ever lived. What was he doing here and what did he have to show him?

While they were walking Ezekiel was taking in all the sights as they walked along. Moshe had a large staff in his hands and he walked quickly as though he were a young man of twenty years. As they walked into the great city Ezekiel was astounded to see that there were many people living in beautiful mansions that spread out throughout the city. There were no cars but the people traveled in beautiful carriages made of ivory and gold pulled by the most beautiful horses that Ezekiel had ever seen.

Ezekiel didn't ask any questions of Moses as they walked through the city. People were walking to and fro and tears ran down Ezekiel's eyes as he heard the sound of children playing. Off to his right there seemed to be a school or a playground where children were playing everywhere. The screams of joy cut through his heart like a knife. He missed Aliya so and wished that she could be with him there. He would take her to play with the other little children in a place where she would be safe.

As the two men continued to walk Ezekiel could see in front of them what looked like the Tabernacle of Moses. Ezekiel had seen it many times in books. But it was more spectacular in person. He couldn't keep his excitement in any longer. "Rebbe, Rebbe Moshe. This is the tabernacle. Oh how beautiful it is."

"Yes. Ezekiel when I went up to the mount to receive the tables of stone from God he gave me the instructions to build this great tabernacle for him. I was to come to the people to receive from them gold, silver and brass. This sanctuary was made so that God would dwell with us. What has happened to our people? God has given our people much more than they could ever use in a lifetime and yet there is no tabernacle on earth unto God. Ezekiel God is not pleased. Your generation has forgotten who you are and what you represent.

Our people spent many years in bondage and God brought them out into the wilderness to take them into the promised land. Our people have gone through much persecution at the hands of the enemy. But we have survived as a people because the hand of a Mighty God has and always will be with them. Please Ezekiel go to Israel and tell the people that there will be more persecution coming before the Messiah comes. If they do not come together and start to worship God like back in the Bible days it will not go well with them."

"But Rabbe I am just a man. They will not listen to me. How will I get them to listen?"

"Look on me Ezekiel. I said that same thing to God. Look at my staff." Moses took the staff and threw it upon the ground and it turned into a snake. He reached down and took the snake in his hand and the snake turned back into a staff. "As God was with me so he will be with you Ezekiel."

"Rebbe I will do as I have been asked. But I am in prison. I don't know whether I will be alive. These people will try to keep me until the day I die so that the people of America will not know what they are planning against them. How will I get out?"

"Do not worry Ezekiel. God will make a way for your release. Don't give up. It's time for you to go back now. Remember God will make a way."

Ezekiel woke up not believing what had just happened in his dream. Was it fake or real he didn't know. But he did feel a sense of peace when he woke up. He had not even noticed that his cellmate had returned from having dinner. The Bible was still draped over his chest.

Ezekiel waited patiently for Officer Zubkov to take him down to solitary so he could see Vladimir. He had not been to see him in over a week. He didn't want the officer to get in trouble. He was the only way that he could stay in touch with Vladimir. If their cover was blown Vladimir might die and Ezekiel would never know what happened to him. His brother was working on getting him to the hospital and he needed the help badly.

Finally the lights went out and Zubkov stood outside Ezekiel's cell waiting for him to get ready. Ezekiel got up from his bunk and put a few things in a sack for Vladimir. His brother would be there to see him soon and he would have more bandages and medicine to take care of his wounds. Ezekiel's heart was beating with every step that they took until they got downstairs in what he called the dungeon. It was cold and dark down there. The air was stale and it was hard to breath. The last time Ezekiel was there Vladimir was coughing and sneezing. He would not be able to hold on much longer.

Vladimir was lying motionless in his cell. He heard every noise and movement which wasn't too often. They brought him food and allowed him to come out and go to the bathroom but that was it. He tried to make friends with one of the officers but it wasn't easy. Finally he found someone who would help him. Officer Gorbachev was a young guy who had a new born baby. He was so proud that he would come and talk with Vladimir sometimes and he even showed him the pictures of his baby girl. He was really a good guy compared to the rest. Vladimir had learned a long time ago since coming to jail that he needed to have help if he would make it. Officer Gorbachev told him that he and his wife were doing terribly financially until he got the job. They were back in their payments and even with the job his landlord wanted to throw them in the streets. He didn't know how he would come up with the back rent. Vladimir didn't know whether to come right out and offer it to him or not. He was in trouble and it couldn't get any worse so he put his cards on the table. "Hey Gorbachev I can get some money for you in exchange for some food and cigarettes. I will give you a number and a name to call. You will get the smokes, food and ask for whatever you need. Don't worry this is how it is done around here. But don't tell anyone about it and I'll take care of you."

The Officer wasn't sure how it worked but he had heard the other officers making deals with the inmates. Why shouldn't he be able to get some things for his family? His newborn needed food, cloths and a roof over her head. It was his responsibility to take care of her and now they might be thrown out on the street despite the fact that he had a job. It would be there secret.

Vladimir heard the sound of footsteps and thought that Gorbachev was coming with some treats. Zubkov opened the door and he looked up to see his friend Ezekiel standing in the doorway. "Oh man. Where have you been? I thought you gave up on me."

"Come on. You should know me better than that."

"Sorry. I was just getting lonely in here. But guess what? I've found some more help for us. I gave my brothers number to another officer. He is young and in need of money for his family. I promised him that I would help him. He will be a great help to me when you cannot make it. You got anything?"

"Nothing much. I spoke with your brother. I just have a few treats. But I wanted to check your back and tell you that your brother is making some phone calls to get you to a hospital. He said that you will probably have to come back here but at least the doctor can help heal your wounds. Vladimir your brother loves you and he is worried about you. He said that he doesn't want you here but you won't listen to him. If he gets you out of here don't do anything stupid."

"Your right Ezekiel. I need to make some changes in my life. Hey there is this guy they call the preacher. He brings Bibles in for anyone that wants one. It's time that you make some peace with God. I will get you one and bring it here for you. We can get you a flashlight and you can read it. Let me fix your back and get out of here before Zubkov get's angry."

Like the dutiful friend Ezekiel changed the dressing on Vladimir's back. It still was not healing well. He really needed a doctor. But Ezekiel was doing as much as he could. It was up to Aleksis now. He hoped that he would be coming soon.

Chapter 19

Aleksis made arrangements with the prison to bring Pastor John with him when he came to visit Ezekiel. Aleksis came to get Pastor John in a brand new Mercedes Benz. He was aware that Aleksis and his brother were involved in the mafia but John wasn't afraid. He was actually very grateful for the help that he was giving to Ezekiel. As a Pastor it wasn't his job to judge people but to do exactly what Aleksis was doing and that was helping someone in need. He truly hoped that he could actually form a friendship with Aleksis and talk with him and Vladimir about God. Pastor John knew that there were many people in the world who had never been taught about God. They were victims of the world that they lived in and once they were caught in the snare it would not be easy to get out of it. He and Aleksis were about the same age but undoubtedly had a very different life growing up. Aleksis didn't come into the church but waited for Pastor John outside. He sent in a young man of about twenty years of age to retrieve the pastor. Pastor John saw him walking up to the church from his office window. He retrieved his coat. He didn't want to keep them waiting. Sergie had been working with Aleksis ever since he was about eleven years old doing small things like cleaning in one of the restaurants that Aleksis owned. He eventually started selling drugs in school to help his family. His mother didn't work and his father was just a laborer and didn't make enough money to feed all of the hungry mouths in the house. It seemed like the harder he worked the less they seemed to achieve. Sergei wasn't a bad kid he just chose the wrong way to help his family. What would become of him now only time would tell. He would surely like to work with a young man like that and see if his life could be turned around.

When the door opened Pastor John saw a young man about six feet tall with a baby face like he had when he was young. But he could tell that Sergei had seen a lot for a man of his years. Somewhere in there was a heart of gold that had been scarred by life. But he did maintain his manners. "Hi Pastor John I'm Sergei. Mr. Voronkova is waiting for you in the car. Are you ready to go?"

"Yes. I'm ready to go." The two men walk outside together to one of the most beautiful cars he had ever seen. No wonder the young people run towards drug trafficking. The allure of the money, cars, a big house and nice clothing was too much to turn down when you live in a slum with more mouths to feed than your parents can take care of. They only want a piece of life that is better than what they have. Pastor John thought about how hard his parents worked on their little fruit and vegetable garden to make a living for him and his brothers and sisters. Life was not easy growing up in Russia. He dreamed of having a big business someday that would make a lot of money so that he could give his children more than he had when he was young. But God called him and instead of the vegetable business he was in the business of people.

Sergei opened the door for Pastor John and he slid into the car next to Aleksis. Aleksis was nothing like what he envisioned. He was an all around nice guy. He had been watching too much television. Aleksis had a big smile on his face and seemed to be glad to see him. Sergei got in the drivers seat and off they went to the prison. Aleksis did have on the tailored suit and you knew that he was a man of great prestige and he had a lot of money. Pastor John didn't want to look conspicuous so he just wore some slacks and a shirt. Aleksis looked like he was going to give the sermon on Sunday morning. Pastor John just smiled. They weren't the hoodlums that he thought they would be. He didn't see a sign of any guns or drugs or anything so he tried to relax. Aleksis took out a box of cigars and offered Pastor John a cigar. "I like a good cigar. Would you like to have one?"

"Thanks but I don't smoke."

"Sorry I should have known that. So how long have you known Ezekiel?"

"Well Ezekiel and I met a few years ago. He and I are in the same businesss so to speak. He is a man of God and so am I. That is what binds us together. We are brothers. By the way thank you for making the arrangements for me to see him. His family is really worried about him. For what its worth he's innocent of all charges. If you can do anything to help him his family would be grateful. I know that you are a man that has a lot of contacts here in Russia. You would be doing something really good for a really good man."

"I know Pastor John. Contrary to popular belief I'm not a bad man. I got into the business when I was just a young man. My mother and father were always arguing over money and at a young age I just wanted to help. So there was a man who gave me money to move his drugs and I did it to help my family. I never meant to stay in the business for a long time but time has a way of getting away with you. After many years I remembered that and took the money that I was making and I put it into legitimate business. I have several clothing stores, automobiles stores, restaurants and other businesses. I have put my children through college because I don't want them making a living the way there father did. This is no life for anyone. My brother Vladimir he is a good soul just like me. We do a lot to help in the community with the kids and all. It is my fault that he is in this business he was just following me. I have to save him now and get him out of this life. I think after his experience this time he will be glad to do something else with his life. It's time for me as well. I'm not getting any younger and I have more money than I can spend in my lifetime."

"That sounds like you are ready to change your life. Aleksis why don't you think about coming to my church one day. Our church doors are open to everyone. You know the next day is not promised to anyone. Do you ever think about where you will spend your eternity?"

"Thanks but I'm not into the God thing. We never went to church. I'm not saying that there is no God. I guess I've never really given it much thought. But no I've not thought about where I will spend my eternity. I thought that after you die that's it. You just go back to the ground."

"Well let's just say that many people believe different things. The point of the matter is those who believe in some type of God no matter what that is believe that there is life after death as we know it. You should at least keep your mind open that this just might be true. And if it is true then what will it be. You see I believe in Jesus. He says that we can have everlasting life. When I die I will go to heaven. I like that idea. I have chosen to believe in Jesus and what he had to say about life. Look at you. There is something in your heart that tells you that the life you have lived is not for your children. Why is that?"

"It's a tough life Pastor John. I've seen what people will do to get drugs. And I've seen what people who sell drugs will do to make money. I don't want my daughters walking the street and selling themselves for a fix. My sons have a brain and I want them to use it instead of a gun to get a point across. This life is not for good people. I have suffered a lot. I want out of this for me and my family. Sergei here is my son too. Unfortunately I showed him the wrong road and now I have to make up for that."

"My point exactly Aleksis. Just think about it. Let me help you. Do you know that you can be born again?"

"Born again? How can a man be born again of his mother?"

"Ahh. That's a good question Aleksis. When we come into this world we are born of our mothers. But to be born again is a spiritual birth. And the beautiful thing about it is that anyone can have it. No matter what kind of life you have lived before God will give you another chance. Please come and talk with me about this. It will change your life and the life of all the people that you know. You can have everlasting life and you can be a light for all the people in your family and the community."

Sergei pulled into the parking lot of the prison. Pastor John was so busy talking that he had not noticed that he was now in another world. The prison was this huge building that seemed to take up more than six or seven square blocks. It was surrounded by barbed wire and there were guard stations at each of the four corners. After they parked the car Aleksis and Pastor John got out of the car. Sergei popped the trunk to retrieve the articles that Ezekiel had asked for. Pastor John had butterflies in his stomach. He knew that he was going to be able to leave this place. He could only imagine what it felt like for those who had to make this place home. Aleksis lead him through to a gate where an officer was waiting to take them into an office where he had to sign some papers to enter the prison. They were quickly searched for firearms and taken into a room where the families met with their loved ones.

All John could see were the faces of wives who were barely holding on while their husbands were incarcerated. It made his heart ache. Now they had to provide for them as well as their children while the husband was in prison. He wished that there was a way that his church could reach out to these women. They were doing well and they could at least give them food and a sanctuary of people who could love them and help them whenever possible. He would have to work on that right away.

The prison was cold, dark and old. That building must have been hundreds of years old. It had seen better days whatever that was. Whoever came up with the idea of prisons? In the Bible days whenever someone committed a crime they had refugee cities where they could run for asylum. These men were being treated like animals put in a cage. He just had to help Ezekiel. This was no place for anybody let alone a man like Ezekiel.

Aleksis and Pastor John made it through the crowd of people to find a seat. It didn't seem like there was any place to sit. An officer came to meet them and took them into a private room. Aleksis told Pastor John to have a seat while he had a talk with the officer. He wasn't sure what it was all about but he knew that Aleksis had power and he was seeing it in action. Pastor John felt like he was about to be interrogated. Is this what it felt like to be in prison? He felt so lonely when the men left the room. It made him feel very uncomfortable. A mouse ran out of a hole in the wall across the floor. He was a grown man but he felt like jumping on the top of the table but refrained just in case someone was watching. But he kept his eye on the mouse.

It seemed like forever before Aleksis and the officer came back in the room. Pastor John had not noticed at first because when the officer opened the door Aleksis followed and Ezekiel came in after him. Pastor John forgot about the mouse and got up with a big smile on his face when he saw Ezekiel. He had lost quite a bit of weight. Pastor John could look into Ezekiel's eyes to see that he was tired and the light that he once had was getting dimmer by the day. He wished that he could just walk him out the door but he knew that he could not. Ezekiel grabbed his friend, put his arms around him and cried like a baby. Pastor John understood the anguish he must have been feeling. After a few minutes the two men's eyes met each other. Pastor John put his arms around Ezekiel and they both sat down next to each other.

Aleksis was such a gentleman. He realized how important this time was for Pastor John and Ezekiel. He just sat on the side and smoked his cigar while the two men talked. Pastor John felt the emotions welling up inside and broke out in tears himself. "Ezekiel please forgive me. You don't belong in a place like this. We have got to get you out of here."

"John I have so much to tell you. But I had a dream last night and God sent word to me that he was going to deliver me from this place. I believe in God and I know that my day is coming. Please do me a favor and tell my uncle and my wife that I am coming home. I don't know when or how but the day is coming and we'll be together again."

The two men's time together was more than John had expected. They had all but forgotten that Aleksis was sitting waiting for news about his brother. Like a true gentleman Aleksis reached into his pocket and gave Ezekiel his handerkerchief. Ezekiel looked up at Aleksis and with the voice of a broken man thanked him for being there for him. "Aleksis I'm sorry. I got caught up in the moment. I saw Vladimir last night to tell him that you were trying to get him to the hospital. He said that he had made a new friend with one of the new officer's and that he would be contacting you. He will be able to get things to him a lot more often than myself. Officer Zubkov has been a great help but I don't want him taking too much chances. If he gets caught Vladimir won't have anyone to help him."

"Thank you. How does he look? Is his back healing well?"

"No not really. I'm doing all that I can do with what you bring me."

"Well don't worry I gave the officer some medicine from the doctor. I should be getting him out of here to the hospital in just a few weeks. These things take time. Even a man like me has to learn how to be patient. If all goes well I might be able to get him out for good. I'm working on something for you too Ezekiel. I will never forget how you have kept my brother alive. You don't know but he means the world to me. Without him life would not be worth living even with all that I have in my life."

"I understand Aleksis. Thank you also for bringing my friend here for me to see also. This will go a long way for me. There is a new guy here called the preacher and he managed to get me a Bible. I cannot live without the word of God. It is a light in this place. I felt like I was falling deeper and deeper into a pit especially without Vladimir to keep me going. Aleksis it amazes me that I could become so close to a man that is so different from myself. Vladimir and I had nothing in common accept that we were in prison together. But your brother saved my life. I don't know what I would have done without him. I will never forget him."

"My brother is a good guy. I was telling Pastor John that it's my fault that he is in this business. He was only following his big brother now I have to save his life or lose him forever. I'm sorry gentlemen but I have a very important meeting with some people and I must be on time. Tell Vladimir that I will be sending for him soon. The officer has the medicine and a few other things for him and you. Don't worry I won't forget you. If I call you friend then you are a friend for life."

John and Ezekiel hug for a few minutes before they leave. It was one of the most painful things that Ezekiel had ever gone through. Seeing his friend was both a happy but sad occasion. He could only go back to his cell and sob like a baby. He wanted so badly to get out of prison but it was all out of his hands. He longed to hold his wife and tuck his baby in bed at night. What could she possibly be thinking? Maybe that her daddy was a bad man and that she would never see him again. He hoped that Raisa had explained things as well as possible to her that her daddy was in a bad place but that he would be exhonerated really soon and be with them in America. She was meeting family that she had never known before and he hoped that this would keep her busy.

Children have a way of making it through tough times much better than adults.

Ezekiel was feeling really depressed and just wanted to tell Daniel that the meeting went well. He took his phone out from the hiding place Vladimir made under the bunk. He checked outside of his cell for several minutes to make sure that there was no one around before he made the phone call. Daniel had retrieved the briefcase from Tsilia and was reviewing the contents when the phone rang. Ezekiel didn't have much time someone could come through at any time. After a few rings he almost gave up when Daniel finally answered the phone. "Hi this is Daniel, make it quick I'm busy." Daniel was on edge Mishenko was working with some shrewd businessman. Any one of them could be the reason why Ezekiel was in jail.

"Daniel this is Ezekiel. I don't have much time."

"Ezekiel what's going on? Are you okay?"

"Yeah. I just wanted you to know that I saw Pastor John today. Now I feel more depressed than ever. Have you gotten any leads on how to get me out of here? Aleksis said that he was working on something."

"Well that's new to me. But if you can call him and tell him to call me. I was instructed not to call him. Tell him to call me and to arrange for a meeting. I'm sure that he can help us but I'm not sure what he might propose that we do."

"Okay. I'll call him tomorrow. Please Daniel get me out of here. I don't know how much longer I can make it."

"Hold on Ezekiel. We have not forgotten about you." The phone went dead and Daniel felt sick in his heart for Ezekiel.

Chapter 20

Aleksis saw the pain on Pastor John's face. He didn't know what to say to him. He knew that the only way to ease that pain was to get his friend out of prison. Aleksis had been to prison many times and knew the suffering of the inmates and how it affected their family and friends. After a long stretch in prison and being away from his children and wife he promised himself that he would get out of the business and never enter prison ever again. He opened his first restaurant and determined to make it a success worked every hour he could to survive the restaurant business. One thing led to another and he opened a hotel and continued opening businesses until he didn't have to do anything illegal anymore. But it was just too difficult to break old habits so he had other people doing the work for him. In any case he kept the promise never to enter prison again.

The drive back home was a lot quicker than on the way to the prison. John realized that he had not said anything to Aleksis since getting into the car and felt bad because if it were not for him he would not have had the opportunity to see his good friend. "I'm sorry Mr. Voronkova thank you so much for taking me to see Ezekiel. Please don't forget my invitation to come and speak with me about anything. If there is anything that I can do to help get Ezekiel out of prison please let me know. When you get your brother to the hospital I hope you won't mind my coming to visit him. Prayer goes a long way."

"I won't mind. I'll be in touch." John didn't go into the church but went straight to his car. He wanted to go and visit with Stephen to tell him that he had seen Ezekiel. Maybe he could call his wife and he could speak with her personally to know that her husband was doing okay. He didn't have the heart to tell them that he had cried like a baby. He wanted them to only know that he was alive and that his faith in God was sustaining him. He had mentioned that he had a Bible. He had not even thought about bringing one to him. But God had already taken care of that through another one of his servants. It was true that God worked in mysterious ways. Ezekiel said that he had a dream. He would have to tell him the details someday when they could see each other on the outside. He would pray tonight that Daniel and Aleksis could come up with a way to get his friend out of jail and to America. If it was one thing that John believed was that if you had enough money in the world that you could do anything. Aleksis had a lot of money and knew a lot of people. It would just be a matter of time.

John called his wife to tell her that he would be a bit late for dinner. She knew where he was going and the gravity of the situation. She had only met Ezekiel one time but she could understand how the situation was tearing his family apart. Stephen was home worrying all by himself. Benjamin had gone back to America to see if he could get the Jewish community involved in Ezekiel's case. The more people working on this the better.

The synagogue members were still coming by to bring dinner for Stephen. He was all alone waiting for the day that his nephew could come home and they could leave for America. The house was filled with pastries, meals of every kind, cards of condolence at the passing of his brother and he spent countless hours reading cards and letters from people who he had not seen for many years. When he really got down he would take out the letter that Mordechi wrote him before he died.

While he had so much time on his hands he took the time to go through his brothers affects. He didn't think that Ezekiel would mind. He had so much on his mind. When Ezekiel got free he didn't want to spend any time going through clothing and boxes. There wasn't much time for Raisa to go through anything but he promised her that they could get anything they needed. A fresh start complete with new clothing, toys and whatever she wanted in her new home. At the moment she was staying at his house and he had enough things for quite a few families. God had been good to him and now he would share that with Ezekiel's family. It was amazing how things were progressing. He had only come to bury his brother and now he was taking care of a new family. Mordechi would want him to do this.

Mordechi didn't have the money that he had so he didn't have much clothing. It only took a few boxes to put them all away. He would take them to a goodwill or maybe someone at the church would like to have them. There were boxes of picture albums that Stephen had not seen in a long time. He cried over the pictures of he, Mordechi and their parents. He wondered where those pictures had gone. He thought that they had been lost when his parents were alive. It was nice to relive for a brief moment the time when they were young and the whole family was together.

Stephen was startled when he heard a knock at the door. He didn't expect anyone so he figured it was a neighbor bringing over some more food. John had not thought to call he hoped that Stephen would be home to receive him. After a few knocks he heard footsteps approaching the door. "Who is that? I'm coming, I'm coming."

Stephen opened the door. "Pastor John. How are you doing? Did you see Ezekiel today?"

"Yes Stephen. Do you mind if I come in for a minute."

"Of course not. You are a member of the family now. Come have a seat. I was just upstairs going through my brother's things. I figured that I should start getting the house in order so that when Ezekiel is freed we can get out of here right away. His wife and daughter are worried sick about him. So what did you find out?"

"Well we went to the prison and Ezekiel was there of course. He has lost a lot of weight and you can see in his eyes that he wants to come home bad. I don't think that he is sick but that place is not fit for any human being to live there. He wanted you to know that he loves you and that he is looking forward to seeing you very soon. He mentioned something about a dream from God. This dream has given him much hope. He doesn't know how but he knows that God is going to deliver him from prison. We didn't have much time but he met a very interesting young man in prison that has been helping him. His brother is the one that set up the meeting for me. I don't know whether you know a Mr. Voronkova but he is not like us but it is amazing how God works through means that we would not think to provide a blessing for us. He has friends in high places and just might use them to get Ezekiel free."

"Well I don't know this name but if he will help my son it's none of my business what he is into. I won't pretend to be a man of God like you Pastor John but what I remember of the Torah God has often times used even the bad gentiles to help my people in a time of crisis. So if God doesn't care then I don't care either. Thank you so much Pastor John for going to visit with Ezekiel. Daniel wanted one of our own to make contact so that we can see for ourselves that he is at least alive. I hope this will be over soon."

"Me too Stephen. Just keep praying. We've done all that we can. Now it is time for God to step in. If he told Ezekiel that he is going to deliver him then he is going to do it. We must keep the faith."

The two men hug and Pastor John makes his way to see Daniel. He was sure that he was waiting for him to come over. Daniel told him that he would be waiting for news from him after his visit. Daniel had retrieved the document from Tsilia and was reviewing some more tapes when he heard a knock at the door. He wasn't sure who it was so he quickly put the contents of the briefcase back into the case. He acted a bit nervous when he opened the door and Pastor John was a bit startled. "Are you okay?"

"Yeah. Sorry I was just reviewing some information that has me a bit worried about what's happening in the world Pastor John. Please come in and have a seat."

"Thank you Daniel. And please call me John. Ezekiel is alive that's all that I can say. He is losing weight and he didn't say but I think that he is feeling a little sick. That place was cold and damp. If we can I can get some blankets for him and the other inmates and that might help to keep them from getting sick. I don't know how to get in touch with Aleksis but if you do please tell him that I will fix up quite a few boxes of blankets and Bibles for the inmates. Ezekiel mentioned that someone got a Bible for him. He is doing the best he can to keep his spirits up. He even mentioned that he had a special dream from heaven that his given him hope."

"That's great." Daniel had a strange look on his face that John was unable to understand.

"You look like you don't believe in dreams or something. But I must tell you that the same God that spoke with Moses on the mountain is still speaking now Daniel. You must keep an open mind."

"No it's not that. I have to tell you that I have been visited by angels as well. There is more but I'm not ready to talk about it all yet. But I do very much believe in angels."

"So what did this angel say?"

"He told me to stick with this case that Ezekiel was a very special person and God wanted me to help him."

"That is great Daniel. Yes Ezekiel is a very special person. I know that he is wondering why he is in this position. Daniel I have to tell you something. When I walked through those doors I was literally scared. If I had not been with Aleksis going to see Ezekiel I don't know whether I could live through what he is going through now. You see some Christians believe that we are living in the end of the world before the Messiah returns. We also believe that there is going to be a time of persecution of the Christian church as well. It's not going to be an easy time. I realized that I was not ready for this persecution. I'm scared Daniel. For the first time in my life I'm afraid of the unknown. I hope this doesn't scare you but they say that we will be put in prison and that many of us will give our lives for the sake of the gospel."

"I understand John. There is nothing wrong with saying that you are afraid of something. I've been dealing with things that I never thought I would have to deal with. I'm very much afraid right now. What if this is all true and Russia is going to invade America? Do you know what this is going to mean for my people and yes all the people who try to come against the new government. I was talking with another Christian friend of mine who had been trying to tell me about some of this stuff for quite sometime now but I thought he was a quack so I didn't listen. Now I have proof of my own of this terrible government conspiracy. I can't tell you more than that. If I do your life will be in danger. I don't want that for you. But I will tell you this that I am already planning on going to America with Ezekiel when he gets out."

"Why what have you learned? Please Daniel I need to know what is going to happen. It is my responsibility to teach my congregation what is ahead so that they can be prepared. If you want I will wait until you are safely out of the country."

Daniel didn't speak for a few minutes. He hesitated to involve John anymore than he had to. After all he was kind enough to go into the prison to meet with Ezekiel. This knowledge was important for the very survival of the Americans and the world. It was more than just a conspiracy about Russia invading America but so much more. This was only a small part.

"Okay. I don't know whether I would want to know but Ezekiel grew up with a young man by the name of Mishenko. Mishenko's father had been working for the government and Mishenko eventually grew up and started working with his father in this business. To make a long story sort Mishenko was involved in some how do you say some shady business with the government. He met a Russian intelligence officer that divulged some very confidential information to him. The officer got caught by the American's and turned over evidence that Russian was in fact planning an attack against the country. I guess the government found out about it and put Mishenko in prison. Unfortunately he also divulged some of this knowledge to Ezekiel. Why God only knows. In any case we believe the bombing was to kill Ezekiel but he had not gone to work that day. Henceforth Ezekiel is now in prison fighting for his life. In the interim one of the members of the synagogue found a briefcase in the ruins of the synagogue behind the Torah scroll case left there by Mishenko. Mishenko was the one that did the upgrades on the synagogue and the school. Upon reviewing the tapes Mishenko has maps of where the bombs were set in America. How he got all of this information I don't know. But he was saving it maybe to get out of the country and tell the American's but he got caught first. He did manage to get his wife and children out of the country. To date no one knows where they are at. I just hope they are safe."

"That's a mouth full."

"Wait a minute it gets worse. I was talking with a friend of mine Jeremy and he says that he got it from a good source that this is not just about Russia and America. This is about a New World Government that is being planned by the major countries of this world. They call themselves the G20."

"The G20. What in the world is that?"

"It is a group of nations that come together every year to make the decisions that will affect the whole world John. I never heard about them either. I don't know where I've been but these people have taken over the whole world while I was sleeping. We are in trouble John. I don't know what we are going to do. We can't stop them and we can't beat them."

"Well I tell you what Daniel. We can't stop them but we can beat them."

"How John? How can we beat 20 of the most powerful nations in the world? Remember what happened in Tianemen Square when the Chinese students rose up against the government? They were massacred right there. These people are dangerous and they will not stop at killing someone."

"The Messiah John. Have you ever heard of Armageddon?"

"Yeah I think so. Jeremy talks about it all the time. What is Armageddon?"

"Well John Armageddon is when the nations come up against Israel?"

"What? Against Israel?"

"Yes Daniel. Hold on now. These nations are going to come up against Israel but God is going to send the Messiah and his holy angels to wage war against these nations. They cannot win against God Daniel don't you see. Israel will be saved. The time is coming. All these things must happen before Armageddon but God is going to give us the victory."

"Oh John I wish that we don't have to go through all of this. Many millions of people are going to be killed."

"Yes you are right. But this is not God's choice. Man has chosen to fight this battle but God is going to end it all. Daniel now is the time for you to accept Christ. If you accept him now he will be with you and you will make it into the new Kingdom of the Messiah. I don't want to pressure you because I know that you do not know much about the Christ. If you could accept him by faith he will make himself real in your life and then you will know through Him that He is the true Messiah."

"I'm sorry John but I'm not ready for that yet. I thank you for your input though. This is all so new to me. I will have to take my time and take it all in. But I will pray that Jesus will make himself real to me if He is in fact the Messiah for whom we wait. I don't mean to offend you."

"No problem Daniel. I am not offended. Listen you know where I am. If you ever want to talk just call me. I must get home now my wife is probably starting to worry."

"Ok. Hey I'll get in touch with you to see Ezekiel again. Thanks for your help."

"No problem." The two men part. Daniel has so much to think about. He had heard about Armageddon but thought it was just some fable the Christians made up but now he wasn't so sure about that.

Chapter 21

John was amazed at how his life had been changed in just one day. He had been studying the Bible all of his life and now what the prophets spoke about thousands of years ago were happening right in front of his eyes. Where had the time gone? He didn't quite know how to take it all in. But he knew in his heart that it was a time to pray for all humanity.

John wanted to be prepared for his next visit with Ezekiel. He noticed that Ezekiel seemed to be a bit sick although he didn't complain. His skin was turning gray and his overall health was not good. He was young and strong but even young people could get sick and die. He did not want to get a message that he had died in that place. He made a plea to the congregation and took up a special offering for medicine, food and blankets to take to the prison. He hoped they could take it soon the men's lives were at stake.

Ezekiel was so happy for the provisions that Aleksis brought for the men of Section 5. Ezekiel knew of two men already that had died from complications from pneumonia. Officer Zubkov was a good man. Ezekiel didn't look down on him for breaking some of the rules. He truly cared about the inmates unlike some of the officers. They used the inmates for their own gain but he helped many of the inmates and saved lives. Ezekiel went that same night to take care of Vladimir's wounds and to tell him that his brother was working on getting him to a hospital. Ezekiel was used to the long walk down the corridor's to where Vladimir was kept. Vladimir had a terrible set back and Ezekiel was scared when he saw his friend. All he could do was to give him the medicine that Aleksis had brought for him. He needed to get to a hospital or else he would die in this place. He didn't even know that Ezekiel was there. He had a high fever and was mumbling under his breath. He was delirious. If Aleksis didn't get him out right away he would be leaving in a body bag. After applying some medicine to his wounds Ezekiel tried to get him to eat something but he couldn't eat. It was hard for Ezekiel to leave him like that but he didn't have any other choice. He would have to call Aleksis right away.

As soon as Ezekiel reached his bunk he had to make an emergency call to Aleksis. The phone kept ringing and ringing. He knew that it was late but he had to get through or Vladimir would die. Finally Aleksis picked up the phone. "Who is this? Don't you know what time it is?"

"Aleksis this is Ezekiel. I'm sorry to bother you. This is an emergency."

"What has happened Ezekiel?"

"Aleksis Vladimir didn't know that I was in his cell. He has a bad fever and is delirious. If you do not get him to a hospital soon he is going to die. You must act quickly." Officer Zubkov took Ezekiel down to the machine shop so that he could make his phone call without waking his cell mate. No one could know that he was helping Ezekiel or he would lose his job.

"Oh my God. Ok I had someone working on it. I will be there to get him tonight." Aleksis started to cry like a baby on the phone. He loved his little brother like his own son. He could not lose him. He didn't realize how bad off Vladimir was.

Ezekiel ended the phone call. He hoped that Aleksis could make this work out. Vladimir was in trouble and he was his only help. The officer escorted Ezekiel back to his cell. Ezekiel didn't sleep much that night worrying about Vladimir.

The next morning came quickly and Ezekiel followed his same routine. He had now been incarcerated for more than three months.

Every Sabbath he made a mark on the wall next to his bunk for each week that passed. Prison life had gotten old quick. His faith was waning and he just wanted to be free. He had forgotten what it was like to be with his wife. He knew that Aliya had grown even in the few months that he had not seen her. Children grew over night and he was missing her more and more every day. He was so grateful that his father was not alive to see him like this. It would have killed him if the cancer had not gotten him first. He missed his father though. He was the rock of the family and always knew what to say when times were hard. He was amazed at the tenacity of the human soul. Some of the men had been in prison several times and even worse had spent most of their young lives behind bars. It was a wonder that most of them didn't know how to live in regular society. They had gotten used to living in prison. How that could happen one could only fathom. Ezekiel was a free man and would not stop until he was free again.

The day seemed to drag on forever. Ezekiel had found peace in reading his Bible, praying and thinking of the day when he would be free. Every day he said maybe tomorrow someone will come to get me. Each day was hard but he knew what God had told him. Officer Zubkov came with great news. Vladimir had been transported to the hospital that afternoon. Ezekiel was elated, worried but then sad at the same time. He would probably not return and he might never see him again. He would have to call Aleksis the next day at work so that he could see how he was doing.

Good news finally came for Ezekiel in a very unconventional way. Ezekiel never felt so down in his life. He felt like if he just killed himself that no one would have to worry about him anymore. He didn't want to leave his wife and daughter but being in prison was taking all the strength he had in his body. Ezekiel had not been able to get through to Aleksis in quite a few days. He hoped that he had not forgotten about him. He promised that he would take care of him if he took care of his brother. If it were not for him Vladimir would have died. He had to be strong. But the thoughts of suicide took over his thoughts more and more every day. One day he was in the common area and one of the inmates said he had a sure fire way to get someone out of the prison. He wasn't talking to Ezekiel so he acted as though he wasn't listening.

Ezekiel knew that he would not get a fair trial and he would be in prison for the rest of his life if he didn't do something to help himself. The inmates boasted that he had never tried it himself but that there was some medicine that when taken the person looked like they were having a cardiac arrest. They would have to take the person to the hospital. They could escape from the hospital if they paid the officer watching over them. Then they would have to get someone to hide them out from there. He said that he had worked in a hospital. The reason why he was there was that he had killed ten of his patients. He was a total psycho case.

Ezekiel had an idea but he would need Aleksis and Officer Zubkov if it was going to work. First he had to find out what kind of medicine the inmate was talking about and have Aleksis do some homework about it and how it should be administered. He didn't want to die trying to escape but if this worked he could have Aleksis have someone pick him up from the hospital and then get out of the country. He could get asylum from the American government. He didn't even know whether he should get Daniel involved but he had to trust someone. All he knew was that he was not going to die in prison.

The first step was to get in touch with someone from the outside. He wasn't having any success getting in touch with Aleksis so he would have to start with Daniel. Ezekiel had a sparkle coming in his eye for the first time in a long time. He was taking responsibility for his own destiny. It would take a lot of prayer but this was a situation that required some prayer and some action. The most important person would be Officer Zubkov and he didn't quite know how to bring up the subject. He knew that every man had a price and if he could meet that price the officer would help him. During his break Ezekiel struck up a conversation with Zubkov to see how things were going. Maybe he had heard something about Vladimir, he was really worried about him. Perhaps Aleksis had been busy and that was why he wasn't answering his cell phone. The officer went outside for a smoke break and Ezekiel followed him out the door. He was just about on his heels when he turned around. "Hi officer. I meant to ask you whether you had heard anything about Vladimir. I have not been able to talk with his brother and I was worried."

"Well the last I heard his brother paid someone to get him free. But if he gets in trouble again he will be back in here without any reservations from the court. He is still in the hospital though. He was really in bad shape. The government looked really bad when the story got out that an inmate was beaten so badly. He got his big break I hope that he appreciates it."

"Yeah me too. Say do you need anything else. I'm trying to get in touch with his brother. He said that he was going to make some phone calls to help me get out of here. I hope he hasn't forgotten about us you know. But then I'm sure you have lots of contacts to help you."

"No not really. That was the best help that I've had in a long time. Hey I have something to tell you. I just didn't know how to tell you. This job is not working out for me. My kids are growing faster than I can make money. I need something better so that I can take care of my family. I'm planning on leaving. I know how hard it was for you losing Vladimir. You're a good guy. I'm sure that you are not guilty of any crime. If there is any way that I could help you I would."

"Has anyone ever been able to escape from this place Officer Zubkov? Please I need help. If you leave me how am I going to make it. I'll pay you whatever if you'll help me get out of here. I have a plan but I need help I can't do it by myself."

"Ezekiel what are you saying? How can we get you out of here? I don't see anyway that we can accomplish that. There has never been anyone that has been able to break out of this prison. There is no way out but through the gate."

"I know but listen to my plan. Think about it. I will get you whatever you want. I heard one of the inmates say that there is some medicine that makes you look like you are having a heart attack. I figured if I took this they would have to take me to the hospital and I would take care of everything from there. What do you think?"

"I don't know Ezekiel. I would have to accompany you to the hospital. I could get that done I guess. But how would you get out from there?"

"Aleksis knows a lot of people. He would have to take care of things from there and get me out of the hospital. That's the easy part. There are so many ways in and out. They could put me in one of those bins that holds the bed clothing. They can sneak me out that way. I plan on leaving the country. I have something I need to tell the world Officer Zubkov. What is happening to me and to other people the world needs to know. What kind of world do we live in where people are wrongfully accused of crimes they didn't commit. My whole life has been taken away and I'm fighting to get it back. Please tell me that you will at least think about it."

"Okay Ezekiel. I'm planning on leaving soon. We'll have to do this soon if at all."

Ezekiel went back to work hoping that the officer would at least think about his proposal but he had nothing to back it up. He had promised that he would do something but he had no money accept for what his father had left him. He was sure that Stephen would not mind using it to get him free. Stephen would get the money together to get him out of the country. He was feeling desperate. It was either this or kill himself and he wasn't ready to die. He had a family and a dream.

Daniel was getting worried that he had not heard from Ezekiel or Aleksis for weeks now. What kind of lawyer was he after all? He had cut himself off from Tsilia even though she was constantly calling him because he didn't want her to get involved any more in this case. He just wanted to get his client free. He couldn't think of a way so he had to just wait until he got a miracle. When Daniel felt stressed he went to the gym for a workout and most times he felt better and clearer afterward. After a good workout he returned to his car. He figured maybe he would stop and get something from the neighborhood restaurant for dinner. He had left his cell phone in the car. There was a message waiting for him. He was hoping that Ezekiel was calling. He couldn't return the call but at least he would know that he was okay. He must have felt so abandoned by everyone. Upon checking the message it was from Aleksis and he said that he would be getting back in touch within a hour. Daniel didn't want to go in the restaurant. He was mad that he had not had his phone with him. He wasn't going to miss this call.

On the way home Daniel was absolutely shaking with fear. What if something had happened to Ezekiel he would never forgive himself. But he had done everything he knew what to do. Ezekiel's case would not be going to trial for quite a few months. He knew they were back logged with other cases but that didn't make him feel any better. Daniel kept the phone in his pocket while he stopped for some dinner and went directly home to wait for Aleksis phone call.

Daniel didn't want to think the worse. Maybe he wanted to plan another trip to see Ezekiel. It was so hard being in the dark. He wished that he could call Ezekiel any time he wanted but he didn't have such privilege. They were still watching Ezekiel but he did have a right and maybe it wasn't the right thing to stay away from him. He would have to take the chance and go and see his client. What would they have to lose? Daniel didn't watch much television but he turned it on to drown out the noise in his head. If he could pack a bag and run away he would but he knew that God was watching him and he feared running away.

Daniel had eaten some pretty bad food and fell asleep watching the local news channel. He faintly heard the phone ringing but woke up in time to catch it at the last ring. "Hi this is Daniel."

"Daniel this is Aleksis. I called to tell you that my brother is out of prison. He has been out for a few weeks now. He was in pretty bad shape but he is finally starting to do better. I have not been able to speak with Ezekiel I'm sure he has thought I have forgotten about him. If he contacts you tell him that I have a mole in my organization. My private phone was stolen. If he calls tell him to not call that number any more. If he calls you give him my new number and tell him to call me. He has done a big favor for me and I want to help him get out of prison in any way that I can."

"I know that it might be too much to ask but if you can go and visit him again or take the pastor to visit. I'm worried about him. His case will not be heard before the court for quite sometime. I don't think that he can make it without Vladimir. They were very close. Vladimir gave him strength and comfort. I don't know what to do Aleksis."

"Don't panic. Ezekiel is stronger than you give him credit for. Remember he has God and that's more than I had when I was in prison. I know that I'm a different person than him. I grew up on the streets and nothing was going to shake me up. But I tell you the truth that there were times when I wish that I had a God to pray to. Okay I tell you what I'll get in touch with Pastor John and Officer Zubkov and we will take some supplies to the prison. This way we can check on him and let him know that he has not been forgotten. I'm still making phone calls about getting him released. I will have to call in quite a few favors to get this done. Vladimir made a terrible mistake in killing that inmate but he was just another drug dealer and the government didn't care about that. Ezekiel's case is different. Let me work on this I'm sure that we can come up with something."

"Thank you Aleksis. Let me know if you need me to do something. If Ezekiel calls I will tell him that you are going to visit him soon and give him your new number."

Daniel was wishing that he had never gotten involved with this case. He had this briefcase full of money and information against the government. If anyone found out about it he would be in prison forever himself. If Ezekiel was going to be released soon he would have to leave this place and he wasn't sure that he was ready to do that. He had just started talking with Tsilia again and for a minute he thought that maybe he had made a mistake not keeping in touch with her. She was a wonderful woman, someone he could build a life with and now all that seemed to be in jeopardy. He would have to call her soon and talk with her about the future.

Chapter 22

Pastor John and his congregation immediately took action putting together personal packages for each inmate at the prison. He really felt that the church had a responsibility to serve the community but had never thought about taking Bibles and supplies into the prison. This was what being a Christian was all about. It was not just about reading the Bible but living it in daily life. He had learned a valuable lesson. Since Pastor John didn't know when he would hear from Aleksis or Daniel he made the decision to call the head of the prison himself. He felt it would be a way that he could make some contacts of his own. Then the church could come in and work with the prison without any outside assistance. He was surprised that the prison officials welcomed the church and he accepted the invitation to come into the prison every couple of months to bring supplies for the inmates. He was told that there were approximately four hundred inmates. He was given a list of items that they would most likely need and he could work from that or bring whatever he could think of. He was surprised that included on the list were playing cards, basketballs, chairs, tables, blankets, towels and any type of personal hygiene items. The list was endless. His church didn't have a lot of money but he could partner with other churches to get whatever the prison needed. Things were definitely bad in Russia.

Many families lived in poverty and certainly could not sustain a family member in prison.

The day came quickly to deliver the packages to the prison. John and his assistant pastor and several other members from the church piled all the packages in three vans that were owned by the church. He wasn't sure whether the prisoners knew they were coming but the guards were aware they would be coming. He hoped that they could set up a few tables and get a chance to minister to the inmates as they came through for their package. He had one package for each inmate. He had not alerted Daniel because he did not want Ezekiel to know that he was coming. What a surprise it would be to see his friend again. He could hardly wait to see the look on his face as he went through the line. Since he did not do the driving he had to get instructions how to get to the prison but it was not difficult. John had been living in Russia all of his life. If they got lost they would just have to stop and ask someone.

Pastor John meant to leave his cell phone in the office so he would not be disturbed but he had forgotten and his phone started ringing. He thought to still shut it off but his wife could have been calling. He had children and things happened every day. The cell phone was a good thing so he could always know what was happening with his family. He was sure it would only take a quick minute to answer the phone. Daniel wanted to let Pastor John know that Aleksis had contacted him and that he wanted to still help Ezekiel. The phone call came just in time before the entourage left for the prison. Pastor John answered the phone. "Hi this is Pastor John."

"Pastor John I'm sorry to bother you but this is Daniel, Ezekiel's lawyer."

"I cannot believe that you are calling. You would never guess what I've worked out."

"What do you mean?"

"Well I called the officials from the prison where Ezekiel is being held. I have arranged for myself and some members to take some provisions for the inmates at the jail. Ezekiel does not even know that I am coming. He will be so surprised. I'm really worried about him and I think this will make him feel better. What do you think? I'm so excited."

"Wow. You make me feel bad. I have not seen my client since he was sent to that God awful place. But Aleksis said that it would probably be better that I not make any waves you know. But this is a great idea. Please do me a favor. Take down this number and give it to Ezekiel. Tell him that the police have been following Aleksis and that someone stole his phone. He said to tell Ezekiel not to call the old number but use the new number. We have not forgotten him but we are still working on getting him out of there. Even if we have to pay some official to help him we are prepared to do that. Tell him we have not forgotten him."

"Okay. Well we are on our way. We have three vans full of stuff for the men. I'll give Ezekiel the message. I'm sure this will make him feel a lot better. I'm just worried about his health and well being. I'll let you know how he is doing when I return."

Daniel couldn't believe his timing. Pastor John was a stand up kind of guy. He would not have had the guts to tell him to do something like this. The police could make lots of trouble for him and his congregation. Daniel would not have wanted to put any of them in danger.

On the way to the prison John remembered how uneasy he felt during his first trip. Just walking through the yard surrounded by barbed wire and guard stations with guns fully loaded. He hoped that he would start to feel better each time they had the opportunity to come and visit with the inmates. Many of the brothers that came with them had never experienced the prison environment. Several of them were picked for the ministry especially because they had experience in psychology and counseling. Maybe someone might want to speak with someone while they were there. It was not just about giving out things but reaching the hearts of men.

It only took a short while to reach the prison. John and the others parked there vans next to each other as close to the entrance as possible. They had a lot of packages to bring in and there was no one outside waiting to help them. The officer closest to the gate came to greet John and the crew. "Good morning Pastor John we were expecting you. Don't worry I will have some of the inmates come out to help you. We suspended the regular work day so that we could accommodate your visit today."

"Wow thank you. What is your name?"

"I am Officer Medvedev. But call me shorty. I'm a Christian too and I like what you are doing. You know I have worked here now for a couple of years and no one has ever attempted to do anything like this. I'm going to ask my pastor to give you a call maybe he might like to help out if you are going to come back that is."

"Yes. We plan to come as much as we can. Anything to help the inmates. I know how difficult this is for them and their families. The next step is to reach out to the spouses and the children to let them know that they have not been forgotten. Times are getting more difficult as we get closer to the return of Christ. It's only going to get worse. The church must step up and take responsibility for those who are in need. We are glad to do it."

"That's great. We can set up some tables in the courtyard. When you are ready we can have them come out by blocks. We have eight blocks with fifty men in each block. That will make it a bit more organized. Some of these guys don't have much manners but for the most part they do okay. Just be firm with them."

John hoped he didn't seem nervous but he was sure glad that there were officers around to protect them. He had heard of prison riots and he sure hoped they didn't have one planned for that day. He told his wife he would be home for super that night. She was worried but this was what he needed to do. His friend was in this prison and this was a way that he could check on him and make sure that he was okay and had what he needed.

Officer Medvedev came through with the help of some of the burliest inmates in the whole prison. If Pastor John was afraid he was terrified when he saw a group of these men coming towards them. But he kept his composure knowing that they were there to help. The men unloaded the vans and they put up the tables in the court yard. The group would stand behind the tables as the men stood in line and came up one by one to get a package. If someone wanted to talk Pastor John and his assistant sat at separate tables on the side to speak with them personally for a short period. There were too many of them to spend a lot of time but he wanted them to know that he would be their pastor and was available to them. He also wanted to make contact with the inmates wives and children on the outside who might need help with finances or spiritual help. It was a God send that Ezekiel ended up in this place. He wasn't happy that he was there but because of it he had learned that there was a group of people living in a place that he wouldn't wish on his worse enemy.

The inmates were being lined up by the officer in charge while the group said a quick prayer that all would go well and a lot would be accomplished that day. Pastor John didn't know when he would see Ezekiel but he kept looking at the line to see if he could spot his friend before he was aware what was happening. He had butterflies in his stomach and couldn't wait to see the excitement on his face.

The first group came through the line. Pastor John noticed that their uniforms were dirty and torn. Some of the men were too big for the uniforms that they wore. He made a mental note to ask the officials if they could buy new uniforms for the inmates. For some of them it was all that they had to wear. One pair of pants and a shirt for the duration of the time that they were incarcerated. His family was not poor when he was young but they still didn't have a lot. He just couldn't imagine only having one shirt and pants to wear all his life. He was sure that they would be happy to have a new set of uniforms.

They were a rowdy bunch of guys. But it was like Christmas for them. Along with the packages Pastor John had bag lunches complete with sandwiches, sweets and soft drinks which was something that most of them had not had since entering the prison. No one could measure the affect that day had on their lives. Men were laughing and joking around with the workers. It was a great day.

Sergei came over to the table to thank Pastor John and his assistant. He had not been in the prison for long but felt like he really needed a sign from God that he was going to make it through prison life. He had felt abandoned by his family and despite reading his Bible he was a new Christian and had lots of questions. He would have conversations with the preacher and that kept him going. This visit really brought home the need for Christian fellowship. He wanted to know if they could somehow come into the prison for Bible study. He knew several of the men that would really appreciate it. Pastor John could not believe what he was hearing a Bible study. He would make a phone call the next day to see if something like that was possible. Before Sergei left the table Pastor John stood up and gave Sergei the biggest hug that he could. He knew that he needed the love of a friend and pastor. Pastor John had gotten through to someone that day and that was what they had come for.

Sergei was Ezekiel's cell mate but Ezekiel wasn't feeling well and stayed behind until the rest of the inmates had gotten a chance to get something from the church that had come in. He had no idea that it was his good friend Pastor John. Aleksis had been good to him and he had really all that he needed. He wanted to make sure that the others had a chance to get something. Visitations from family members were few and far and in between for most of the inmates. Sergei came back to the cell with a large package full of good things and a bag of lunch. For the first time in weeks he had a big smile on his face. This made Ezekiel smile too. The whole prison really needed something like this. Instead of fighting the inmates were smiling, laughing and being kind to one another. Something great had happened that day.

After almost three hours of work the workers were starting to pack up the tables that had nothing on them any more. They couldn't believe that they had given out just about all of the packages that they brought with them. Pastor John had spoken with many of the inmates and was planning on coming back for Bible study if he was allowed by the officials. He had a feeling that this was going to work out. What an amazing time they had that day. But he had not seen Ezekiel yet and he was worried that he might not come out. What was he going to do? He had been there before but he didn't want the officers to know that he knew him personally. They only had a few packages left what could he say to get him out there.

Just when he thought that all was lost he saw Ezekiel standing at the end of the line. A well of emotions took his breath away. Ezekiel looked even worse than he did the first time he saw him. He was trying to make eye contact without anyone noticing. Ezekiel had decided to come out when Sergei told him that he had met one of the nicest men that he had ever met. Ezekiel just wanted to see the face of the man that prayed with Sergei and set his soul free for the first time since he came to Section 5.

Ezekiel could not see clearly the tables that were in front of him because of the other inmates that were in front of him. Pastor John stood up in front of the table so that as Ezekiel got closer he could see his friend as he turned the corner. When Ezekiel saw Pastor John he couldn't believe his eyes. He wanted to run to him and hug him but he was confused and elated all at the same time. What was he doing here? He could get himself in trouble if the authorities knew that they were friends. He made eye contact and smiled but Pastor John could see the pain in his eyes. Seeing his friend brought pain to his very soul. Oh how he wanted the day to come quickly when he could see him on the outside and they could sit together in the little restaurant that they loved to both go to for lunch. They could talk about God, family and the future of their families and the world. He yearned for his wife's cooking and the smell of his little girl tucked closely to her father's chest.

The rest of the inmates came forward to receive their packages. It was ashamed that it all had to end so quickly. The last package was given and Ezekiel walked over to the table. Pastor John should have alerted his assistant but had not completely thought everything through. Pastor John reached out and took Ezekiel's hand in his hand. He could not resist hugging him. At this point he had hugged quite a few lonely souls so nobody would notice that this was any different. Pastor John asked his assistant to go and help the others break down the tables and get ready to return to the vans. This would give him a moment to speak with Ezekiel. After he had left he and Ezekiel sat down at the table. "We don't have much time. Don't worry your cover is not blown. Nobody knows that we know each other."

"This is crazy John. You could blow my cover and even more get yourself in trouble."

"Listen stop fussing already. Take this piece of paper. It has Aleksis new phone number on it. He is being watched by the authorities and someone has stolen his old phone. He wants you to know that he has not forgotten about you."

It was too much for Ezekiel to handle and he fell into the pastor's arm like a bowl of noodles. The tears flowed freely and the stress of the whole situation just came pouring out of Ezekiel's heart. "I don't know how much more I can take. I just want to die John. I just want to die."

"Now you look at me. Look at me Ezekiel. Don't talk like that. We are going to get you out of here. Just hold on. I will be back soon to see you. Maybe Aleksis might come and maybe not but I'm not going to forget you. You are my brother and I love you. Your time is coming. I don't know how but you are going to get out of here. Hold on please. Don't let go. Most people faint just before the deliverance comes. Don't let them win."

Ezekiel was still a basket case but tried to get himself together. It was so good to see his friend. This was an answer to prayer. But now Ezekiel had Aleksis phone number and he wanted to set up a meeting so that he could get Ezekiel out of prison.

Officer Medvedev gave the two men a little time but ended the conversation. It was time for the workers to leave but the mission was accomplished. Pastor John hugged Ezekiel one more time and left the compound with the other works. His heart skipping a beat as he walked out the doors, through the yard leading to the gate and into the safety of the vans.

Chapter 23

zekiel didn't feel as free as Sergei. He wished that it was so but he became tormented in the worse way after seeing John. Like a scared child he wished that he could find peace in the arms of his friend. When Ezekiel was just a young boy he remembered the day when he got lost from his mother. One minute she was right in front of him but in the store he saw a rack of bicycles and couldn't resist touching the beautiful red bicycle that he wanted so badly. In just a moment he was separated from her and when he turned around to tell his mother what he wanted for his birthday she had walked off. She had not realized that Ezekiel was no longer walking beside her. She was frantic. Ezekiel never felt so scared in his life. He ran from aisle to aisle looking for his mother.

In tears Ezekiel saw a nice lady that had a badge on her shirt. He knew that she worked there and maybe could help him find his mother. The young lady saw the distress in the boy and made a call over the intercom at the store. Ezekiel's mom arrived within seconds to find her little man in tears thinking that he would never see her again. Ezekiel had never felt so abandoned and out of control in his life. That same feeling was welling up in him that day. His throat was tight, beads of sweat burned his eyes, he was having a panic attack. Gaining control again seemed so far away from him he just fell to the floor of his cell and passed out.

When Ezekiel came to he was in the infirmary and a nurse was looking down at him. It startled him for a minute. He couldn't believe that he had passed out. Tears were still flowing from his eyes. "Mr. Ezekiel are you okay?"

"I think so. What happened?"

"It seems like you passed out Mr. Ezekiel. We'll keep you here for a few days to make sure you are feeling better to return back to work."

Ezekiel didn't make a fuss. He didn't want to be in the infirmary but it gave him a chance to ask the nurse some very important questions. Officer Zubkov was off and had not told him whether he was willing to help him or not. He had a substantial amount of money but he wasn't sure what his services would cost if he were willing to help him with his plan. But now he knew why he was not able to get through to Aleksis. What was the police looking for? He knew that they were drug dealers so it must have been about that. He would now have to wait a few days before he could call him. The nurse had given him some medicine that made him feel very sleepy but it was also very relaxing so he didn't mind.

Ezekiel slept for quite a few hours. When he woke up the attending officer had brought him a tray of food. He didn't much feel like eating but attempted to eat a few bites. He was feeling weak. The infirmary was a far cry from his cell but certainly not a hotel room. They were in need of supplies. He hoped that it had seen better days. Maybe Pastor John could get some supplies to make the place look more like a place for sick people. A new coat of paint would do it some justice. Being in the infirmary made him feel worse. He would have to act like he was much better by the time the nurse returned the next morning. He needed to get access to his phone. Aleksis was waiting for him to call. Ezekiel said his prayers and tried to sleep the best that he could considering the circumstances.

Ezekiel woke up in the middle of the night to use the bathroom. The one great thing about prison was that there was no privacy at all. There was always someone watching when you went to the bathroom or took a shower. The infirmary was amazing because there was a bathroom complete with shower. Ezekiel would miss being able to go into the bathroom and actually close the door once he was put back in his cell. The officer must have walked away from his post because he never came in while Ezekiel slept or when he got up to use the bathroom. Ezekiel wasn't very tired but tried to go back to sleep. He heard some footsteps outside and thought that the officer was finally coming back to check on him. An amazing feeling swept over Ezekiel like a bad cold. It was an amazing power that made him actually feel sick to his stomach. When he looked up there was a man dressed like he was going to a very important business meeting. He walked into the room and stood just a few feet away from the bed that Ezekiel was about to lay on. He didn't say a word he just smiled at him. All Ezekiel could think was what was this man doing here. He had white hair and looked like he was around sixty years of age. He was very handsome and had the air of an English gentleman. But who was he and what was he doing in the prison that time of morning? There was an airy feel about him and Ezekiel became afraid.

"Don't be afraid Ezekiel. How are you doing?"

"I'm doing fine. Who are you?"

"I have come to help you Ezekiel. I have friends in high places and we can get you freed from this place. You are a very special man Ezekiel. I know who you are."

"Who am I?"

"You have been commissioned by God to do great things in the earth. But I have more power than he and I can give you great power and wealth. There is nothing that you cannot have."

"There is no one that is more powerful than God. You must be an angel of darkness."

"Well I would not say that. I am the Baron De Rothchild. I hold the 13th chair of the Druidic Counsel. I am the CEO of Earth Inc. Join us Ezekiel and I will train you to take my position when I step down."

"I don't want anything to do with you. You are of Satan."

When Ezekiel said that two angels dressed in white robes that stood as high as the ceiling stepped out of heaven. Ezekiel was frozen in place he couldn't move a muscle. All he could think was these are two of the most beautiful angels I have ever seen. One had blue eyes that sparkled

174

like crystals and the other had green eyes that pierced through the soul. With swords drawn they lunged at the man. When he saw them he turned into the most ugliest creature that Ezekiel had ever seen. The creature turned to run away. The two angels didn't utter a word but disappeared as quickly as they came. He was so afraid that he lost control of his bowels. Ezekiel passed out on the floor he was so afraid.

When Ezekiel came too he was still shaking and wondering whether he had really seen that man. He found some paper towels and wiped up the mess he had made on the floor. How would he explain this to the nurse in the morning. His pants were wet. Finally the officer had returned to his post and Ezekiel told him he had an accident and he gave him some clean pants and Ezekiel went into the shower to bathe. The bath was the best thing for him at that moment. Just the water falling over him made him feel alive again. He had never had an experience like that nor did he ever want to have one again.

After taking a shower Ezekiel went back to sleep and the morning came quickly and Ezekiel was feeling much better. Maybe it had been just a terrible dream. Nevertheless he would tell John about it the next time he saw him. Maybe he would understand what this all meant. He had to stay focused on getting out of prison to be with his family again. The nurse brought him a tray for breakfast and he ate heartily so that she would feel that he was doing better. He didn't want to spend another night in the infirmary. He needed to make a phone call to the outside.

Ezekiel finished his breakfast and tried to make small talk with the nurse as she performed her duties that morning. She really wasn't very busy. The only patient she had was him. So her morning duties were no more than come in give him breakfast and sit down doing her nails. He didn't care though she could do what she liked. If he were paying the salary she would be fired. She was nice enough though. After breakfast she came in to check on him and see how he was feeling. "Mr. Ezekiel how are you doing?"

"I'm doing much better. I had a bad dream last night. The devil came to visit me. What do you think about ghosts Ms. Anastasya?"

"Well you know I didn't much believe in ghosts until I started working here."

"You don't say. What changed your mind when you got here."

"Well the word is that there was a man that was murdered right here in the infirmary by one of the guards. Ever since then he kind of hangs out here. He just won't leave this prison. He walks around the place scaring people to death."

"So what does this guy look like anyway?"

"Well he was about my height around two hundred pounds and he was about thirty years old and he had a hideous scar on his face. He was here for rape and murder. They say that officer came to work here just to get revenge on this guy. You know there are a lot of stories about this place that give me the creeps."

"What kind of stories?"

"Well they say that Stalin's son was put here in this prison for charges against the government. Can you imagine Stalin's own son. I'm sure that created a scandal. But then his father was no choir boy either. Everybody knows that. Also they say that after the war many of the Nazi officers that were caught were put here. Back then the KGB were known for their ruthlessness. They say that there are rooms in what we call the dungeon where they used to interrogate these guys about what happened during the war. It is said that many of them died during interrogations they were so cruel to them. But the most interesting was this guy, very brilliant guy who later became a well known poet. He wrote his poems while he was in prison about life and the terrible atrocities that the government lodged against its own people. I read a few and they were awesome. He really had a pure heart although he was here for murdering a close relative. They said he just lost it. Can you imagine that?"

Ezekiel wished that he hadn't started talking with her but he had nothing else to do. He was still afraid from last night. What if that man came back what would he do? He needed to get out of that prison because something was happening to his mind. He didn't want to forget who he was and end up a basket case in prison for the rest of his life.

"Well I don't know but maybe there is such a thing as ghosts. In any case let me ask you a question since you know a lot about this place. Has anyone ever escaped from here before?"

"I'll tell you a very interesting story that happened a few years before I got here. There was a man who said he was in here by mistake. He said that he was innocent of his charges but the court didn't believe him and he was to be here for like ten years. So he and another man decided that they were going to break out of here. This place to tell you the truth is so lacsadaisical and corrupt that it wasn't difficult to do. Like for example the man that just got out of here to go to the hospital I know for a fact that his brother has connections. He'll never see the likes of this place again. If you have some money you can get out of prison no matter what crime you committed. Trust me."

"You mean Vladimir?"

"Yeah that's his name. I keep my eyes open you know. If a person wants out they can get out of here. But let me finish the story. These two men worked in the bakery where they make the bread right. They made arrangements with the guy who brings in the supplies by truck. He brings all supplies in through a back door. They paid him so that when he left they could be smuggled out in the truck. Well it worked just fine because the officer never checked the truck before it left the property. But when they realized they were gone the police looked everywhere for them. Eventually they were caught and brought back to prison. You know Mr. Ezekiel the thing most inmates do that is stupid when they escape is stay in the country where they can be caught. They don't have the resources to get out of the country. It's easy to get out of prison if you have a full proof plan. But then you have to get out of the country. This way they will never catch you and bring you back."

Nurse Anastasya was frank and to the point. Ezekiel would need a full proof plan and a way to get out of the country. He had a plan and wanted to get out of the country but he would need a lot of help.

"Yes you are right about that. Nurse Anastasya do you think that I can go back to my cell. I have by Bible there and I really miss not having it with me. I am feeling a lot better now and I'm sure the officer can put me on light duty just in case I feel light headed again. I love your company but it was really lonely here last night by myself. The officer in charge was no where to be found the whole night."

"I know. Don't tell anyone but he goes somewhere and sleeps for the whole night. He has two jobs you know. People think that we make a lot of money but we don't. I have two jobs as well. It's the only way to make ends meet in Russia these days. This new government was supposed to focus more on the people and build the country up. But that's not happening. Many are starving Mr. Ezekiel. When you get out of here take your family somewhere else and make a good life for yourself. I don't know why you are here and I'm not one to pass judgment on anyone but Russia is not a good place to raise a family. The country is plagued with corruption. I understand why some of our officers here in the prison are out for themselves. They do what they have to do to survive. Trust me he's only trying to take care of his family."

"I understand Nurse Anastasya. I won't tell anyone. Can I go back now?

"Sure Mr. Ezekiel. Just promise me you will take it easy. If you feel bad you just come back and see me. I'll take care of you."

Ezekiel couldn't get back to his cell quick enough. On the way he saw Officer Zubkov. He looked like he was really glad to see Ezekiel. "Hey are you okay? Sergei said that you passed out yesterday."

"Yeah. I'm doing better. I think I had a virus or something. The nurse gave me something that knocked me out and I slept like a baby but I wanted to get out of there. I had been trying to get in touch with Aleksis but can you believe someone stole his phone. In any case I need to get in touch with him. Have you thought about what we talked about?"

"Yeah. I have postponed my last day so I can help you. I'm sorry but I really need the money too. My wife is expecting a new baby. I wanted to just die when I found out but what could I say. She has always wanted children but this has got to be the last one. I just can't afford it."

"No problem. I understand. I'm going to call my lawyer and Aleksis and work this out. What I plan is this there is a drug that I can take but it will make me seem as though I am paralyzed. When this happens you will have to transport me to the hospital. After I get to the hospital I will be pronounced dead at which time I will be hiding out until I can leave the country. You see if they think that I am dead they will leave me and my family alone. Then I can go to America without them looking for me ever again. What do you think?"

"Wow. How did you think that up?"

"That guy who calls himself the mercy killer was talking about it in the courtyard. He killed a lot of people that way. But as long as I get to the hospital in time they can keep me alive. It's not meant to kill only to paralyze. They use it in the hospital during operations. I'm gonna have someone look it up. Listen don't worry. If everyone does their part it will work and I will be a free man."

"Well let me know what I need to do. Hey I need about one hundred thousand for this. Hey I'm putting myself on the line for you. And let's do it quickly. I can get you to the hospital and then you will need a doctor waiting to do the rest. I guess we can do this. I wish you all the best Ezekiel. You don't deserve what has happened to you. I would like to know that you have been released from this place before I leave."

"Thanks. I'll let you know. If I can get to Aleksis tonight and he can get the medicine and the doctor we can do this within a week. I need to make a phone call. Aleksis is waiting for me. I just made a friend with the nurse. They have a toilet in there maybe she will let me use it. Will you escort me so that no one will be conspicuous."

"Sure. You have your phone?"

"I'll have to get it first. Give me one minute. The good thing about the infirmary is that the nurse is there during the day and at night the officer sleeps during the night. There is no one else there so I can be alone."

Ezekiel retrieves the phone and some other things from his cell. He figured he was going to be out of there soon so he took everything he wanted and what he wanted to get rid of. His plan was to fake being sick for as long as he could and it wouldn't look strange that he had gotten sick and need to be hospitalized. Now he had to take care of things on the outside.

Chapter 24

Officer Zubkov escorted Ezekiel back to the infirmary. Nurse Anastasya was doing what she did best, nothing. She was sitting at her desk reading a book when they came in. Ezekiel acted as though he wasn't feeling well again and the officer just went with the act not really knowing what the script was for the play. Nurse Anastasya came running over to Ezekiel and caught him just before he hit the floor. Officer Zubkov put the bags down he was carrying and helped her put him on the cot. "Ezekiel is still not feeling well. He thought it would be better to get some things from his cell and come back here. He said you did a really good job taking care of him."

"Sure he can stay here as long as he wants. As you can see there is no one else here but me. Don't worry I'll take care of him."

Officer Zubkov went back to his post and Ezekiel sat up for a while talking with nurse Anastasya. He felt that he could trust her. She really didn't care about much. She was just making a living like most of the staff at the prison. Ezekiel had to wait until she either went out or left for the night before he could make his phone call. He had slipped the phone in his pants leg and hoped that it didn't fall out. When she left for the night he could find a hiding place for the phone. He was getting closer and closer to a solution to his problem. All he needed now was for Aleksis to make the connections for him on the outside at the hospital.

If he could get a doctor to meet them when they got to the hospital he could pronounce Ezekiel dead. He could revive him on the way to the morgue and then Aleksis could make the arrangements to have him picked up and sent to the funeral home where he would stay. Ezekiel didn't have all the particulars worked out yet. How would he get from the funeral home to the airport? Where would they fly to? Would the American's give him asylum? It would take some time but time was not on his side.

It was just about lunch time and nurse Anastasya brought Ezekiel a tray of food. She told him that once lunch was over that she would have to give out meds. Not even ten minutes had lapsed since Ezekiel came back to the infirmary when another officer brought in the preacher. He was lying on a gourney looking like he was at deaths door. Nurse Anastasya told the officers to put him on the bunk next to where Ezekiel was sitting. Ezekiel had not known that the preacher had terminal cancer and had spent a lot of time in the infirmary. He was coughing and his color was gone. The doctor had given him only a few months to live but the court didn't care about the fact that they were sending a dying man to prison. For what? He was about to die. Why would they not allow him to be with his family these last few days of his life? The system was cruel.

Nurse Anastasya put in an IV to keep the preacher hydrated. His pulse was faint but this had happened before and she watched him closely and brought him back from the very brink of death. Ezekiel felt bad because he didn't realize the work that one nurse was doing all by herself. He guessed she deserved to have some time to rest in between patients. The preacher could hardly maintain control of his body. He was shaking like he was cold. Sweat poored down his face like a running faucet. The pain was unbearable but the nurse didn't have the kind of drugs that he needed. She could only give him something to put him to sleep so he didn't have to face the pain. The cancer had spread to all of his vital organs and it was just a matter of time. Why should a man have to die in a place like this? He wished there was something that he could do. The nurse had a line of men waiting outside for their medications. While she was busy Ezekiel got wet towels to wipe the brow of this young man that was literally dying before him. The preacher opened his eyes periodically to look at Ezekiel. He tried to speak but Ezekiel could barely hear what the man was saying.

"Is there anything that I can get for you?"

"Please if I die in here tell my wife that I will see her in heaven and not to worry about me. Can you remember that?"

"Yes I can remember that." It was all that Ezekiel could do to stop from crying. Looking at the preacher reminded him of when his father died in his arms. He didn't know what Christians did before they died. Did he need to talk with someone? Maybe they could get Pastor John to come in and give him his last rights before he died. He had somehow made connections with the prison office. Maybe his wife could come in and see him before he died. He would make sure that he made a phone call that night to see what he could do.

He stayed by the preacher's side all day. He could at least take out his Bible and read to him. If it were not for the preacher he would not have his Bible. It really had given him a lot of comfort at times when he felt all alone and that he could not make it alone. Ezekiel thought that he would just read from the Psalm. It always gave him peace when he read it. As when his father died he read Psalm 23. The preacher opened his eyes and smiled.

"Ezekiel you are a man of God yes?"

"Yes. You know I don't remember what your real name is? I don't want to keep calling you the preacher."

"My name is Samuel."

"What a great name? The name Samuel means "Heard of God" or "God has heard". Another translation can be "Son of El" or "Son of God". Samuel was the last of the judges and the first prophet. Samuel was the one whom God sent to anoint King Saul and King David. You must be a very special man."

"I don't know about that but ever since I was a young boy my mother told me that God came to her one night while she was pregnant and he told her that I would go to the people and preach is message. I have done that all the days of my life. I don't know why this has happened at this point in my life Ezekiel but here I am. But you know I am not afraid. I have fulfilled my destiny here on this earth and now I will fulfill my heavenly calling."

"I know what you mean Samuel. I don't know why I am where I am at today either but here we are two men of God going through perhaps one of the biggest tests of our lives."

"Ezekiel this is the final test for me but I believe that you have so much more to do for your people. Just remember don't give up. You have all that you need to fulfill your destiny. When you feel weak just pray and God will give you the strength to make it the rest of the way. I have been through many things in my life and prayer makes all the difference. Remember the scripture that says "if my people which are called by my name shall humble themselves and pray and seek my face, and turn from their wicked ways; then will I hear from heaven, and will forgive their sin, and will heal their land.""

"Yes I know that scripture. This is the word of the Lord after Solomon had anointed the temple that he had built unto God. You know you remind me of a good friend of mine. We used to talk about the Bible together. I really miss him."

"Good friends are hard to come by. When you find a good one you should treasure it for life. I miss my wife and friends in my congregation. I'm sure you feel the same way also. This is the time when you really treasure your relationship with God even more. You see God is with you even when men cannot be with you. He says that he will never leave us nor forsake us."

"You said a mouth full. Maybe this is one thing that I need to learn from this. That God is my rock and my salvation. He wants me to do something and I must fulfill this for him just like Moses fulfilled his calling and all the other prophets before him."

"That's good." Samuel was feeling weak so Ezekiel just sat with him while he fell back to sleep. He was contemplating what Samuel had told him. It gave him much strength. He felt sick in his heart that he could get comfort from a dying man. Ezekiel started to believe what Samuel was saying. Although it was sad that he was in prison but he was in a way glad that he was there to deliver this message to him at a time when he needed a true friend.

Ezekiel had not been taught to hate the gentiles but he had not made an effort to get to know them either. Now he had met two preachers that had made a profound impact on his life. His life had been forever changed. He was being called by God not only to help save his people but to warn the gentiles as well.

Nurse Anastasya had disappeared for a while but returned with two trays for her guests. Samuel was still sleeping when she arrived but the noise she made when she walked was enough to wake the dead. Nurse Anastasya was unlike any woman that Ezekiel had ever met. She was young, beautiful and very sweet. Instead of wearing a uniform like the other officers she wore a white dress, stockings and shoes. But for some reason she wore these shoes that had taps on the bottom so you could hear her a mile away. Ezekiel was afraid to ask her what the significance was all about. The thought was overwhelming him so he just had to ask. "Anastasya please tell me why you wear those taps on the bottom of your shoes."

"Oh Mr. Ezekiel you should eat to get your strength back. I'll try to make it brief so you can eat your dinner. Now don't laugh. But I have an email friend who is in the military in America. She told me the story about how they wear these shoes like these. They are called cloriforms. These shoes are so awesome. They don't have to shine their boots like we do here. These shoes have a natural shine. She sent me a picture and I absolutely thought they were made in heaven. She was nice enough to send me a pair. But she didn't tell me what they sounded like when you walked in them. But I kind of like it because no matter where I am in this God awful place they know that I'm coming. I feel like an American soldier. I hope that one day I can leave Russia and go to see my good friend in America. So it was a gift from a friend."

"Oh that's nice. I was just wondering. I hope I didn't offend you in any way."

"No Mr. Ezekiel. How is Samuel doing? I'm sorry I have been busy today. That doesn't usually happen. Actually I have made friends with his wife. I call her every time he gets sick like this. I think that he will be leaving us soon. I'll make sure that she gets here to see him. It's really sad that they won't let him out of here. He really needs to be spending his last days with his family."

"Yes you are correct about that. Maybe you know someone that can help."

"No not really. I try not to get too involved with the inmates and their families. But Samuel is different. He doesn't belong here and he is dying. I do have a heart you know."

"I know Anastasya. I know."

"Well Ezekiel its time for me to go home now. See that Samuel eat as much as he can. Watch over him because the officer on duty tonight will most likely be sleeping or playing cards or something. If he get's sick he'll call me and I'll come in to take care of him."

Nurse Anastasya left for the night and not a moment too soon. Ezekiel didn't wait to eat his food. Samuel was asleep but he wanted to make his phone call before he woke him up for dinner. Ezekiel went into the bathroom and closed the door. He pulled out his phone. Who should he call first? Perhaps it would be best to talk with Aleksis first and tell him his idea and see what he thought about it. He couldn't do it without him. Aleksis was a mafia boss and had all the connections he needed to pull this thing off. He would need a plane to get out of the country. How he would repay him he didn't know but he would tell him what he wanted.

The phone rang several times before Aleksis answered the phone. "This is Aleksis who is this?"

"Aleksis this is Ezekiel. I got your number from Pastor John. How are you, how is Vladimir? Tell him I miss my friend. I'm gonna get him for leaving me without saying goodbye." Aleksis started laughing like he was talking to his long lost friend. Ezekiel was amazed. He still could not believe that he was getting all this help from the gentiles. But then even during the holocaust the gentile people risked their lives for the jewish people.

"Ezekiel. I'm sorry about my phone. The police have been watching me. I had someone right in my own organization giving information to the police. Don't worry I've taken care of it. Things are back to normal. I'm doing good and Vladimir is doing better every day. He was in bad shape. I could not believe what they did to him. I wish I could take care of those officers that beat him. But I'll never get justice. So tell me what can I do for you?"

"Aleksis I can't stay on long. I've been sick and I'm in the infirmary. In any case I want to break out of this place. I have a plan and I wanted to speak with you about it."

"Okay. What's the plan?"

"Well there is this guy in here that killed a lot of people while working in the hospital. You might have heard about him. In any case he says there is a drug that I can use that will make me almost clinically dead. I have asked one of the officers to escort me to the hospital. I will need someone at the hospital waiting to bring me out of the coma. Then I will need someone to transport me out of the hospital to the funeral home. After that I will need a plane out of the country."

"Ezekiel are you crazy. This will take a lot of planning. But you know it will definitely work. These people are not as smart as you think they are. Did you ever here about the guy who hypnotized the officers in the prison and walked right out of the prison?"

"No. Stop it. That cannot really be true."

"Yes it is true. I can show you the story in the library books. This really happened. He did it many times to the government. Let me work on it. This is going to cost a lot of money. Do you have any money Ezekiel?"

"Well I have to pay the officer to bring me to the hospital. I will get in touch with my lawyer. I do have some money. He will talk with my uncle about the rest. He is not a rich man but I know that he has some money and will use it to purchase my release. I will get in touch with him and you get things going. I will call in a few days and you can tell me how much we will need."

"Okay Ezekiel. You saved my brother's life. I will save yours. In my line of business my word means everything. I made a promise and I plan to keep it. You call me in a few days. Maybe three or four this might take a bit of planning. But we can get you out of there. No problem."

Ezekiel felt like he had finally accomplished something. Now he needed to call Daniel to see if he could get some money. He had some but it would not be enough. The plane alone would cost a lot of money to fly them to America. Ezekiel checked really quickly outside to make sure that Samuel was doing okay and that the officer was not outside. The coast was clear and Ezekiel made his way back to the bathroom to make his final call for the night. Daniel's phone rang like no tomorrow. He had received a call from Simon and was on his way to his house when the phone rang. It always seemed to ring when he was enroute somewhere but he had a lot going on and couldn't afford to miss any phone calls. He put the phone on speaker so he could continue driving. Simon sounded like he had swallowed a canary. He had found out something about Mishenko that he had to tell him. "Hi this is Daniel whose this?"

"Daniel this is Ezekiel I don't have much time."

"Ezekiel. Are you okay? Did you get the number from Pastor John?"

"Yes. Thank you so much. I have a big request."

"Anything Ezekiel. What can I do for you?"

"Well first you must promise not to discuss this with anyone."

"Of course Ezekiel. I'm your lawyer remember."

"I know but this is big. Well I'm tired of waiting here for my trial. I've decided to bust out of here. I just can't take it anymore. I didn't do anything wrong Daniel. This is what I need. I spoke with Aleksis and he is going to help me get out of here but I need some money to pay some people and for a plane to America."

"Ezekiel do you know what you are saying? You will be an escape prisoner. They will be looking for you. We will never get you into America."

"Daniel that is the beauty of my plan. See Aleksis will get me some medicine that will make me look like I am really dead. The officer will transport me to the hospital where there will be a doctor to pronounce me dead. He will draw up the papers. Then he will revive me and have me sent to the funeral home. You will let them know that I will be coming. I will wait there for Aleksis to come and pick me up and take me to the plane that will bring me to America. I know it's a lot to take in but we can do this. He is sure that we will have no problems. He is working on the particulars. I need you to tell my uncle the plan. I need as much money as he can come up with. He must tell the funeral home not to tell anyone about the plan. He can fly out with me. I don't even want my wife to know until I reach America. It will only make her worry. I won't even contact Pastor John until I have reached America. I don't want to put him in any danger."

"My God Ezekiel. How did you come up with this plan? I tell you I don't blame you for helping yourself. I have done a terrible job."

"No Daniel. There is nothing that you or anyone else can do. I have to do it this way or else be in prison for the rest of my life. I don't know anything. I can't help them. Personally I would spill my guts if I had any information."

"Ezekiel how much time do you have to talk?"

"Well I'm in the infirmary. They have a private bathroom here. The nurse is gone, the other patient is asleep and the officer is awol. I'm okay I think."

"Well let me tell you something that I have not told you. Simon found a breakcase that Mishenko left in the back of the Torah cabinet. He had gone to the synagogue to see what could be salvaged. He found this briefcase and turned it over to me. Until now I have looked at some of the information and thought that once we got you out of there you could take its contents to America. He had a tape in there that mentioned that he had information on a Russian invasion on America. I think this is what they have you in prison for. They think that you know about all this stuff."

"I cannot believe it. Well we had better take that to America and turn it over to the government. They will definitely let me in then."

"Wait I have more. I'm on my way to Simon's house now. He says that he has uncovered some more information. Maybe this might help as well. Also there was a large amount of cash in the briefcase. We can give it to Aleksis for the plane and whatever else he needs. Don't worry. Keep the money that you have saved and use this money. At least Mishenko is helping in a way to get you out of this mess he put you into."

"Well I'm not mad at Mishenko. He didn't mean for all of this to happen. He too has lost his life and much more. He is stuck in Siberia for two more years. I hope that the government will still let him go."

"You are a good man. Is there anything else that I can do for you?"

"No not at the moment. Oh wait a minute. There is a preacher man that is here in the infirmary. I need for you to get in touch with Pastor

John. Tell him that he needs to go to the officials of the prison to get a visit with his wife. He is dying of cancer I don't know how much longer he has to live. Please it's a matter of life or death. He needs to come in as soon as possible. They can get in touch with his wife."

"Okay. I will telephone him tonight. Perhaps he can come in within the next couple of days. Ezekiel call me in a few days so we can speak again. If anything changes call me any time."

Ezekiel went back outside to see whether the officer had returned and the coast was still clear. He could see that Samuel was waking up and he went over to put a cold compress on his head. He still had a fever but it was breaking. He sure hoped that his wife and Pastor John could come very soon to see him. He would also see if he could bring some medication for the pain. He was in very bad shape.

The prison must have received some food from one of the inmates because Ezekiel could actually identify what was on the plate. This night they were having potatoes, chicken and vegetables. This was the best dinner he had since coming to prison. Most of the time it was some kind of slop that he wouldn't feed to his worse enemy. First he would try to get Samuel to eat some food. He really needed something to give him some strength. He ate a few bites but couldn't keep it down. His insides were sore and his throat too. He could drink liquids though. That helped a little.

Samuel went back to sleep and Ezekiel ate his dinner and layed down. He would nap a bit and keep watch over him through the night. The officer was either sleeping or playing cards. He could care less whether Samuel lived or died. Ezekiel wasn't sure how long he had slept when he woke up to a noise in the room. He opened his eyes and looked around but he saw nothing. He went over to the infirmary door to see whether the officer had returned but there was no one there. Samuel was sleeping quietly. He was so still that Ezekiel checked his pulse to make sure he was still alive.

Ezekiel went to use the bathroom. He heard another noise while he was in the bathroom. When he came out of the bathroom he saw in front of him a ladder of light that went straight up through the ceiling. Ezekiel was so amazed at what he saw that he stopped dead in his tracks and just looked at the ladder. He wondered where was this light coming from and even more important where was it going. Then he saw off to the side four men in the room. Without even speaking he knew that the four men were Abraham, Isaac, Jacob and Joseph.

Ezekiel immediately fell to the ground on his knees sobbing and weeping before these men, the patriarchs of the jewish people. He could not understand why God was sending these important men to speak with him such a lowly man. Each of them had eyes of fire. Abraham looked at him and smiled. "My son do not be afraid. I have a very important message for you. My name means father of a multitude. From my loins came the nation of Israel. We have come to ask you to take a message throughout the world. There is a great persecution that will be coming to the nation of Israel. It will make the Holocaust look like child's play. Many of my children refuse to return to the land that has been given to them by God. They have received much treasures from God and have made new homes throughout the world. But they do not know that they are in more danger in these places than in Israel. Please tell the people of the world to prepare for the coming persecution and to take my children in and give them a safe place of protection."

Ezekiel did not say a word. He was frozen in place. The next man who spoke was Joseph. He had on the clothing of a king. Ezekiel could hardly believe his eyes. There was an amazing feeling of power coming from this man. His face was young but very mature. He wished that he had the privilege of living when Joseph lived. He wanted to know so much about him. He had so much he wanted to ask about his day. Joseph walked towards him and said "I am Joseph. My name means one who will increase. The name Pharaoh gave me means savior of the age. God increased me and I became the savior of my age. I was sent before my family to provide food during a time of great famine in the land. A great famine is coming in the land. Ezekiel you must get prepared.

As in my day God will provide wealth to build his Kingdom if we seek his Kingdom first. You will see miraculous things like when Moses and the nation of Israel were on their way to the promised land. God provided manna from heaven and he provided quails when the children asked for meat. He even gave water from a rock. You too will see the hand of God moving in mighty ways for his people.

Ezekiel we can only do so much for you. We are praying for you constantly because things will be worse than you can ever imagine in the world. Many will die if you do nothing. You must prepare. Be a savior to your nation."

As soon as Joseph finished speaking Ezekiel couldn't get in a word edgewise before Isaac spoke to him. He smiled and said "I am Isaac. My name means laughter. My mother laughed when she was told she would have a son in her old age. Ezekiel God gave many prophecies to the prophet Daniel which he was told to shut up the words and seal the book even to the time of the end. This is that time. Many will laugh and scoff at the prophets that God will call in your time to reveal what has been shut up in the books.

The word through the prophet Joel is this I will pour out my spirit upon all flesh; and your sons and your daughters shall prophesy, your old men shall dream dreams, your young men shall see visions; and also upon the servants and upon the handmaids in those days will I pour out my spirit. And I will show wonders in the heavens and in the earth, blood, and fire, and pillars of smoke. The sun shall be turned into darkness, and the moon into blood, before the great and the terrible day of the Lord come. Ezekiel follow the word of the prophets that are here on the earth now. God is sending forth his messengers in the earth to save the world. Only those who follow the word of the Lord will be saved."

Ezekiel was trembling and crying now. He didn't want to hear anymore but somehow knew that he would have to hear from Jacob before it would all be over. This was all too much for him to take. His life was in a mess and now God wanted him to take a message to the world that the jewish people would go through something worse than the Holocaust. The most painful time in the history of his people would be repeated. What was coming? He couldn't imagine anything worse than that.

Jacob came forward to comfort him as he lay in a pile on the floor crying like a baby without its mother. He was scared and wanted nothing more than to just die at that moment. Jacob put his arms around Ezekiel and said "Ezekiel I know this is too much for you to handle. I am Jacob and my name means supplanter. My destiny was to become the father of the nation of Israel. My name also has another meaning, that of a circle. My life went around in circles until God took hold of me and changed me. You can only achieve what you were called to do when you connect with God and when you walk under and open heaven. After many years of testing finally I came to Peniel when I wrestled with the Angel of the Lord. It was then that I died a death to self. He gave me a new name, that of Israel that meant a prince with God or to rule with God.

Today Ezekiel here in this prison like Joseph you wrestle with God about why you are here and the destiny that he has placed before you. Do not wrestle any longer Ezekiel. Embrace who you are and your destiny. Like Moses you have been called to speak the word of the Lord to a people who have forgotten God. It will not be easy but many lives are at stake. The time is short."

Jacob put his arms around Ezekiel and hugged him like a small child. Ezekiel was so weak he could not stand up. Jacob raised up and walked towards the other men. The ladder had disappeared and then a door of light opened before them and as quickly as they came they disappeared. Ezekiel lay on the floor still amazed at what had just taken place. He had a knowing that something had taken place that would forever change his life.

Chapter 25

Daniel pulled into Simon's driveway. He didn't know why he wanted to see him but he was sure it was something he did not want to know. His mansion looked even larger this time. It was something the way the lights hit the building or something. He had the water fountains going and Daniel just knew that Simon was into something. But it was none of his business so he didn't ask. Daniel didn't have to knock on the door, Simon was waiting for him when he walked up the cobble walkway. He thought that was odd but then Simon was an odd kind of guy. He looked like he had been up for days, his clothes didn't smell very fresh and he had been drinking. He wasn't sloppy but you could smell it on his breath.

"Daniel I'm glad you could come. I have some really crazy information for you. You will never believe what I've found out about this case. Come on into my study and sit down. Have you had dinner yet?"

"No but I'm not really hungry. I will take something to drink if you don't mind."

"No problem. I have a bar right here. Make yourself comfortable."

"Daniel please let me tell you an amazing story about Russia that you might not know."

"Okay."

"During Word War II Stalin knew that it was just a matter of time before Hitler invaded Russia. He was a brilliant man and decided that he had better prepare for the day before it came. It is common knowledge that he built several military bases below ground so elaborate that the Russian Army could retreat to these underground bases and fight the enemy from underground. There are remnants of these bases that still exist today. When the Germans invaded Russia the army fought with everything that they had. But at a certain time they believed they might be taken over so they were ordered to blow up the underground bases so that it would not be found by the German soldiers. Today thousands of Russian soldiers gave their lives to keep the secret of their fareless leader."

"I believe that I heard something about that. I just never took the time to follow the story. It's an amazing story. But what does that have to do with this case."

"Follow me for a minute Daniel. Along with the bases that Salin built he also built large waterways into Russia as well. In addition to the waterways and the military bases he used places like cathedrals, sports stadiums, apartment buildings, prisons and most importantly the metro system to hide things under the ground. When he built something you had better believe there was something else under construction under the ground. Much of what he built still remains today. If you go into the metro railway there is an area that is marked off and no one can go into this area. The story is that Stalin was fearful that he would be captured and so he built this elaborate city under the ground. There was built what is called Metro 2 and it goes from the Kremlin to the underground city. Included in this city was a palace for Stalin, a bank, a military installation, a prison where many people who went against the government were tortured and oh let me not forget the treasures that he confiscated from Hitler. Are you feeling me?"

"I'm sorry but no."

"Don't you see. The reason why they put Mishenko away was that he had been shown the secret city. No one can see the secret city. Mishenko saw that Stalin had in his possession billions of dollars worth of art, gold and silver that was plundered from the jewish people during the Holocaust. He wanted to get the treasure and somehow return it to the jewish people. It's a wonder that he had not been killed. He knew that no one would believe him so he stole some of the treasures and the only reason he is still alive is because they don't want anyone to know and also they want to retrieve what was stolen. They have Ezekiel because they think that he knows where the treasure is being held. You got it."

"What in the world? How did you find out about this? Simon are you telling me all the truth?"

"Yes I'm telling you the truth. Didn't you look at the contents of the briefcase?"

"Well yeah but I have not gotten through it all. I've been working on the case. I figured that if we could get him out he could take the briefcase with him to America and let the government sort it all through. So you think that Mishenko actually saw this secret city and there is a large amount of treasure there. That sounds so amazing."

"Yeah. But they will never believe that Ezekiel doesn't know where it is. Oh I forgot to tell you that he does say where the loot is being kept. I say we get the loot and get Ezekiel and get him out of the country. At least he'll be a rich man."

"Are you crazy? They'll kill us all. I just want to get Ezekiel out of here and back with his family. Now where is the treasure Simon?"

"Now come on Daniel. You would not know about this if it were not for me. You have to give me a cut for my trouble. I want to get out of Russia too. I can use some help. I'll have to leave everything behind. My wife will be okay. I'll miss my kids though. I'm sorry but I'm in a tight spot myself. I've gotten in with the wrong people so to speak. This will be the break that I need."
"Okay Simon. I don't know what we are going to do with all of this. I will get back to you on what we will do. Of course you could do it all by yourself but obviously you want some help for some reason. So I guess you are not as bad a man as I think that you are. You are still thinking about Ezekiel."

"I love Ezekiel like a brother but I'm trying to save my own life too Daniel. Please don't judge me harshly for this. Mishenko moved some of the treasures to a cave that was dug underneath the synagogue. I guess he learned something from Stalin. I didn't want to move it without some help. I had told Ezekiel that I would pay for the rebuilding of the synagogue and the school. I figured we could sell it and build one bigger and better than the one that Mishenko built. At least in a way the money from the jewish people would go into doing something good for those who lived on after them."

"Simon I guess we won't be able to get the treasure out of the country. Who knows what belongs to who. I think that I can sell it to someone. I'll make a phone call and get back to you on that. Don't do anything or speak to anyone about this."

"I won't Daniel. I hope you are not mad with me."

"No just make sure that you rebuild the synagogue and the school. What you do with the rest is up to you. I don't want anything to do with it."

Daniel felt kind of hollow inside. If this got any bigger he would get on a plane and never return. He just could not handle another thing. He would call Aleksis and see if he could come with him and Simon to see the treasure. Maybe he could find someone to buy the treasures and the money would be used to build the synagogue and school. Ezekiel would be freed and back with his family in America. The only loose end would be Mishenko. He wondered if there was some way they could help him. Only time would tell.

While Daniel drove home he felt like he was riding in a tunnel. There was so much all around him that he couldn't hear and he couldn't see but what was in front of him. It was all coming down too quickly. He felt the need to drive over to the synagogue. Simon had it boarded up so that no one could get in. He was making sure the treasure was not found. It was amazing how it was all under their noses. Daniel picked the lock that Simon had on the building. A small trick he learned when he was young. He went inside the synagogue and he could see that Simon had really started cleaning the place out. Where was the opening? Was there some kind of trap door that led to the treasure? He wasn't sure whether Simon had indeed found it because he really didn't say. But according to him this was the scene of the crime. He wanted to know what he was going to tell Aleksis. If he could see the treasure he would know more about what was involved. So far he had no reason to mistrust Aleksis but then again he was in the mafia. He could try to kill them all and then where would Ezekiel be? He would have to trust someone. The jewish people had a right to that treasure. Aleksis and Ezekiel were in prison because of it. Something good had to come of the time they had paid.

The briefcase was behind the Torah cabinet. Maybe Mishenko left a map of some kind and that was how Simon knew that the treasure was buried underneath the synagogue. He would have to go home and check every piece of paper and every tape that Mishenko left behind. Daniel had not been to synagogue in quite a few years. He just started walking around to see if he could remember where everything was. The synagogue itself had only one floor but the school had two stories. The synagogue was such a beautiful building. Mishenko spared no expense in its building. He did remember that there was a stock room in the back of the synagogue. He walked to the front of the synagogue. The storeroom sat really in the back of the altar where the Torah cabinet sat. It was one of the largest Torah cabinets that Daniel had ever seen before. It was ashame that it was nearly demolished like that. It was obvious that Simon had spent a lot of time going through the synagogue. As he walked into the storage area there it was a door that led down into the cave that Mishenko built. There was another lock on the door but Daniel was not leaving until he saw what Simon had seen. His heart was beating and he was afraid of what was behind the door. But if this was what this was all about he wanted to see it for himself. There was no light switch. Simon had used a flashlight that he left in the storage room. Daniel turned on the light and walked carefully down the staircase. It was quite old but it was still holding up pretty well. Daniel could not believe what he was seeing.

The cave was not very large but large enough to house a treasure unlike any that he could ever imagine. Mishenko had it all put in as though it were a museum. A person could actually live down there. There was the most elaborate furnishings than Daniel had ever seen. It looked like it was taken from a person or persons who were very wealthy. There were chairs, couches, paintings in crates and on the walls. Large tables had golden candelabras, silver candle holders, crystal and silverware fit for a king. What stood out in Daniel's mind was the crates full of pictures, nothing but pictures of families. Some of them had names and dates on the back. Daniel recognized that these were families that had most likely been killed in the Holocaust. Why would Hitler keep all of these things? Stacked as high as the ceiling were crates of gold, silver and other things that were confiscated from the jewish people. The hardest thing to see was a crate full of prayer books, yarmulkes, tallits, torah scrolls and tefillin all for jewish prayer. Why did they keep these things and even more importantly why did Stalin choose to keep them as well? These would only be important to a jewish person. Daniel fell to his knees and cried like a baby. In this cave was the memory of so many people he was overwhelmed. It was like it was a shrine to the jewish people. Their prayers were being uttered through the souls captured in the pictures. This was a testament that the Holocaust really happened and no one would ever be able to say that it didn't.

The crates were stacked as far and as high as the eye could see. There were crates with gold jewelry, diamonds and precious stones of all types and sizes. The bulk of the treasure was in gold bouillon coins and bricks. The total had to be in the billions of dollars just in this one cave. He could only imagine what Mishenko left behind. There was no way that he could possibly get it all out of the caves all over Russia that Stalin had built. And what had the Americans and the others unfolded that Hitler had pillaged from many of the countries that he invaded. The thought of it was staggering. Daniel started to feel creepy so he headed back up the stairs locking the door behind him. No one could know about this. He would see if Aleksis could help Simon get the money so they could build the synagogue but he hoped that Simon would lock the place up and never let anyone in again. It was a sacred place.

Something felt wrong about moving the contents of the cave. Mishenko wanted to return the artifacts to the jewish people. Daniel wished that it all could somehow be taken to one of the museums either in Israel or America where the pictures could be retrieved by family members who had lived through the Holocaust. Family heirlooms could be once again passed down to the next generation.

Daniel stood in the synagogue for sometime contemplating the impact that millions of people had lost their lives in a war that still had so many skeletons in the closet. How many of their ghosts walked the halls of this secret city in hopes to one day have a resting place. Daniel prayed that they would not go to hell for invading the privacy of such great one's as these. The one's whose blood was shed because of the greed of Hitler and his henchmen.

Chapter 26

Daniel was beside himself. Through all of this he knew that he had to get back to God. This was more than he could deal with and he knew that he needed God's guidance to make it through and to the next step in his life. What that step was he wasn't really sure. He needed to get in touch with Aleksis and speak with him about Ezekiel and the treasures that Mishenko left behind. Although he and Mishenko lived on opposite sides of the tracks he needed him to get Ezekiel out of jail. He promised the angel that he would do everything he could to see Ezekiel through. This was the last but the biggest step to date. Daniel took a deep breath as he dialed Aleksis private number. It was almost as if he was waiting for the phone to ring because it maybe rang one time before Aleksis was on the line. "Aleksis this is Daniel, Ezekiel's lawyer. Am I disturbing you? If so I can call back at another time."

"No Daniel. I need to talk with you as soon as possible. I'm sure you have spoken with Ezekiel about his big plan. He has a lot of guts. I'm at the hospital with my brother. If all goes well I can get him out in one week. I will speak with my pilot and he will make the arrangements to fly him to America. As long as he has his papers that will not be a problem. I will fly in with him. I have lots of family in America and contacts in America. My good friend went to America many years ago after he was released from prison. He said that the government was always watching him and he couldn't take it any longer. He has a very big business there in America. I myself don't want to tangle with the American system. I don't want to go to prison again. Here I have the contacts I need to keep my business going. Sorry I'm rambling. What can I do for you?"

"No you are fine. I'm glad that you have already taken care of his plans. I will call his uncle and the funeral home in the last minute. I don't want the plan to slip out. You know when people get excited they will start talking and saying things they should not say. His uncle is a good man and the funeral director will understand the situation. But this is something different Aleksis. I hope no one hears this conversation and you must promise me that you will take this to the grave."

"Well what is happening, I promise?"

"You might know about a case that happened quite a few years ago a young Jewish businessman was sent to prison on charges of espionage. In any case he is the reason why Ezekiel is in prison now. He apparently not only did Mishenko have information about a coming war between Russia and the United States but he was also taken to Metro #2 to the hidden city that Stalin built. Do you know anything about it?"

"Know about it. Many have been taken to the city. I wish that I could see the city. Stalin was a crazy man but he was a genious. Can you imagine the treasure that is under there?"

"Well yes I can as a matter of fact."

"What do you mean?"

"Well this businessman somehow stole some of the treasure. He wanted to retrieve some of what was stolen by Hitler from the Jewish people. I know where some is. My partner wants to sell it to build another synagogue and school for the Jewish people. They blew up the first one that Mishenko built. Do you know anyone that might want to purchase it? If not for anything else most of it is not for sale but the gold we need the money for the synagogue."

"Well this is amazing. I don't have words. Can I see it?"

"Yes. But no one but you. I know that you have a driver. If you can trust him then that will be okay but no one else."

"When can we meet?"

"Right now is fine. I don't have anything to do. I have to pick up my associate but we can meet you in one hour at the synagogue. But you should dress very casually and not park anywhere near the synagogue so you will not be seen. It will be dark by then so no one will notice us."

"Okay I'll be there in one hour."

Daniel made a quick phone call to Simon and asked to pick him up in one hour to meet with Aleksis at the synagogue. He informed him that he had seen the treasure and that they would have to make a deal with Aleksis. He didn't want to sell any of the personal items only the gold. Simon agreed to hold onto the personal items and that the cave would be sealed up and never opened again. Daniel didn't know whether to believe him but he had no choice.

Simon was waiting at the door when Daniel pulled up. Daniel didn't want anyone to notice them at the synagogue at night so he drove around the block several times to make sure they were not being followed. They parked the car a few blocks away near an all night restaurant. Simon and Daniel went into the restaurant and ordered coffee. The two men sat in the booth for about twenty minutes as they sipped the hot coffee. Daniel couldn't believe he was even in that restaurant with the likes of Simon. And to boot he was meeting a mafia guy and his driver to negotiate the purchase of the gold that Stalin took during the war from Hitler. His mother would turn over in her grave if she knew what he was doing. But why not use the gold for the synagogue? And Ezekiel had a sure way of getting out of prison to America without the government looking for him again. It would all be over soon and maybe he could go back to his boring life. He had not given it much thought but he was feeling like it was time for him to get married and start a new life if Tsilia would have him. He was feeling confident that she had a thing for him. He would have to do something or else lose her for good.

"How did you know when it was time to pop the question to your wife?"

"Huh. What do you mean?"

"Well there is this girl that I like but we have not been in contact for quite a few months. I took her out a few weeks ago. I think that she likes me and I finally realized that I would be blessed to have a woman like her as my wife. How do I pop the question?"

"Daniel you are a funny man. You must not have dated very much."

"No I really have not dated much. I've been a batchelor for a long time now. I never did very well with women. I get butterflies when I talk with them. There's nothing wrong with that. At least I'm not like most men. They don't appreciate women. My mother taught me better."

"Hey let's talk and walk at the same time. We don't want to miss out visitors."

"Yeah your right. I just wanted to make sure that no one was following."

The two men walk to the synagogue. There was no one in sight so Simon opened the lock. It would be easy for one of them to peak out the door and see Aleksis when they walked up to the door. In no time Daniel saw two men walking around the corner. The close was clear and he hoped that it was Aleksis. He had no idea what he looked like. This was so stupid but here they were. They walked right up to the door and Simon let them in. "Hi I'm Simon and this is Daniel."

"I'm Aleksis and this is my driver. Let's make this quick. It's hard for me to do anything these days. The government is looking at me closely but I'm much smarter than they are. Where is the treasure?"

"Come this way."

The four men walk to the room in the back. Simon opens the lock on the door and steps gingerly down the stairs with the flashlight in front of him. There was a light but Daniel had not noticed it when he went down the first time. The light helped him to see that there was even more than he had seen with the flashlight. Aleksis had a weird look of excitement on his face when he saw all the treasure in the room.

"What in God's name?"

He immediately walked towards the back of the room where he saw the gold. Next to it was a large golden menorah that stood almost as tall as he was. He brushed his hands over the menorah to see if it were in fact real. He turned around and looked at his assistant. His assistant was looking at the box full of diamonds and precious stones.

"Father. Look at this. Your wife would love to have something as beautiful as this. I have never seen such valuables before. It looks like they belong to a queen or somebody."

"You might be right. As Hitler wages war against many countries he plundered the treasures of Austria, Czechoslovakia, Poland and other nations. These treasures also came from the jewish people and other prominent families like the Rothchilds. These pictures and furnishings come from museums and art collections that go back several hundreds of years. History says that the American General Patton and President Eisenhower found in a salt mine tons of gold, manuscripts, the Guttenberg Bible, mosaics panels and stacks of paintings, sculptures and other stolen artifacts. It took hundreds and hundreds of trucks to cart all of the artifacts from the salt mine. This doesn't even touch what was found. Today there are still caves being found in Berlin where Hitler, Hermann Goering, Field Marshall Kessilring and Von Runstedt kept the treasures that they stole. Combined they could have supported many wars. Your friend was a brave man taking this stuff. I must tell you that as amazing as this all is I cannot move any of this. But I can move the gold."

"What do you mean? Well the government is watching me as it is. But I can take the gold but not anything else. Don't worry you have enough money in just the gold to rebuild many buildings ten times over. I will take just one brick and one coin. I will contact you with the value of them both. Then we will have to figure out how many you have and we can come up with a price. We must go now. Daniel I must call you about the other matter we have been talking about. Don't worry it will be soon."

Simon seemed to be a bit upset. He wanted to get as much money as possible. His greed was showing but he didn't press the issue. They all walked up the steps and out into the street to their separate cars. Neither Daniel or Simon said anything for a while. Daniel really didn't want to sell anything so he was happy with the deal. Simon on the other hand wanted to sell some of the treasures and not just the gold. But he knew that Daniel was not going to help him any further. He would have to settle with what they agreed on. After all the treasure would still be there and no one would know but him and Mishenko that is. He could wait until Mishenko came out of prison and see what he wanted to do.

Daniel couldn't wait to drop Simon off at his house. He didn't like how he had reacted when Aleksis offered to take the gold but nothing else. He knew that he was a crook but he couldn't prove it. What was he thinking getting involved with him in the first place? He was a crook and nothing else. If he didn't need him he would never have told anyone about the treasure. Whether he did the right thing or not was not going to be his problem. After this he wanted nothing to do with him. He was only glad that he had at least given him the briefcase because Ezekiel would need the contents to share with the American government and the cash would help pay for his passage out of Russia forever.

Ezekiel's day was finally coming and they had to make it look like he had really died. It was his responsibility to make sure that his uncle and the rest of the community had a funeral all arranged so that the government would not be looking for Ezekiel ever again. The clock was ticking and his day to leave Russia was just around the corner.

Chapter 27

Aleksis was keeping his part of the deal and now Daniel had to get in touch with Stephen to keep their part of this elaborate scheme to get Ezekiel out of prison and to safety in America. Daniel's first stop would be to see Stephen, he must get prepared to leave the country. He also would have to set up a private funeral with just a few people. He didn't want too many people to be involved in the scheme. The few could inform the rest of the community that Ezekiel had passed away and this would be best for everyone. It probably would not be good if they knew too much. The little the better.

Daniel just went to the house. Stephen had not been going out very much. He was spending time these days cleaning up the house for the day that he and Ezekiel would leave for America. When Daniel showed up at the house Stephen thought the worse. Stephen invited Daniel to come in but he had moved most of the personal items out of the house. He figured that he would leave and go home to wait for Ezekiel's trial. Raisa and Aliyah were worried about him being there all alone. He seemed to have aged several years since Daniel saw him last. The two men sat down in the living room together. There were boxes of every size all over the living room. Daniel could see that he had been working very hard getting the house together. There were just remnants of the family that once lived there. He must have been thinking the worse since it had already been about six months since Ezekiel was incarcerated. He was a good man Stephen. He had raised his family and now had taken on raising his brother's family. This could not have happened at a worse time in his life.

Stephen didn't have much to say. Daniel had his foot caught in his mouth. He didn't quite know how to explain this all to Stephen but he had to have his help. After some small talk it was time to get it all out. "Stephen I have something very important to tell you."

"I know. I figured you didn't come by for no reason. Is Ezekiel okay?"

"Yes he is doing fine. Please don't worry. But this has to do with him. Ezekiel called me the other day and he told me that he just can't take it in prison any longer. He feels that even when he has his trial that they are not planning on releasing him from prison. I believe that what he says is true. I've been struggling with some type of defense but they are not interested in my defense. I thought that maybe somehow if we could find the right people we could pay for his release. Amazingly so Ezekiel befriended a man who is a part of the Russian mafia. He took a liking to Ezekiel. When the man killed another prisoner he was beat up pretty bad and Ezekiel risked his life to help him when they put him in the hole."

"Wow. My boy he is such a good man. Look at him in prison and he still has a heart to help someone in need. That's my Ezekiel. But what does this have to do with his release. Do you think this man can help get him released? Oh Daniel tell him that I will give him whatever he wants. How much money do we need?"

"Hold on a minute. There is so much more to tell you. Some I will tell you now and some I will tell you when we get out of Russia. What you need to know now is this. The man has a brother who is very well connected. He will help us arrange for Ezekiel's release. But there is something that I have not mentioned."

"What do you mean?"

"Stephen we are going to fake Ezekiel's death. He feels like it is the only way to get him out. This is what we have to do. Ezekiel is going to take some medicine that will make him seem as though he is dead. He will be transported to the hospital where a doctor will pronounce him dead. We will need him taken then to the funeral home and the next day we will have his funeral. Of course he will not be in the casket. After he is buried we will have a plane waiting to take you to America. You must tell the people at the funeral home that no one is to know that Ezekiel is not in the casket. Just invite a few people to make it look legitimate. Does this make sense so far?"

"Yes. This feels like when many people did whatever they had to do to save themselves during the Holocaust. I'm not ashamed to do this Daniel. I want to get my son out of prison. I don't care what we have to do or how much we have to pay. I wish we could have saved some of those innocent people who were killed during the Holocaust. Let's do it. I will call them as soon as you tell me what evening for them to be there. They will not have a problem helping. I will invite just a few people to make it look good. We stick together."

"Thank you Daniel. I'm sorry that this has taken so long. But dealing with the government is not easy. It's not what you know but who you know. I think you already understand that."

"Yes I do. I will not tell his wife yet about this. I think that I must wait until we are in fact in America and then she will see her husband for herself. If something goes wrong it will just kill her. Daniel don't tell Ezekiel but Raisa is pregnant. She is due in just a few months. I don't want to upset her neither do I want to upset him. If we make it they will both be overjoyed at the birth of their first son."

For the first time that day both men broke out in laughter and Stephen took out a bottle of wine to make a toast to Ezekiel's release and the birth of his grandson. This was his family and he was going to do everything he could to make sure they were safe and taken care of. It was the least he could do for his brother.

Daniel was somewhat amazed at Stephen's reaction. He thought that he would want no parts of a breakout but it was just the opposite. He understood how he felt though. The pain from the Holocaust was something that none of them could ever forget. They would have all paid any price to be free. Ezekiel's incarceration was just another way by which an innocent man was being robbed of his God given right to freedom. The meeting was a great success and afterwards Daniel left feeling like he had accomplished something by giving an old man hope that he would see his loved one again. He had suffered so much in his life and this news gave him hope and joy.

The plan was all in place now. Daniel would try to wait patiently for a call from Aleksis and from Ezekiel. Aleksis said that it would probably take a week to get everything in place and then Ezekiel would be on a plane to America. Daniel had to think whether this was the time for him to leave Russia or not. He really wanted to patch things up with Tsilia but would they spend the rest of their lives in Russia or make a change too for American life. They were both good lawyers and could make a good living in America but it was all happening so quickly. Maybe they should take some time to talk it all over after he got Ezekiel in America and situated. He didn't have to worry.

Daniel had a lot on his mind and thought maybe it would be nice to go and sit at the small park near his home. He could use the fresh air. He parked his car in the parking lot that led into the park. There were families having lunch. The children were running and playing. He could not even remember what it was like to be young and free. No cares in the world. He found a park bench where he had a good eyes view of what was happening in the park but at the same time he had enough distance to have some peace to himself. He thought he would have to bring Tsilia there for a romantic picnic. Women liked stuff like that. She was a tough attorney but she was a girl nevertheless. He wanted to spend the rest of his life doing nice things for her. What was in the future for them? Maybe children, a nice home and of course the dog. This was the American dream. He wanted to give her everything he could. So it was settled he would convince her that it would be a good thing to leave Russia and start a new life in America.

As if from no where a man dressed in a white robe came and sat down beside him. He tried not to look but when he looked at the man his face shine like the sun. His hair was white and his feet were like brass. When he turned to look at Daniel his eyes were like blazing fire. Daniel was mesmerized but scared at the same time. The man opened his mouth to speak to Daniel. "Daniel do you know who I am?"

"No I'm sorry I do not know who you are?"

"Daniel I am Jesus the Son of the Most High God. I have a very important message for you."

"Jesus. Are you the same Jesus whom I have heard about?"

"Yes I am. Daniel you sit here contemplating on whether you should leave this place and what will be the sum of your new life."

"Yes."

"You like many others you think that happiness is in the things of this world but you will not find happiness nor find peace and joy in the things of this world. Only I can give you peace and joy."

"What do you mean?"

"Daniel all that you see in front of you will soon be destroyed. In the beginning when God created the heavens and the earth he gave man all that he needed to be complete. But when man decided that he would turn away from God and what God instructed them to do this is the cause for all of the pain and suffering in the world. Man does not live by bread alone but by every word that comes from the mouth of God."

"I understand what you mean."

"Daniel I am that bread. Your fathers were given bread or manna from heaven when they lived in the wilderness on the way to the promised land God provided this for them to sustain life. But I am that bread from heaven. If you partake of me you will never hunger nor thirst again."

"How can I receive of this bread that I will no longer hunger. I feel a hunger and a thirst inside that I cannot quench."

"Daniel I am the way, the truth and the life and no one comes to the Father accept by me. In order to enter into the Kingdom of God you must be born of water and spirit."

"But how can a man be born again after he has already been born of his mother? Can a man be born of his mother and father again?"

"No Daniel you must be born of the spirit. I will put my spirit in you and you will then be born into new life as a child of God born of the Spirit of God. Then and only then will you be in the Father and the Father in you."

"I would like to be born again."

"My Son you must go to one who is called Pastor John. Speak to him and he will pray with you and baptize you in water. Then I want you to go to the nations of the world especially Israel and tell them of me. The time is coming soon when I will return to the earth as I did two thousand years ago. I came then to give of my life on the cross so that all men could have everlasting life in the Kingdom of God. The second time I will come to judge the nations and to take all those who follow me to a place in heaven that I have prepared for those who love me. In my fathers house there are many mansions. I have gone to prepare a place for you that there you might be with me always."

"I will go to see him."

As quickly as Jesus came he quickly left like a vapor of air. Daniel was stunned and didn't quite know what to think. He understood though that something had happened and he didn't want to let go. The power of Jesus eyes made him want to know more about him. He felt such love from him that he had never experienced before. He wanted to be in heaven with him in the place that he had prepared.

Daniel took out his phone and dialed Pastor John's number. No one answered at first but then he heard the voice of an angel. "Hello this is Hanna, John's wife. Can I help you?"

"Well this is Daniel. I'm a friend of a friend. Is John available?"

"Sure let me get him. He's just in his study."

It seemed like forever before John came to the phone. "Hey this is John. How can I help you?"

"Hey John it's only me Daniel. I really need to speak with you. It's an emergency."

"Ok Daniel. Hey my place is not far from the church. Or if you'd like I can meet you at the church, whichever you prefer."

"It doesn't matter really. But maybe it would be good if you can come to the church. I have a lot of things to tell you."

"Sure. Please is Ezekiel okay? I hope nothing is wrong."

"No really everything is great. But this is an emergency. Only you can help me."

"I'll be there in about fifteen minutes. You come right over."

John was starting to panic even though Daniel said that nothing was wrong with Ezekiel. But what was the emergency. He never heard such pain in Daniel's voice. He figured he had better get right over there and start praying just in case. He might need strength to deal with whatever the situation was at hand. He kissed his wife and told her that he would be back in just about an hour or so. He wasn't sure what he was going to hear when he got to the church. It had been a tumultuous time. His good friend was in prison and it had caused John's life to be changed forever.

John could practically walk to the church from his house. He wanted to get there before Daniel so that he could open the church and pray before he arrived. He walked as quickly as possible hoping that he would not be stopped by anyone on the way. He knew so many people that walking down the street was difficult. He was somewhat of a celebrity in his neighborhood. He knew the names of all the children and the families because they attended his church. The school teachers knew him on a personal basis because his children went to the school. They were just one big happy family in that area. John wondered whether the life that they lived would soon end. Ezekiel's situation opened his eyes that his world was very small and that he needed to look outside of himself to find the other world's that existed just outside his community. This was a good time because he only got a couple of waves from two little old ladies sitting on their porch. He had gotten to the church in no time. There was nothing going on that afternoon so it was quiet.

No soon as John entered his office that he heard someone calling his name. Oh no he thought he didn't get a chance to pray and Daniel was on his way. He thought someone had seen the door open and wanted to talk or pray or something. He already had an appointment. He went to the door to see Daniel coming through the door like a mad man. His eyes were glassy like he had been crying. Shaking like a leaf he fell into John's arm like a scared little boy. "Daniel what is wrong with you? Are you sick?"

"John please I need to talk with you. John I, I saw Jesus."

"What are you talking about? Come and sit down right here and tell me what happened."

"I was sitting in the park on the bench. I have had a really bad week. I don't know whether I can make it through this case much longer John. This whole thing with Ezekiel has done something to me. I don't know whether it is good or bad but I just know I don't want it any more. I need to be free from this. But one day two angels came to me and told me that Ezekiel was special to God and that I needed to stick with him and help him through this."

"Take your time Daniel. Look at me Daniel. I understand what you are facing. I've had situations like this too in my life that just drained me of everything I had in me. And every day it seemed to take more and more until I had nothing else to give. You will make it through this."

"Well tell me what is going on with me. I'm seeing angels and then I was sitting on the park bench and this man came up to me and sat down and told me he was Jesus. He told me to come to you and ask about being born again. I was so mesmerized by him. He looked young but he looked very old. I don't know a lot about Jesus but this guy I know has been trying to tell me about him over the years. I didn't really believe until I met him for myself. My heart was somehow changed and I believed what he told me. What am I to do now?"

"Daniel let me tell you this. I believe that Jesus is the Messiah, the Christ, the Son of God. He came two thousand years ago to give his life as a sacrifice so that all mankind could live. In the time of Moses a sacrifice had to be given for the sins of the people. The sacrifice was offered up to God and he forgave the people's sins. Well Jesus came to be the final sacrifice, the Lamb of God for the sins of the world. Now we no longer have to give a sacrifice but the price has been paid by the blood that was shed on the cross. Does that make sense?"

"Yes. I think so. It's been a long time since I went to synagogue but I do still come for Passover and the other feasts. I think that makes sense."

"Okay. So all you need to do is accept Jesus as Messiah and the sacrifice he made for you. You will then be immersed in water or baptism. This signifies your death and resurrection into new life. He will then put his spirit in you and you and you will be born of the spirit."

"That's what he said. For some reason I wanted it. Just looking into his eyes John. I'm not flakey but he had the most beautiful eyes I have ever seen. There was such love in them. But at the same time there was this agony in his eyes as well. What does that mean?"

"Daniel look at the world today. Jesus is God in the flesh come to tabernacle with his people here on the earth. Do you really think that he is happy with what he sees happening on the earth that he made? The earth is the Lord's and the fullness thereof. He has put his heart and soul into making all that is in the earth. He loves the earth and the people but they have fallen away from him. It pains his heart to see husbands and wives killing each other. The children don't even know God anymore because the parents do not teach of his ways. Mankind rapes the earth by killing off the beautiful birds, animals and the fish of the sea. This is not what God envisioned for the beautiful garden that he created. And then many people say there is no God. How do you think that makes him feel? He cries for us and he's pleading for us to turn from our wicked ways back to him."

"I'm sorry John but I've been a bad person. I have not done right by God. I want to change and follow Jesus. I want to be in his Kingdom when he comes. Can you baptize me in water and pray for me?"

"Yes Daniel. Let's pray together and I will baptize you right now. I promise you that it will change you life. Please come to church regularly and we can study the Bible together so you can learn more about being born again. If you have a spouse bring her along."

The two men bow their heads together and John prays the prayer of faith for Daniel to receive Jesus as Lord and Saviour. The church had a baptistery and he baptized Daniel in the name of Jesus. Daniel had made a choice for Jesus that day. Daniel cried like a baby. He didn't know why he was crying but for the first time in his life he felt cleansed.

Chapter 28

Daniel had just had an epiphany and had forgotten to tell John about the plan to get Ezekiel out of jail. After his baptism John invited him over to his home to meet his wife and have a small celebration. He realized how fragile Daniel was at the moment and wanted to lend his support to the new convert. While Daniel was drying off in the bathroom John called ahead to tell his wife that they were having a guest for dinner. She was excited that Daniel had given his life to the Lord and had something special waiting for him.

The walk to the house was a special one that day. John was bringing home his new brother in Christ Jesus and he was beaming. When he left the house he had no idea what Daniel was so upset about but his fear turned into joy. Daniel was still somewhat quiet but had to tell John what they had planned. Ezekiel loved him and would not want to leave America without at least saying goodbye. He could be at the funeral home when Ezekiel arrived and that would give them some time to spend with each other before leaving. It was the least he could do. John had been a source of strength and encouragement for the whole Jewish community after the bombing opening up his church despite everything.

Daniel looked over at his friend and smiled. "John I have something important to tell you."

"Well you certainly have a lot on your mind today. What is it?"

Daniel stopped walking to get his attention. "Please stop just for a minute."

"Okay. You have my attention?"

"I wanted to tell you at the church but so much was happening so quickly. I need to tell you that Aleksis is going to get Ezekiel out of jail."

"Oh my God. That is great. But why the long face?"

"Well we believe that Ezekiel will never get a fair trial. We are going to plan his death and break him out of jail that way. In this way the government will think that he has died and we can get him safely out of the country without them looking for him. I know that it sounds crazy but John it's the only way. Aleksis is setting things up on his end. I have already told Stephen and he is setting up the fake funeral. I want you to be at the funeral home the night Ezekiel is transported so that you can see him before he leaves for the States. Do you understand? You can never ever tell anyone what we have done."

"I understand Daniel."

John felt like the wind had been knocked out of him. He turned and started walking towards the house. He didn't say much after that. He was happy for Ezekiel but he was sad that it had to come to this. He felt that he would never see his good friend again in life. He missed him and now this. The rest of the walk home felt like an eternity.

Hannah had the table set with all kinds of goodies for her husband and their guest. The two men walked through the door but they both had long faces and Hannah did not understand. Something had happened but she knew to wait for John to tell her what was happening. John introduced Daniel to his wife. "Hannah sorry we are late. This is Daniel the man I told you about. This is a day of celebration. Daniel has given his life to the Lord."

"It's nice to meet you Daniel. You have a very important name in the Bible. Perhaps one day God will call you to be a prophet for our people. Here sit down. I have a surprise for you after dinner. I hope you are hungry I have made lots of good things to eat."

Daniel had not had a home cooked meal in a long time. He usually ate out at the restaurant down the street from the house. He was a batchlor and wished that he had a beautiful wife and family like John. But soon when this was all over he was going to ask Tsilia to marry him. He hoped that she would say yes. He had not thought of it but where would they have the wedding. Now that he was a Christian should he have it at the synagogue or at the church. Well since there was no synagogue that was easy to answer. But perhaps he could have Pastor John and the Rebbe do a service for him. That would be great. He could share it with the church and the synagogue members. He felt light hearted for the first time in weeks. The table looked so beautiful he couldn't help but comment on the hard work that Hannah put into the dinner. "Hannah the table looks wonderful. I will have to return the favor one day. I'm not married but I do have a friend that I would like you both to meet. She is a lawyer too. You both can tell us the secret to the perfect marriage."

This broke the ice for John. He blushed at Daniel's comment. "The perfect marriage. Yes I have the most perfect wife in the world. She is always there for me and the kids. I hope that she thinks that I am the perfect husband."

"Yes you are John. He keeps me on my toes. And he always compliments me about the house and everything. A wife really likes to hear that."

The evening was going very well but John felt a sorrow that he would be losing his friend. How could he be so selfish? He was home with his wife and his children were safe. His wife was in America and his daughter had not seen her father in quite some time. He could only imagine what she could possibly be thinking? She was so young and certainly missed her father. If this was what Ezekiel wanted then this was the right thing to do. He would say a prayer that all would go well and Ezekiel would soon be free.

He had not spoken with him since the church came to the prison to bring the inmates packages. He could see the tears in his brother's eyes and the pain was slowly killing his spirit. The next time he would see him would be on the outside. John seemed to be daydreaming at times and Hannah noticed but tried to cover for him. She knew that something was on his mind but that he would surely tell her later. He was under a lot of pressure with the church and the new ministry feeding the poor at the prison and connecting with their families. She tried to help all that she could but she had to make sure she was there for the church and the children. John had more energy than she did. She couldn't keep up with him.

After dinner Hannah went into the kitchen to put the food away and wash the dishes. The kids had gone over to her moms and she was glad for the peace and quiet in the house. She and John didn't get a chance to have much time to themselves since the children were born. She loved them but it was never a dull moment in the house. Daniel and John went into the living room to sit and talk for a while. After each baptism at the church each new convert was given a cross and a Bible. Hannah had just gotten a new box in so she quickly took one out and put it in a small box and covered it with some nice wrapping paper she had from birthday's and set it aside for Daniel. She would give it to him before he left so that he could open it at home. He didn't stay long after the meal. John called out to her that Daniel was leaving but that he wanted them to come over and meet his friend for dinner one evening. Hannah came out to say goodnight. "Daniel I have a little present for you. We usually give these to all that get baptized at the church. Open it when you get home. I hope you like it."

"Oh wow. That is so sweet Hannah. Thank you so much. John I will be in touch soon. Maybe in another week we can get together for dinner at my place. Sorry I forgot to mention that Ezekiel says there is a guy in prison with him that is dying. He wanted to see if you could get in touch with his wife and perhaps come and visit him before he dies."

"Really. I will call the officials today and see what I can do. Thank you for the information. If you need me for anything just let me know."

Daniel left and Hannah waited to see if John would tell her what was bothering him. He was sworn to secrecy but he knew that his wife would not tell a soul about Ezekiel's dilemma. He had not kept anything from his wife from the day that they were married. But was this different? She waited patiently to see if he would say anything but he said nothing. Instead he was very quiet and withdrawn. She just couldn't take it any longer. When she finished the dishes she came into the living room to speak with her husband. "John you seem to be quiet and withdrawn all evening. This is just not like you unless you have something on your mind."

"I'm sorry honey. I am sworn to secrecy on this one. I'm not sure whether I should go back on my word. This is really important."

"Oh. Does it have anything to do with Ezekiel? I know that you have been really worried about him."

"Well yes it does. Give me just a bit of space. I can't tell you right now but maybe in a few weeks. Don't worry. He is doing okay."

"Okay honey. I will pray okay?"

"You are certainly the best wife ever. Remind me to buy you a nice gift or something."

"Wow I will definitely remember to do that."

Daniel felt terrible that he had to tell John what they were planning. But he would have been upset if he did not know. He would have been asking questions as to where Ezekiel was. This was best then he would not be worried about him. He could not believe what had just transpired in his life. He needed to tell Tsilia about it but it was really late. He would call her the next day to tell his good news. He hoped she would be happy about it. They had not ever talked about God. She knew that he was Jewish but he had never asked her whether she believed in God or not. This would be really important if they were to be married and have children. He would want her to share the same beliefs but he knew that he could not force her.

It seemed as though people were watching Daniel because his phone always rang no soon as he reached home. He was an important person these days so he carried the phone with him everywhere. The phone was ringing and he looked at the number to see that Aleksis was calling. This was important so he answered it right away. "Hi Aleksis what's going on?'

"Nothing much. Just to let you know that I have a price for the gold. But we can take care of that later. I have everything taken care of for Ezekiel. I really want to get this done. I have a buyer for the gold in America but like I said let's get Ezekiel out first. I will go and see him tomorrow. If John wants to come he is more than welcome. In any case I will drop off the medicine that he will take. If you want to call him and give him the info that is fine. This is what he will do. According to the doctor the officer must be ready to bring him immediately to the hospital. He will have one and a half hours from the time he takes it to get him to the hospital and to the doctor. The doctor will take care of everything from there. He will transport him to the mortuary in the hospital where my men will be waiting. They will transport him to the funeral home. He will have to stay there for a few days while we get the plane ready with the gold. Then we will be ready to go. Have I left out anything?"

"No I don't think so. So you will go and see him tomorrow?"

"Yes. I will tell him that he is to take the medicine the following day. He will have time to tell the officer and everything else is in place. The evening that Ezekiel is brought to the funeral home we will meet at the synagogue to pick up the cargo and transport it to the plane. All things considered we will be leaving the following afternoon for America. Don't tell Ezekiel but I have a surprise for him. My brother is out of the hospital and wants to see him before we leave. He wants to go to America with me but I need him to stay here to run the business for me while I am away. He misses Ezekiel and wants to personally tell him thank you for saving his life. Remember don't tell him if he calls you."

Daniel had to sit down. It was all happening so quickly now. Ezekiel would finally be free in just a few days. He usually did the calling so he would just have to wait until he saw Aleksis the next day. He would call John and tell him to meet them at the funeral home. He had a lot of calls to make so that everyone would be ready. First he would call Stephen because he would be taking care of the funeral and leaving the next day with Ezekiel. He didn't know about the gold but that was okay. There was not enough time to tell them about everything. He would speak with them at the funeral home after transporting the gold. His head was spinning.

"Aleksis just in case I forget thank you for helping us with this. I could not get him free without you. We are truly indebted to you and your brother."

"No, no. I am glad to do it. Prison is no place for anyone especially a man like him. He doesn't deserve this. I hope the rest of his life is better than this."

"Yes me too. Please call me again after you meet with him tomorrow. I'll take care of things on this end."

"Okay."

Chapter 29

Aleksis met with his doctor friend and picked up the medicine for Ezekiel. Now it was time for him to go to the prison and give him the important instructions. Ezekiel had not called in a while for anything for the prisoners so Aleksis just picked up some things that he thought the officer might want. Aleksis had done well but he promised himself that he would never forget where he came from. He was assured that this would work without incident. There was no need to inform Ezekiel that he was coming. He didn't want him to get cold feet. The plan was that after he left the prison that Ezekiel would inject himself with the dose that the doctor had already put in the syringe. The officer would be standing by because time was of the essence that he get Ezekiel to the hospital as soon as possible so the doctor could pronounce him dead and the rest would be easy. He had a special surprise for Ezekiel. Vladimir healed very quickly and was back at home. He and a friend would be waiting for Ezekiel at the hospital. His brother would be there at the hospital to see that everything went without incident. Vladimir was worried about the plan but couldn't think of another way to get Ezekiel free. With all the clout they had no one wanted to touch this case. Aleksis understood what the problem was after seeing the contents of the cave. The government wanted the stolen items back and was holding Ezekiel in hopes that he would drop a dime on where it was being held. Mishenko had uncovered lots of Stalin's secrets and Ezekiel was a pawn to get it all back. Unfortunately Ezekiel had no idea about the cave or its contents.

It was time for the show to begin. Aleksis and his driver set out for the prison the next day. By that night Ezekiel was to be a free man. Everyone involved had marching orders and Daniel was praying every minute that all would go well. Ezekiel had no idea that Aleksis was coming that day. He was still in the infirmary when he arrived. Aleksis sat in the waiting room while Officer Zubkov went to retrieve him from the infirmary. Within minutes a man walked through the door that Aleksis did not recognize. Ezekiel had lost so much weight. He had really been sick and the stress of the situation had taken its toll on him physically and emotionally. It was a good thing that he had come, he might not have made it much longer. When Ezekiel saw Aleksis it was like a light went off and he knew that his day had come. Aleksis tried to be a tough guy but when he saw the state of his friend tears rolled down his cheek. "Ezekiel."

"Aleksis." Ezekiel nearly fell into his arms. Tears rolling down his cheek Aleksis caught him before he fell to the ground. They both sat down on the bench in the waiting room.

"Ezekiel what has happened to you. You look like you are on your way out. Are you sure you can do this?"

"Aleksis my good friend died the other day of cancer. His wife came to pick up his body. I fell apart after that. He was a good man and he died in this place. It's not fair. I think that I'm losing my mind."

"No Ezekiel. You are going to make it through this. Don't let them win. You hear me?"

"What are you doing here? Is it time?"

"Yes Ezekiel. I have spoken with Officer Zubkov. You must administer this dose of medicine as soon as you get back to the infirmary. He will be standing close by. The nurse will alert him that you have fainted and are very sick. He will take you to the hospital where a doctor is waiting for you. He will pronounce you dead on arrival. After he has taken you down to the morgue he will revive you. My men are there to make sure everything goes well. The funeral home will be called and they will have your funeral. Your uncle knows what is about to happen. He will be waiting to take you to the airport where I will take you to America. You must be strong. This is your day Ezekiel. Even Vladimir is praying for you. I don't know but you have changed him. He is a new man."

Ezekiel smiles at this comment. It gives him the power to go on. He thinks about his wife and daughter. They are waiting patiently for him and he is not going to give up on them. He looked at Aleksis and said "let's do it."

"Okay. Here is the medicine. Don't wait just do it. I'll see you in a few days."

Aleksis didn't stay long. He gave Ezekiel the medicine and left. It would be up to Ezekiel now. Officer Zubkov escorted Ezekiel back to the infirmary. He talked to him only briefly. He needed to be standing right outside the infirmary when Ezekiel injected himself with the medicine. He would have only a short period to hide the needle before the medicine took effect. He didn't want the nurse to find it. Officer Zubkov could retrieve it from his pocket and throw it away after they left the prison.

Nurse Anastasya was doing what she did best, nothing. She had a hard day when the preacher passed away. He had a horrible time and his poor wife never got a chance to say good bye. Ezekiel will never forget the look on her face when they came to pick up the body. This was not the way she envisioned the end of her loving husband's life. They had built a life together and had children. It was their desire that they would grow old together and see the children grow, get married and have children. But that had all changed in the twinkling of an eye. Now he was gone and she would have to raise the children on her own. He didn't want his wife to have experience the hurt and anguish of losing her husband like that. It was time for him to leave this place and go back out into the world. He was afraid to admit that the alternative of spending the rest of his life in prison was not a good one. Nurse Anastasya was sitting at her desk and the officer was standing outside of the infirmary. Ezekiel took out the syringe and injected himself with the medicine. He immediately put the syringe in his pocket. He could feel the medicine working right away. He stood up to walk over to where the nurse was standing. The officer was in eyes view. As he got closer to the officer he could feel his throat tightening. He started to get dizzy and his legs felt like they were about to bunkle under him at any moment. He cried out to the officer to make sure he was paying attention. A small screech alerted the officer and the nurse that something was wrong with him. The nurse ran over to Ezekiel right away. He had been sick and she thought it was the same thing again. When she reached Ezekiel he was out cold. She felt for a pulse and there was no pulse. What was happening? This was unusual. Was there something going around? She got really scared. The officer came running.

"What's going on? Is he sick again?"

"Yeah but he doesn't have a pulse. He needs to get to a hospital right away. I'm not sure what's happening. I'm not gonna have another person die on me. Get him out of here right away." She was feeling sick.

Officer Zubkov put Ezekiel on a gourney and rolled him out to a van and put him in the van to escort him to the hospital. No one stopped him because this has happened before. They had just escorted Vladimir to the hospital. No one was the wiser. Officer Zubkov was just to take him to the hospital. He was driving, sweating and trying to watch Ezekiel the whole time he was driving. The hospital was only a few minutes away. That doctor had better be there or else Ezekiel was doing to die. When he pulled into the emergency area it was almost like he was waiting outside. A doctor was standing at the door and he hoped he was the guy. Aleksis probably told him to watch for them. He came running over just as the van pulled into the parking lot. A whole crew of people actually were waiting. Officer Zubkov never felt better. He was free and had been paid a lot of money. Now he could take care of his family and get a few things he just wanted. He wanted to uphold the law but he kind of fell into this. He hoped that he would never have to do something like this again.

The hospital team pulled Ezekiel out the back of the van and put him on a hospital gourney. They started taking his vitals as they rolled him into the hospital. The Officer just left the van there and went inside with them. He had to get the paperwork for the prison officials to make it legitimate. All had gone well so far. They rolled Ezekiel into a room and he stood outside to watch and wait. No one would enter that room until he had that paperwork and his work was done. After only twenty minutes the doctor came out and they had pronounced Ezekiel dead. Officer Zubkov could not believe they had pulled it off. The doctor came out with some papers and he was ready to get in the van and go back to work. He might not ever know whether Ezekiel had made it out of the country but Aleksis was a big man and he knew what he was doing. His job was done.

The doctor gave him a wink and they put the sheet over Ezekiel's head and a nurse rolled him out of the room to an elevator down to the morgue. When they arrived downstairs they were to revive Ezekiel and he would be transported to the funeral home where he would stay until he left Russia. Vladimir and another man was waiting in the room to see Ezekiel. Vladimir thought that his friend would be moving around soon and that they would finally be reunited. There was so much that he wanted to say. To thank him for saving his life. This was to be a big surprise for Ezekiel. He had been through so much.

The nurse gave Ezekiel another injection that would bring him out of the coma like state that he was in. When he gave him the injection Ezekiel did not respond. He didn't know why Ezekiel was not responding. He had given him the right dosage. Immediately panic set in and he called the doctor to come downstairs that something terrible had gone wrong. By the time he arrived the nurse was pacing up and down and up and down the floor. "What happened?"

"He's dead doctor. He's really dead. I don't know what happened."

"What do you mean he's dead? Vladimir reacted without thinking and started choking the nurse.

"What did you do? What happened? Why is he not coming out? You had better do something or else I'm going to kill both of you right here."

The doctor started panicking too. "Stand aside and let me see what's going on?"

Ezekiel had left his body and was now standing in the room looking at himself. Vladimir was beside himself. His friend was there waiting for him. He didn't know what had happened. Why did he die? What went wrong? He would never see his wife and daughter again. This was not supposed to happen. But all he could do was stand there and look down at himself.

All of a sudden two angels came into the room. They stood looking at him like everyone else. The doctor had started doing CPR on Ezekiel but nothing was happening. One of the angels came to the head of the table and while the doctor did compressions he put his mouth over Ezekiel's and breathed into Ezekiel's body. As quickly as he breathed Ezekiel started to cough and was breathing again. His spirit went back into his body and he opened his eyes. Vladimir cried like a baby and the doctor's life was spared.

"Ezekiel are you okay?"

"Vladimir yes I am fine. The strangest thing just happened. I was looking down at myself. I really died Vladimir. But you know it didn't feel like I thought that it would. It was actually kind of peaceful. I just worried about my wife and daughter. I don't want to leave them. Man it's good to see you. Are you feeling better?"

"Yes. Don't worry about me. Let's get you out of here. Your uncle is waiting for you. The funeral director is on his way to pick you up. We had better leave as soon as possible. Aleksis will be worried. He is waiting for me to call him as soon as we have left this place."

"Thank you." Ezekiel turned to the doctor and the nurse who stood speechless. "Thank you for everything."

Vladimir and Ezekiel slipped out through the back door where the funeral director was waiting. The two men hugged as the car slipped into the night. Vladimir went home to let Aleksis know that everything had gone well and Ezekiel was free.

For the first time in almost a year Ezekiel felt like he could breath but his ordeal was not over yet. He still had to board the plane and get into America. Aleksis was sure that he wouldn't have any trouble. All he could think about now was being with his family again. Ezekiel had not seen Shalom since his father died. It was so good to see his face. It was both wonderful and painful at the same time. There was no time to talk until they arrived at the funeral home. Ezekiel layed down in the back of the car in a coffin. It was the eariest feeling he had ever had. Not long ago he had died and if it were not for the angels that came to breathe the breath of life into him he would have been dead in that coffin for sure. He lay there thinking about all the things he would have missed. His daughter was so very young and had not even grown up yet. He promised his father that he would take his family to Israel and he wanted to keep that promise. And most importantly God had called him to speak to his people about the future.

After some time the car came to a stop and he could hear Shalom talking with his father. The door opened and Shalom and Stephen pulled the coffin out of the back of the car. Ezekiel had no idea that Stephen was waiting at the funeral home for him. He could feel the bumps of the casket being layed upon some wheels. It was smooth now being rolled into the funeral home. They wanted to make sure that if anyone was watching they would not see him. Shalom opened the lid and Ezekiel sat up so he could get out of the casket. He was excited when he saw his uncle Stephen standing there waiting to help him get out of the casket. It was a very strange meeting but a happy one. "Uncle Stephen I didn't know that you were going to be here waiting for me. I'm so glad to see you."

"Ezekiel I'm glad to see you too. I'm so glad that you are okay. I have so much to tell you. I'm sure you are tired. Are you hungry? If so I can go and get something for you to eat. There is a room in the back where you can sleep until the funeral is over tomorrow. Then we will be leaving for America."

"You know its funny but I have not eaten a good meal since I entered prison. Please get me some real food. Uncle Stephen how is Raisa and Aliyah?"

"They are both doing great. Hey why don't you ask them yourself. Let me call the house."

Stephen took out his cell phone to make a long awaited phone call home. He had not told Ezekiel that his wife was expecting he thought she should tell him. The phone rang several times before someone picked up the phone. "Hello."

"Hello. Raisa is that you?"

Raisa started screaming and crying on the phone. Stephen's son and daughter came running to see what was happening. She started screaming Ezekiel is on the phone, Ezekiel is on the phone. Please get Aliyah.

"Ezekiel I'm sorry. I knew that you were coming out today but I didn't know that I could get so emotional when I heard your voice. Oh honey I miss you so much. We are getting Aliyah to speak with you. She is sleeping but if I don't get her she will be very angry with me. Hold on a minute."

"Daddy, daddy. I miss you so much. When are you coming to America?"

"Sweet heart I will be there in just a few days. I'm so sorry that I have been away from you for so long. I promise you I will never leave you again."

"It's okay daddy. I know that you cannot help it. Me and mommy are doing good. Daddy we are expecting a new baby. Did mommy tell you?"

"A new baby. What are you saying Aliyah. Put mommy back on the phone."

"Yes Ezekiel we are expecting a new baby. He will be here in just a few months. Stephen wanted me to tell you. I'm glad that you will be here for the precious arrival."

Ezekiel felt like he was going to pass out. If he had missed the birth of his son he would have wanted to die. He couldn't wait to see them both. He was ready to go home right away. But they had to put on a good show. He just realized that Daniel was not there. He would ask Stephen about him.

"Raisa I'm sorry I have so much on my mind. I cannot take it all in. It's late you had better go. Stephen is going to fill me in on what we must do before we get on the plane. I will see you very soon. Take care of yourself."

"Okay Ezekiel. I will see you soon."

Ezekiel was so overwhelmed that he just hugged his uncle and Shalom. Stephen went to get Ezekiel some real food while Shalom took him into the back room where he could lay down and wait for him to return.

Chapter 30

Aleksis and Daniel had a private meeting at his home the evening that Ezekiel came home. There was the final business of payment for the gold that Aleksis bought from the treasures Mishenko left in the cave. The payment would be more than enough for Simon to rebuild the synagogue and school. Some of the families had medical bills to pay so a lot would be accomplished with the money. Aleksis had done very well for himself. Daniel never wanted to live a life of crime but Aleksis had done a good thing for Ezekiel and his family. He learned that it didn't pay to judge people for the life that they lived. He would have to stand before God on judgment day all by himself. God was all about forgiveness. Maybe one day Aleksis and his family would give their lives to God and repent for the things that they did wrong in life. God was faithful to give everyone that chance.

Daniel didn't want to waste much time because he needed to speak with Ezekiel about a lot of things. He had to drop off the briefcase with him so that he could use it as leverage with the American government for his asylum. He was just ecstatic that his client was free and on his way to building a new life for his family. It was certainly a long and arduous ordeal for anyone.

After a brief meeting Daniel took the briefcase containing the money and dropped it off at Simon's house and reminded him to be at the funeral the next morning. He had never been at a fake funeral before but there was a first time for everything. It was time now to head over to the funeral home to see his brother. After all that had happened Ezekiel was more a brother than a client to Daniel now.

It had been almost a year since the ordeal started. When Daniel looked at Ezekiel he could not believe how much weight he lost. It was like seeing a skeleton with some meat wrapped around it. He could barely walk. When Daniel walked into the back room he was laying down stuffed with the food that Stephen brought him. He had not had a good meal in a very long time. The men in the room all turned to look at Daniel. Ezekiel looked at him through two dark eyes that had no light. It would take some time for him to heal from what had happened in his life. But he was tough and his family would give him the strength to persevere. The two men hugged and tears filled their eyes. "Thank you Daniel for helping me."

"No thank you. You have taught me so much about strength. I wish I could have done more. There is so much that I must tell you."

"Well sit down. There are no strangers here."

"Okay. Ezekiel there is so much that I have found out about why the government put you in prison. It seems that Mishenko had more information about Russia than meets the eye. This briefcase was found behind the torah cabinet by Simon. He was the one that gave the information to me. You can take your time going through it. Also included in the briefcase is some money that perhaps he put aside to take care of himself if he got the chance to defect from Russia. Use it for your family I'm sure that after everything he would want that. Also this is going to blow your mind. Underneath the synagogue is a cave full of treasures that Mishenko stole from the government. I have asked Simon to seal off the cave so that no one could get into it because there are many relics from the Holocaust like pictures of people's family, gold, things that were stolen from these families. I will tell you this though that we sold some of it for the sake of having the finances to rebuild the synagogue and the school. It's up to Simon now. I don't want anything to do with it. I think that it is sacred ground. I don't want anyone else trampling over the souls of these people. I know this sounds crazy but it is all true. Do you have any questions?"

"I can't believe this. What in the world was Mishenko wrapped up in? He was just a businessman as far as I knew."

"Well yes he was a businessman but he got to know some very important people. Unfortunately they had big mouths and they took Mishenko down to the secret city built by Stalin many years ago. He saw what was in the city and other caves around Moskow. He stole a lot of the treasures and put it in a cave under the synagogue. I believe that he was put in prison for this. He is still alive because they have not found the treasure. They think that you know where it is. I wish that I did not have to tell you this. It must stay in this room and never to be spoken of again."

"But why did he do this?"

"I really think that in his own way he wanted to give it back to the Jewish people. I don't know how he planned on doing it but I think that he wanted to tell the world what he had seen. This was his way of having proof that the city existed."

"Wow. This is too amazing. I don't think that I can handle any more Daniel. I will take the briefcase and give it to the American government and they can figure it all out. I just want my freedom and to take my family to Israel. I have to warn them."

"I understand Ezekiel. I will be here tomorrow. After the funeral you and Stephen will board a plane for America. Aleksis will let me know when you have reached America. I wanted to come with you but I think that I will say good bye to you now. Keep in touch. If you ever need anything don't hesitate to get in touch with me. Oh Pastor John will be here tomorrow. After the funeral he would like to come back and say good bye to you as well. He and I have become good friends. He loves you very much. He is glad that you are leaving but he has mixed emotions."

"Thank you Daniel. I will never forget you. I'm sure we will see each other again. Remember "see you in Jerusalem.""

"Yes my friend "see you in Jerusalem.""

The two men hugged. Daniel looked at Stephen. He had aged so quickly in just a few months. But now the old man could take his son home.

Chapter 31

A small group of people filed into a funeral home to pay their last respects to one of their sons. Pastor John and his wife sat in the back row of the home. Although everyone was aware that Ezekiel had not really died there was this feeling that something had been lost that would never be regained. With the bombing and incarceration of their son the innocence of the community had been lost forever. Rebbe Isak had healed from his wounds and came to say good bye to his good friend Stephen and Ezekiel. They were his family and it would be hard to go on without them. The Jewish people had fought a terrible fight during the Holocaust. Those who had survived hoped to build a new life for their children hoping that they would never suffer again. But unfortunately the war was not over and a new fight was just on the horizon.

Mordechi and his brother Stephen had a life long dream to take their families to Israel, the place given to them by God so that they would never have to live in a land where they were not loved and appreciated. Now Mordechi was dead and his brother took on the role of patriarch of the family. Ezekiel just went through the fight of his life and there would be many more before his life was over. Now it was time to reunite the family and complete the dream of his father.

They didn't have a traditional funeral since it was only for show. After the ceremony Pastor John and Rebbe Isak went into the back room to say goodbye to their old friend. Ezekiel was overwhelmed when he saw the Rebbe especially because he had not seen him since the bombing. He looked great and had recovered fully. He was waiting for the rebuilding of the synagogue and the school that was crucial to the life of the community. As he hugged his friend he remembered the good times and the bad times but hoped in his heart that the future would be brighter.

Pastor John stood on the side waiting his turn to hug his good friend. He had learned a lot during Ezekiel's incarceration and hoped that he would be as strong as his brother when the time came when all Christians throughout the world would be persecuted for the name of Christ. It was just overwhelming that he might not ever see his good friend again. Words could not describe his sadness. His wife was waiting so he didn't say goodbye only farewell until they met again hopefully under better circumstances. Ezekiel promised that he would write and call as much as possible. It would not be a good thing to ever try to come back to Russia ever again. Maybe John could come to America at a future date.

Stephen and Ezekiel were rushed out of the funeral home by some of Aleksis goons for the flight at the airport. Stephen glanced over at his son to say this is it. We are on our way out of here finally. Ezekiel only stared out of the window at his beloved Russia. It was time for him to move on from here and face the task that God had in front of him. He knew that it would not be easy but nevertheless like so many of his forefathers before him he could not say no to the pleadings of God because the future of his people depended on it. Like Jeremiah he said "hineni" "here I am send me". It would be a privilege to be the prophet of God he was called to be. The tears began to roll down his face.

Aleksis was waiting in a plane at a private airport for Stephen and Ezekiel. As he boarded he turned and looked at his home one last time and boarded the plane never to return again. His wife and daughter were waiting. Destiny had called him to a higher purpose.